DARK WARRIOR:

TO TAME A WILD HAWK

FROM THE DARK CLOTH SERIES

BOOK ONE

BY LENORE WOLFE

TRIQUETRA PRESS

This is a work of fiction. Names, characters, places and incidents either are the product of the author's imagination or are used fictitiously, and any resemblance to actual persons, living or dead, business establishments, events or locals are entirely coincidental.

Triquetra Press

First Printing January 2011

ISBN-10:1460944224

ISBN-13:9781460944226

Copyrighted ©2011 by Lenore Wolfe

All rights reserved.

The scanning, uploading and distribution of this book, via the Internet or via any other forms without the permission of the publisher is illegal and punishable by law. Please purchase only authorized electronic editions and do not participate in or encourage electronic piracy or copyrighted materials. Your support of the author's rights is appreciated.

If you purchased this book without a cover, you should be aware that this book is stolen property. It was reported as "unsold and destroyed" to the publisher and neither the publisher nor the author have received payment for this "stripped book".

to my family
much love and joy x x x

Look for Dark Warrior: Kid

Dark Cloth Series Book Two

To be released 2014. A Western Romance

All Kat wants to do is marry the man of her dreams. But Lady Fate seems to have other plans....

Other Works by Lenore Wolfe

Doorway to the Triquetra

Children of the Atlantis Series Book One

To be released June 12, 2011

Paranormal Fantasy

Look for the free sample chapter at the end of this novel.

The Fallen One

Children of the Dark Mother Series Book One

To be released 2014

Paranormal Fantasy

A Tribute Novel

Solstice Fire

Daughters of the Dark Moon Series Book One

To be released 2015

Paranormal Fantasy

She dreamed of him....

and he came to her....

To Tame a Wild Hawk

by Lenore Wolfe

Prologue

We are born of ashes—and as the young boy stared at the ashes covering the palms of his hands, at six years old, he knew—to ashes we would return. They had appeared to ride from hell through the haze of the fiery sun as it lit the prairie grass around them. Flames from the setting sun licked at their feet, the thunder of horses' hooves hitting the ground as though the Gods of thunder played the drums—burning the sky down around them.

Screams of women and children filled the hot prairie air, and they ran without direction but could not escape. They could not evade men on horseback, who rode them down and shot them with no more emotion than they would show a wild animal. The men from the wagon train swore viciously and shot back at their invaders, diving behind anything that offered them cover on the barren, prairie grasslands. Horses' high-pitched whinnies rose above the melee, and they lunged in fright and pain when a stray bullet struck them down or caused them to stampede out of control.

The boy could not tear his gaze from the scene before him. He wanted to. His eyes refused to obey. Everything around him moved as if in slow motion. He could not understand what was happening—to him—to his friends—to his loved ones. He could not understand *why* this was happening.

A bullet struck the ground at his feet. He stood, staring at it. It befuddled him, refused to give word or heed to the reality happening around him. As he stared at it, stillness settled within him like fractured pieces of time. A voice that seemed to come from nowhere, yet everywhere, yelled, run! And in blind panic, he obeyed.

He ran past a wagon, the thud of a bullet, slamming into the side and splintering the wood, causing him to flinch. A long sliver struck him in the cheek as he dove into the bushes at its rear. Then, the sight of a man on a pony caught his attention—and, once more, all he could do was stare.

He stared, paralyzed, as the man shot a boy in the back, heard the heart-stopping scream of the boy's mother and saw her go down beside her son, an ugly red stain covering her chest. He swallowed hard at the bile that burned its way up his throat. Tears pooled in his golden eyes. Much later, he would recall how the mules brayed in panic and broke loose from their harnesses, trampling any who got in their way. But, for now, he did not see them. Later, he would remember the wagons tipping over in the frenzied melee, crushing the few who hid beside them. He would dream of this, have nightmares of this. But, for now, he saw only *the man*.

"Papa," Jordy McClain whispered.

He squinted, through the haze of dust, at the man who took careful aim, one-by-one, killing their friends. Giving a small cry, he leaped up. His only thought that somehow *he must stop his papa*. But a bullet slammed into the dirt beside him, and he hunkered back down. Dust spiraled all around him, choking him. He covered his nose and mouth with a mud-streaked hand. He mustn't sneeze. If he did, they would kill him, too. Maybe if he got really little, they wouldn't see him. He hunkered down and got as small as he could.

A child ran, screaming, past his hiding place, and Jordy couldn't help himself, he stood to help her. In the next instant her small body jerked backward as if pulled by an invisible thread. His knees buckled. He slid to the ground in a heap. Open mouthed, he stared at the man who held the gun. "Papa," he mouthed. Paralyzed, he watched his father wrack another bullet into the chamber; watched as he lifted the rifle and took aim. Jordy's gaze followed the direction his father pointed the gun.

No!

The bullet slammed into Yellow Wolf's back. As if in slow motion, their scout spun around and fell to the ground. Tears streamed down Jordy's face, leaving dusty tracks in their wake, and this time he did scream, "Yellow Wolf. No, no, no!" He realized what he had done, caught his lip between mud-streaked teeth, covered his mouth with his hands and whimpered, but no one paid him mind.

To Tame a Wild Hawk

The prairie grasslands carried the last screams of the dying across the plains. Jordy placed his hands over his ears and rocked back and forth from his hiding place in the tall, prairie grass. Then, even the screaming stopped, and he sagged in the silence. The men looted the dead and shot those who moaned. Jordy's breath left his lungs and lodged in his throat. Papa? Tears rolled down his chubby cheeks, leaving a trail of wet dust in their wake. He swallowed at the huge lump in his throat. How could his papa do this?

And as he peeked through the prairie grass, there stood a man in the middle of the melee. He stood, out of place, in his long, fancy coat, even to a six year old boy. As Jordy squinted through the smoke and dust, he realized the man was looking for someone.

A terrible feeling crawled through his tummy.

Jordy hunkered down as far as he could get in the grass as the man's gaze turned directly to where he hid.

The hair stood up on the back of the boy's neck.

The man had no face.

Worse, instead of a face, he seemed to wear some kind of mask, which looked like a face—*but was not a face at all.*

Jordy wanted to scream. He felt as if he were having a bad dream and couldn't wake up. He'd swear he was awake, that everything was real—yet not real.

Not real at all.

He let out a breath when the man turned to the men, who were, by now, showing signs of wanting to shoot each other, if their raised voices and arguing were an indication.

The men hollered at his father, and his papa shouted back at them. Jordy bit his lip until he tasted blood as they mounted up, and he didn't breathe until they rode out. More tears rolled down his face. His papa hadn't looked around for him—*not once.*

He curled up into a ball and cried. His throat burned, and something squeezed his heart until he thought it would burst. He wished his ma was here. But she was gone. She had died in childbirth, changing his father. His papa had become angry and drank a lot after she died. And he wouldn't even look at Jordy's new baby sister. Then, one day, his papa had packed Jordy up and headed west, leaving his baby sister behind with his Aunt Sarah. He didn't know how to get back to her. He was all alone.

Lenore Wolfe

Yellow Wolf was dead, now, too. The Cheyenne scout always talked to him when he hurt. But he never would again. With deep, wracking sobs, he cried for some time, rocking back and forth. He must have fallen asleep. Because, the next thing that he knew, he heard the sound of a lone horse coming his way, and he held very still.

For those who would listen, who could tilt their head and hear it, the wind blew a death song across the prairie. It lifted and danced among the grass tops, its sad and mournful song.

To the Cheyenne Warrior, looking out over the massacre of the wagon train, the voices of many joined in that song. He rode his pony with the ease of his people. The richness of his ancestry etched in the lines of his regal bearing. His pony picked its way amongst the dead as if to show his own reverence for what had taken place here this day. The warrior tilted his head as if listening to their story. For, indeed, there was a tale to tell.

He heard their sorrowful song because he had learned to listen. Their broken bodies cried out to his spirit. Their sightless eyes stared up at the heavens. Women, who'd fallen by their children. Men, who'd fought to save their families. Horses, dead under their saddles, and mules and oxen, fallen right where they'd stood, still in their harnesses. Wagons, tipped over.

Women's trunks, strewn all over the ground.

The warrior dismounted and walked amongst the carnage. He reached to pick up a pan, looking around. It saddened his heart. It was a sight he had witnessed many times.

Spotting a thatch of dark hair amongst the corn silk color of the prairie grass, he walked silently towards it. As he got closer, he could make out the figure of, what looked to be, a young boy. He picked up the slight sound of movement and sat down against a busted wagon wheel, his back to the child. He plucked a blade of grass and rolled it back and forth between his thumb and finger. "Only a white man would do such a thing as this to his own people." He waited a second, and when the boy didn't respond, he added, "A civilized man would never do such a thing. There is no honor in the doing."

Without looking, he sensed the child's fear, felt the boy shrink from him. "You can come out now. They are gone." Again, he waited a moment. "No one here will hurt you. Besides," he paused and glanced back, "that is a mountain cat bed you lay in. She might be upset when she returns and finds you in her bed."

To Tame a Wild Hawk

The child sat up. He was pleased to see the child was, indeed, a boy. The boy looked around for the cat—then back at him. The boy's green-gold eyes locked with his, clenching his jaw, perhaps to keep from betraying his fear. He would make a good son.

"Are your people, your parents, here?" He waved his arm to indicate the dead.

The boy shook his head.

He studied the boy, puzzled. "I am Standing Bear, son of Swift Knife." He placed his hand on his chest. He waited. "Where are your parents?"

"Dead."

He heard the hesitation in the boy's answer. It was a lie. What was the boy hiding?

A young hawk soared above them. Swooping down, it landed on a log near the boy. For several long seconds, the hawk's cold, proud eyes riveted to the child's green-gold ones. Then, in the same mysterious way the hawk had appeared, it flew off. A good sign. He would call the boy, Hawk. But, for now, he'd wait for the boy to accept the future set before him.

"You can come with me. You will be safe." He walked to his pony and waited.

He watched as the boy's golden gaze darted over the melee and lit on the Cheyenne scout. The child's eyes filled with pain. The scout was the boy's friend. Perhaps the scout had taught him about the Tsistsistas. Perhaps he had taught him the civilized people were different from the whites. "I will not harm you. The Cheyenne will not harm you. You will be safe." Something in him yearned to help the boy.

The boy's golden gaze shot up and met his, and the child, again, set his jaw. Many things crossed through his eyes, and they darkened to a deep shade of green as he looked back at his murdered friends—fear, panic, pain, and something else.

Hate.

The boy hated the white eyes. He was too young to recognize the emotion for what it was. But someday he would. Standing Bear looked out over the dead, littering the ground. He knew hate.

The boy would not rest until they no longer cried out to him in his sleep.

Chapter One

Cheyenne, Wyoming – Late Summer of 1871

Dancing rays of heat coiled up from the dirt packed street beneath the hot, Wyoming sun. A cowboy sat with his chair tipped back on a boarded walk against one shaded wall, his feet propped against a post, his Stetson pulled down low, over his face.

The ladies stayed inside the shielding walls of the buildings, lining the streets of Cheyenne. In summer, the time-weathered, boarded walls of the buildings provided shade. In winter, the walls provided shelter from the endless winds, which blew snow around but did little to hold in the heat or keep out the cold. In cthe cold, the ladies huddled around the large, pot-belly stove, or the stone fireplace, drinking tea. But, today, they mainly sat in the small diner, sipping lemonade and gossiping about their men—and the latest fashions.

The town boasted several saloons, where cowboys got drunk and stumbled down the, as of yet, untamed streets of Cheyenne. Twice a year, at spring and fall roundups, they went down the streets, shooting and hollering, waving their pokes of money, proud and happy to have survived another year. But, today, the town sat quiet, baking in the endless rays of the sun. An occasional frisky breeze, which should have felt good, only kicked up dust when it did a little dance, spinning sand in small circles, which would have been mesmerizing if it weren't for the grit it left behind in your teeth.

Beside the town's main mercantile, Cord's Mercantile, sat one of the town's hotels. The mercantile, a single story building, held canned goods, pots and pans, slabs of bacon, and clothes. The latter, you could buy already made up. Even so, there were also a few bolts of fabric, since a woman usually sewed her family's clothes, herself. The hotel was a tall, two-story, building, where the clerk was seen occasionally, his glasses sitting nearly on the end of his nose, sweeping the endless dust which coated the boarded walk.

Upstairs, in one of the hotel's well-kept rooms, Amanda Kane sat with her feet soaking in the coolest water she could find in this, what did they call it, oh yeah, God-forsaken land.

She'd propped her head on her arms over a small table. She had always hated being inside, but there was no help for it in this sweltering heat.

Three layers of pristine, petticoats were pulled high up on her thighs.

She hated them too.

She sucked in another breath of the hot, dry air. Her dark curls cascaded down around her face and over her arms. Several damp tendrils clung to her forehead and neck. A healing crystal, from around her neck, dropped forward, sending tiny prisms of light dancing across the room.

She pulled the petticoats higher still, sending the tiny bells, sewn into her skirts, singing. These wretched skirts, she thought, shoving irritably at her long, dark locks in a desperate attempt to escape the heat they held around her face. The bells sang with each movement, so tiny, the sound nearly imperceivable. Despite her agitation, she never failed to calm with their music.

Her gaze traveled the length of a crack in the floorboards. Again, and again, she followed the crack. In the heat, the boards had turned hard. Tough. Tough, like the life one leads out here in the untamed west. Was that why her father had betrayed her? He hadn't believed she could run the ranch alone. Through his death—her papa had won.

She felt the stage roll into town before she heard its wheels crunching the ground beneath. She closed her eyes, a single tear breaking free and dropping to the water below.

Outside, the driver pulled the team to a halt—the harnesses jangling as the driver yelled, "Whoa! Easy now. *That's it.*" The great beasts shaking their heavy coats, sending the metal jangling, once again.

To Tame a Wild Hawk

Mandy barely heard the hesitant knock at the door. She knew her childhood friend had come to warn her of McCandle's return. "Come in," she managed through her dry throat. She couldn't have said another word. She couldn't swallow past the lump that had formed there. She lifted her head and met her best friend's gaze.

She didn't want to see pity there.

Meagan's crystal blue eyes held the pain that, Mandy was sure, mirrored her own but bore no trace of pity. "He's standing outside."

Mandy thought of the sapling trees, their leaves yielding against destruction. They'd sway with a gentle breeze—and bend to a great wind. Her gaze dropped, once again, to the floorboards. She could be tough, like these dried boards. Tough like the west. Or—she could bend like saplings. Strong. Strong—even in the meanest wind.

She followed the tough, worn boards to the window, leaving a trail of wet footprints in her wake. He stood there, beside a man dressed in a black, tailored jacket, looking up, his cold, green eyes searching for her, his hand on his Stetson as he met her gaze. His unusual green eyes had shown warmth when her father was alive, but she knew him well and was not deceived. As a child, he'd been mean. He'd never lost that growing up, And now, as a man, he had a hole in his soul where his heart should have been.

Be careful, child, the Grandmothers warned. You are in danger.

The voice of the *Grandmothers* sounded clearly to her. They had always spoken to her this way, from beyond the veil. This had been the way of it since she had spent four years with the Lakota tribe. They had called her the *gift of spirit* and taught her their ancient ways. They had said, her path was destined, and she was given to their brethren tribe, the Cheyenne, to be returned to her people. They had said, *one day her visions would help their people to cross into an unknown land to escape the white eyes, saving thousands of their men, women and children.*

They warned her now, and this danger she knew well. What she did not know, what she could not see—was how to stop it.

She held the steady gaze of the man standing outside, and she knew, her only hope lay in breaking free.

Therein was the danger. Breaking free would probably mean her life.

You hold the shields, child. They will keep you safe. Listen, and you will know.

Know? Know what? How to fight the most powerful man in Wyoming territory? How *could* she fight him? She knew what her father could never know—what he could never see. She knew that behind the kind, gentle eyes he'd shown her father, lay a man who would do anything, go to any length, to get what he wanted—and he wanted her father's ranch. For it lay between him and the railroad he was bringing to town.

Her father had only seen a powerful man. "Why would he need this small ranch?" her father had argued. "He already owns half the land from here to Colorado!"

Because of the railroad, papa. It's the railroad he wants—and you're in the way.

This man, who would take what he wanted if she couldn't stop him, stalked through the doors below, shaking her out of her thoughts. She glanced, once more, towards the stranger who watched him go, then looked—directly at her.

She backed into the shadows of her room, not taking her eyes off him. Goosebumps swept up her back, causing the little hairs to stand on end.

The man appeared to have a face—yet no face—rather, his face appeared to be a mask.

She wanted another look, but he turned away, his face now hidden in shadows beneath his dark hat.

The front door slammed, reminding her of *who was heading her way*. She scrambled for her shoes, listening as he stormed his way up the stairs. Taking a deep, cleansing breath, she tied the laces of one shoe. His heavy tread led to her door where he violently banged, until the hinges threatened to tear from their foundation. She tied the laces of her other shoe and stood. But he wasn't waiting. He stormed into her room, sending the door crashing against the wall.

Mandy swallowed her frustration. "Well, hello, McCandle, nice of you to *wait* to be invited in." She used a calm tone she knew would frustrate him. She had to keep him off kilter, off balance. It was the only way.

He strode across the room in purposeful steps, stopping directly in front of her, his pale, green eyes, cold. His gaze traveled the length of her, leaving the promise of retribution in their wake. "I was just at your ranch."

He'd had the stage stop by her ranch. Why didn't that surprise her? He had always wielded his power in such a way. She raised a brow at him. "Yes?"

"Your men met me at the gate with shotguns," he sneered. "Do you really think you can stop *me?*"

To Tame a Wild Hawk

He grabbed her chin. She knew there would be small finger marks from the force of his grip.

She clenched her teeth. "Let go of me, McCandle."

He lowered his head to just above hers. She didn't look away but held his gaze.

"Where are the old bats?"

"Bats?" She raised a brow. "You mean my teachers?" He snarled at that, and she held back a smile. She really shouldn't irritate him this way. But she couldn't help herself.

"Teachers. You mean *witches.*" He raised *his* brow, his eyes narrowing. "You will not see them again," he said, his voice low and mean.

Mandy couldn't believe his gall. He'd always talked to her this way, as though he had a right to, as though he owned her. It threatened her, how certain he was, how sure of her surrender.

She fought to keep her center, to stay calm. The room slanted and transformed. Mandy no longer saw McCandle but the vision before her.

Blinding rays seared a scorching path of hot dust. A pony picked his way amongst the stones, leaving little of his trail in his wake. With each unshod step the dust rose and settled, nearly obscuring his path. Mandy knew the pony remained unshod because no sound of steel, hitting stone, rang out.

An unshod pony and a man. . . .

The room came sharply back into focus. She met the disconcerted, pale-green eyes of McCandle, and knew. . . .

A man.

A man, clad in the buckskins of the Lakota—who rode an unshod pony. . . . "I will not need your help, McCandle."

McCandle's gaze narrowed on her. "What the hell! Where were you just now?" He reached behind her head. Grabbing a hand-full of her locks, he twisted until he held her head painfully angled back, his eyes mere inches from her own. "Answer me, damn you."

She met his green eyes, boldly. "The *Grandmothers* have shown me the way. You seek retribution—and retribution there shall be." She sensed the stillness from her center. Let its calm radiate upward, and envelope her. "But," she enunciated, "it will *not be yours.*"

Lenore Wolfe

He let go of her as if stung, not breaking contact with her gaze even as he backed his way out of the room. She looked away, and he stood for a moment just beyond the door, close to escape, yet something stopped him. She hoped he would not realize what it was that allowed him to regain his senses so easily. His lips turned up in a sneer. *"Witch."*

She looked at him but did nothing more this time. Contact with him had left her weak. It was all she could do not to let it show. He held power, and his power would have to be squashed before he realized what it was he held. It was not the power of the railroad, or his money, that made him dangerous. With some patience, perhaps he would never know where his *true* power lay.

To her relief, he stormed back down the hallway, slamming out of the building. She sank to the bed.

When she opened her eyes again it was dark. Deep shadows lay around her. The promise of something, unknown, hung suspended in time, like a prism out of her reach.

She sensed his presence in the room, this buck-skinned man with the designs of the Lakota and closed her eyes. Quieting her thoughts, she went still, so she would know where he crouched. After a moment of trying, she gave up. He would not reveal himself unless it was what *he wanted*.

"You came," she whispered this.

"Did you think I would do anything else?"

"You are not Lakota but white eyes. Yet you carry the design of the Lakota."

"They are my people," his voice was quiet.

He had moved closer to the bed, and she had not heard, nor sensed, his movement. He would make a dangerous enemy. But he would not be *her* enemy. They carried a destiny of a different sort, the two of them.

And she was unwilling to follow *that* thought.

She bit her lip, trying to stop the trembling. "I have seen you for many years, in my visions, in my dreams, but I have not known what they meant."

"Do you," he paused, "not know? Did you not ask the *Grandmothers?*"

She went still. "No."

To Tame a Wild Hawk

"Why not?" he whispered this close to her ear, now. She could feel his breath on her hair. She could smell the scent of him. It was intoxicating.

She sucked in a breath at her thoughts.

She moved, sensing, more than feeling, a deep loss—a longing that sat at the edges of her life, just outside the reach of her memories. She missed him, missed him so much it tore through her heart, raged through her soul, leaving her in tatters. "I—I do not know." She was unaware of what it was she'd answered. She couldn't even remember the question.

She knew he smiled.

He'd moved away. She missed him here, too, now, her mind—sharp with how much, as though she'd lost him again. She'd known him in her dreams, it was true. She could remember past lives they'd shared, just not the man who'd caused her such pain. Her dreams so pure and rich, she sometimes had difficulty telling which was the lie—and which the dream.

"Perhaps one day, you will know."

She centered her breathing and changed the trail he'd taken. "You still seek a warrior's revenge." It wasn't a question, and she did not question how she knew. The Hawk was well known in these parts as the boy who grew up with the Lakota, and it was rumored wherever he went, a gunman followed.

"Life is a continuous circle, and many paths are entwined."

She sensed his pain. The cry of his people rang in her ears. "The path crossed, crosses between you . . . and me." She nearly sat up. "So the man you seek—*is here.*"

He did not answer. Her eyes flew wide. *"McCandle."*

She closed her eyes, sensing his affirmation. "How is it you are to help me?"

"Do you not know?"

She opened her eyes, staring into the dark. "No," she said simply.

"Your father has stipulated in his will, you will marry or lose the ranch?"

She sucked in her breath. "My father threatened as much, but I have not listened to the will to know that he stipulated anything."

"You shall marry," he stated as though it were fact.

"McCandle?"

"No."

"Then, whom?" She asked this, though she knew the answer. She waited to hear it anyway, holding her breath. And for reasons she couldn't fathom, the answer terrified her more than McCandle.

"Me."

She sat straight up in the bed. "What!" It wasn't a question.

The room slanted, once again. The buckskin clad man stood before her. This time, she saw her own wedding.

"Know your destiny, child."

She shook her head. "I cannot *Grandmothers.*"

"You must. For in it lies the future of the people."

"That is so unfair, *Grandmothers.*"

"You will not be unhappy." He stood so near her, now, his words were whispered against her lips. "In fact, I would say you will be most happy." The last was pressed against her lips.

"Hawk?" But even before she could regain her senses, she knew he was gone.

Mandy scrambled from the bed, grabbing a cloak.

Outside, she didn't bother to stop to light a torch; a full moon lit her way. She followed the path out of town, on foot, not stopping to saddle her horse. She had to see the teachers—now.

Dawn streaked the sky in pale, rose lights by the time she reached the little village, caught in a beauty of spirit, next to a serene flowing river. She made her way to the tipi setting near the edge. She passed several of the people and smiled in greeting as they hurried this way, and that, to start a new day. The teacher pulled back the flap and came out, even before she reached her tipi.

Mandy stood before her, tears in her eyes, and greeted the frail, old woman with respect.

"You fight with a primitive fear," her teacher said after a moment.

"How can I do this?"

"Would you rather you married McCandle?"

"I would rather I didn't marry at all."

To Tame a Wild Hawk

"It is not the way of your people that you run a ranch on your own. You would have many enemies seeing a woman as prey, stealing their way, as your people are want to do."

Mandy fought back the tears. "I do not know him. He does this for his revenge."

"Child—*you have always known him*. Listen with your heart—you will know."

"How soon?"

"How much time did your father give you? How much time will McCandle?"

Mandy sighed in frustration.

"This is your destiny, child." The old woman turned back to go inside. "We must return to the people. It is too dangerous now. Listen child—hold your personal crystal and listen with your soul. You have known him since the beginning of time." She closed the flap behind her, leaving Mandy to make the long journey back.

Dawn streaked the sky when Mandy reached a place sacred to her. She had found herself drawn here—to this place of peace. She went to her sacred space, a medicine wheel, known only to her. She went in through the east door and sprinkled tobacco behind her to close, symbolically, the door. She sat in the north and listened with her soul. Finding the center of her being, she sat in the manner she had been taught, where life could carry a continuous circle around her. Light filled her—healing light—light of understanding. Once again, she saw her own wedding, and she sensed a deep peace. She knew she would help to protect the secrets of the people. She saw the way of protecting the teachings. She saw her children around her.

But the way of the Hawk remained unclear.

Chapter Two

It was late in the afternoon when Mandy returned to town. The town remained quiet, just as the day before, laboring too hard under the heat wave to want to resume its usual bustling activity. The tiny bells in her skirts trilled as she walked, her thoughts deep in the center of her being, least she give way the urge to panic. She let her thoughts remain there, quiet and near her soul.

She walked past the little white church at the end of town. A cemetery lay peacefully sheltered in the shade at its side. She stopped for several moments, gazing towards her father's headstone, absorbing the love he'd held for her in the memory of his smile, before heading for Cord's Mercantile to pick up supplies for when she would return to the ranch the next day.

The bells on the door sang out as she entered the store, and she smiled in greeting to Cord. Meg stood before the bolts of fabric, picking out one for a new dress. Seeing Mandy, she set down the fabric and hurried to her friend.

"Where have you been?" she whispered. "I was worried."

Mandy hugged her friend. Spices, and sachets stuffed with flowers, wafted throughout the store, giving her a slight sense of melancholy. "I had to see the teachers." She reached out and squeezed Meg's hand. "I am sorry I worried you."

Meg smiled her acceptance of the apology. "What are you going to do about McCandle?"

Mandy moved to the rows of canned and jarred goods. The cans lined the shelves from the top to the counter. Heavy legs supported the open counter to take the weight off the shelves, and the skillets and china plates lay in front of them. Underneath the counter lay an assortment of butter churns, canning jars, milk pails and tools. Herbs and spices lined the shelves nearby.

Mandy picked out a can of peaches. Looking at the can, she frowned. "The *Grandmothers* tell me I will not marry McCandle."

Meg sagged against the counter in relief. She looked down at the iron pots, but Mandy knew she didn't see anything. Her thoughts were busy like a runaway freight train.

"Did they say *how* you are to escape him? I wish I could be as sure, as you are, of the *Grandmothers*' predictions." She put a hand on Mandy's arm. "How can you escape him? How will it ever be all right?"

Mandy met Meg's blue eyes—the depths much like shards of cracked glass. She loved the color. Looking into her friend's eyes, she always remembered the crystals. She saw the worry Meg held for her, shinning clearly there. "I am to marry someone else. I cannot explain, but McCandle will not win this time."

Meg wasn't fooled. "I can see you're not completely at peace with this."

Mandy picked up the cans of peaches, two at a time, and set them on the counter. "I'm completely at peace with the *Grandmothers* wisdom," she said, "but I cannot reconcile what it is I am supposed to do."

Meg picked up a couple cans and helped Mandy carry them to the counter. "Would this have anything to do with Hawk being in town?"

Mandy stilled and looked directly at her friend, as always, unsettled by her friend's innate insight. "Yes," she answered simply, watching Meg's face.

"He is the boy raised by the Lakota. The boy they call white Indian." Meg looked down. She raised her eyes and met Mandy's gaze. "The man in your visions."

Mandy sighed. "Yes." She resumed her quest for supplies, this time starting in on cans of baked beans.

Before Meagan could retort, the bells on the door rang, again, announcing another customer. Mandy turned to greet the new arrival and gasped before turning away.

The man's eyes were sharp with cruelty, unmistakable here in the west. She could only pray the trouble he sought did not lay here, in Cord's

To Tame a Wild Hawk

Mercantile, for evil rolled off him. Cruelty and evil were close, but different. Cruelty could be fought on a physical plane. Evil, however, was another matter.

His hair was long. He wore a close cut beard and a suit, currently layered in trail dust. She looked at Cord, but his eyes were on the cruel ones of the intruder. Her own widened in amazement at how calm he appeared and, in some way, his calm reached out to her.

When the stranger's eyes swept the store, Cord glanced at her, trying to warn her, with a slight jerk of his head, for them to run.

But the strangers deep, gravely voice growled, "She stays." And for the quiet way he'd stated it, something told Mandy not to put him to the test.

Cord tried a different tact. "Can I help you?"

"Yeah," the man answered so pleasantly, Mandy glanced at him in surprise.

A southern bred gentleman, she thought. Somehow, she questioned whether the southern bred manners extended beyond his soft voice.

"I want tobacco and new clothes to replace these. . . ." He gestured at his dusty suit. The stranger's icy, blue eyes lifted and moved between Mandy and Meg before settling on Mandy's face. "Oh, yes," his gaze narrowed on her, "and add her to the list."

A chill ran up Mandy's spine, and she stared at him. The danger she'd sensed lay at odds with his quiet voice. Something told her they were standing in the middle of quicksand, and someone was going down. His eyes remained like slices of the cold, blue sea. His hand snaked out and yanked her to him.

"Now, see here Mister. . . . " Cord started, and Meg made to step up too. The muzzle of a gun, pointing at him, brought them both up short. They had not seen the man move, but there was the gun just the same.

Yet the man's gaze never left Mandy's face.

The bell clattered again, and the stranger stepped behind Mandy, an arm snaking around her waist and yanking her to a granite-like chest. As the door swung shut, she heard the man's snarl in her ear, "Say hello, mister."

Chapter Three

It was, now, Mandy's turn to stare. And she stared, struck dumb, at the man who stood before them, now. He was a gunman. He stood not a dozen feet away, his hat low, concealing his face. But Mandy had a curling sensation in the pit of her belly, warning her of visions, unknown. He lifted his head as though in slow motion. Mandy stood, spellbound, caught in a murder's embrace, yet suddenly, aware of only one man. Shock set in as recognition slowly dawned, and came crashing around her head. He caught her gaze with his piercing, golden one, and Mandy would not have remained standing if not for the sinewy arm of the man holding her—with a gun to her head.

Hawk.

She heard the piercing cry of a red-tailed hawk as sure as if she were standing outside. She felt the wind batter his wings, felt them brush against her face.

The sun sliced through the span of his feathers as they swooped forward. Its, razor sharp, talons spread out, like the predator he was reaching for his prey.

Death was sure to follow.

She came rushing back into her body, staring at his clothes. For several seconds, no one spoke. She could hear only her own harsh breath.

Hawk.

He wore a suit. She could not reconcile this.

From her conversation with Hawk, last night in her hotel room, she realized the gunman, holding her captive, worked for McCandle.

Hawk continued to watch her in the way of his namesake. His gold-green eyes held a lethal calmness. His stance emphasized deadly power, coiled in his large frame. Her gaze dropped to his hands, then to the pistol strapped to his side. The warrior sought revenge, but Hawk used the way of his white heritage.

Grandmothers—I do not know this man.

Listen with your heart, child. You know him well.

She drew in a shaky breath. Her legs felt like the jelly she helped her Aunt Lydia can, every fall. She knew from the pinpoint lights behind her eyes, if this man didn't let up on her ribs, soon, she was going to pass out—and then, he would undoubtedly kill her.

She looked up to find Hawk's gaze riveted on her face. His gold-green eyes flickered over to Cord, and something, unnamed, moved between the men before taking in Meg, then settled back on Mandy.

His gaze moved over her with sensual ease. She flushed, then realized, he was baiting her. He wanted her angry. He wanted her ready. "What have you got yourself there, McKinney?" he drawled with lazy ease.

Mandy had to look at him, twice, to be sure that western twang had really come from him. Like the trickster coyote, he had many faces, but then, his words brought her back with roaring clarity. McKinney! *The McKinney.* The cold-blooded bank robber and killer of everyone who got in the way, *McKinney!* Her gaze clashed with Hawk's, once again. She would be ready.

She had to be.

She glanced at Meg, trying to convey, as best she could, to be ready.

McKinney snickered at Hawk's question. "Just a piece of fluff I plan to amuse myself with." He gave her ribs another painful squeeze. "She's a might skinny for my liking, I prefer my women a little more—filled out, but she'll do."

"Over my dead body," Mandy's voice was a hiss.

McKinney chuckled and gave her ribs, yet, another painful squeeze. "That can be arranged," he whispered this near her ear, his voice sensual. He could have been talking her out of her dress for the way he said it.

To Tame a Wild Hawk

Hawk's cold eyes took in McKinney for a moment and lowered to her, catching her gaze with his piercing one. Raising a brow, she heard two words ring clearly in her head.

Death wish.

McKinney pulled her tight against his chest. She felt his coiled hate beneath his mask of calm disdain—felt his curled anticipation. He was awaiting a *bloodbath*. He was looking forward to it. It was heady, nauseating in its beauty. Like a great cat tearing apart its prey. The taste of blood sending the great cat's senses taunt with knowledge of the upcoming feast.

"She's pretty though, isn't she Mister? You can have the one over there if you'd like." He nodded toward Meg.

"Oh, I don't know," Hawk's golden gaze pinned McKinney, once more, "I don't expect you'll be enjoying much of anything after today."

McKinney grinned, mean and nasty, and drained away the last of Mandy's fear. She centered herself and the room slanted. She saw herself held there, trapped in McKinney's embrace. She saw these things through Hawk's eyes.

And she waited.

"I'd nearly given up catching you," Hawk was saying. "I was even going to let you go. Imagine my surprise when you up and started to lead me here. Decided to turn yourself over to me or was your boss afraid I'd give up?"

McKinney laughed. He stood relaxed, nonchalant, as if he hadn't a care in the world. Except that he was holding Mandy prisoner, and he held a gun to her head, he sounded as though he were discussing the weather. It was infuriating. "Nope. Just got tired of waiting for the boss to give me the okay to kill you." He shrugged. "Nobody troubles me and lives to tell about it." He shrugged again, his smile easy. "Not even you."

"It's been a long time," Hawk said. Mandy realized he, too, was smiling. His eyes were pools of liquid gold. "Looks as though it's finally over. You're the end of the line."

McKinney snickered. "You haven't got me yet Hawk, and you'll never be free. You're good," McKinney said, sounding as though he were having a civil conversation . . . until you heard the words. "Real good. Too bad you have to die today."

The time was near.

Mandy let the mask, she had learned to wear so well, slip into place, the mask of the rancher's daughter, the mask of a western female, who now owned, and ran, a ranch. "Let go of me," she spat. "Then, you and your friend here can get on with your game. I have better things to do with my day." She stomped her foot. "Release me this instant!"

The hand around her waist squeezed tighter, and she flew into a wild fury. "Damn you, I said unhand me this instant!"

"Mandy!" Cord sputtered.

"I'm sorry. But if this foul brute doesn't release me this instant. . . . "

McKinney swung the gun first at Cord, then back. "Be still!" He actually laughed, and once more placed the gun against Mandy's head.

Mandy didn't know if it was the laugh, out of context with its surroundings, but she felt the warning clear to her toes, and quieted. McKinney was insane.

Hawk raised his brow, and she knew he asked if that was the best she could do. She shrugged her shoulders but, apparently, it was enough. Hawk's gun cleared leather in a blink of an eye. The shot clipped McKinney's ear. "Let go of her, McKinney."

McKinney didn't even blink. "Huh-uh, me and this pretty little thing are going to have a real good time."

What happened next was a blur to Mandy. McKinney swung her, leveling his gun at Hawk as he dove for cover. The bullet blasted into a jar and glass shattered everywhere. Cord dove to the floor, and Meg beat a hasty retreat behind the mounds of fabrics. Then, she saw Cord take after Meg—and breathed a sigh of relief that he meant to keep her friend safe—she could concentrate on the gunman—and the Hawk.

Mandy's ears roared from the gun's loud explosion so near to her ear, and her eyes watered from gun smoke.

"You don't even know why you're here, Mister!" McKinney bellowed this like a madman, hauling Mandy off the floor in his rage.

The switch in demeanor, from calm to rage, scared her more than his soft, southern voice. She didn't know which personality was worse, McKinney calm and insane—or enraged.

"You don't even know why I led you here." He looked down at his clothes, looking repulsed. "You've been a damn pain in my ass. Look at me! I haven't had a bath, or a decent meal, since I took this damn job. I'm going to have to kill you, Mister?"

To Tame a Wild Hawk

"Why *did* you take this job?" Hawk asked this from behind the counter of canned goods. "Who put you, and your renegade friends, up to visiting that particular plantation?" Hawk enunciated.

McKinney laughed at this, the calm, southern gentleman firmly back in place. He shrugged. "It was war. It was easy money."

There was a poignant pause. "You all took turns with a young, pretty blond there," Hawk's voice was flat. "You used her up and left her to die."

"So what?" She felt McKinney shrug. "It was—just a job." McKinney grinned. "A job meant to get you—here. And it worked." McKinney shifted Mandy's weight against his hip. She knew he was now looking for an angle. "You shouldn't have let it matter so much. Now, look where you are."

"I could have killed you an instant ago," Hawk drawled, softly. "But it's funny. I wanted you to know why you're about to die." He didn't say anything else for several seconds, and for the first time, Mandy felt the unease in McKinney.

"Do you even remember the six-year-old boy you tied to a tree because he tried to help his ma? I found him two days later. They we're all dead—all but the little boy. He died in my arms from the wounds you and your men had inflicted on his body." Hawk paused, then bit out, "Six years old. Did you see him as a threat?"

"I remember." McKinney shrugged. "The woman was real good. The kid? Well—the kid—was a pest."

Hawk walked out from behind the wall of supplies—his gun leveled at McKinney. It was clear he was through talking.

McKinney laughed. But it was equally clear he was grasping for the same level of levity he'd used earlier. He seemed to realize this at the same moment Mandy did—and switched tactics. "You stupid fool! The only question is, why was it so easy to get you to come back here? What could the woman, and the boy, possibly mean to you?"

Mandy waited for an answer. She *wanted* to hear his answer, but it never came.

Hawk's face went impassive, his gaze riveted to Mandy's. *Life is a continuous circle, and many paths are entwined.*

Mandy peaked up at McKinney. His eyes were brutal. Even to a man who knew the unforgiving in an unforgiving territory, they breathed the unforgivable. The unseen. His laugh was cruel, like a man who saw, clearly, the moment when he knew he tasted victory. "Bet you want to know who hired me."

Hawk's eyes were cold as the northern sea. His gaze dropped to Mandy's.

Mandy met his gaze, remembering her words to him at the hotel. *The path which has been crossed, crosses between you and me—and your revenge.*

Mandy braced herself. "He knows, McKinney."

McKinney's arm slacked in surprise. "Wh-hat?"

Mandy's gaze never left Hawks. "He knows." She went completely still—waiting.

McKinney's jaw jerked up-and-down like a cow chewing its cud, unable to reconcile his loss of control.

"Let her go, McKinney," Hawk's voice held no more emotion than he would show to life for one so without.

McKinney snarled, but his words lay limp between them. "What? You going to kill this woman too?" His gun left Mandy's head with lightening speed.

But not fast enough.

A gun exploded. Blood spattered all over Mandy. She heard a gurgle of surprise from McKinney, and he abruptly let her go.

She stumbled forward.

She turned as though in slow motion, her hands to her mouth from what she saw. She bent and ran for the back door.

Meg followed and held her while she sucked in deep breaths of fresh air into her lungs. When they heard the volley of shots from the front, they both ran on shaky legs back to the front of the store.

"Now what's happening?" Meg yelled at Cord.

"They were waiting for him," Cord shot back and dove to stop Mandy from going out the door.

Mandy fought him, staring out of the window in horror, wanting to turn away but unable to obey her brain's simple command.

Cord worked to restrain her. "Were you saying something about death wishes?" he said to Meg, grabbing Mandy around the middle and yanking her away from the door.

To Tame a Wild Hawk

Meg raised a brow. "Who? Me? No. I believe that is what Hawk said." She indicated out the window.

Mandy wouldn't contemplate how they had heard those words until much later. But, for now, Hawk stood on one side of his horse. The horse, wounded, buckled, as though slammed from some unseen force, and went down. Hawk, himself, had been shot at least once that Mandy could see.

One man lay in the street, another on the opposite sidewalk. Neither was moving.

As Mandy watched, Hawk dropped another from the roof, with the rifle he'd removed from his scabbard. Then, all was quiet, except from his horse's pained cries.

She watched as Hawk stroked the horse—tears rolling down her face. He was saying, goodbye. He drew his pistol, and she turned her head. She heard the shot; felt the deafening silence that filled the empty space left behind, where only moments before chaos had been the driving force. Only then, did she realize how bad Hawk, himself, had been shot.

She shook off Cord's hands and raced out the door. When she was within a few feet of him, she stopped. Hawk's gun hung loosely in his grip as though his world had collapsed. His shoulders were pressed down as if by an unseen weight. "How is it I did not sense the trap?" he got out between clenched teeth when he noticed her. The gun slipped from his fingers. His knees buckled, and he went down beside his horse.

Meg yelled for the doc at the gathering crowd.

Mandy knelt over Hawk. There was a bullet in his shoulder, but he also had one that appeared to have passed through his right side, and there was blood everywhere. She brought his head to her lap. "It is McCandle," she whispered. "He's been in touch with someone. I'm sorry—I did not realize to what extent, until now—I sensed something new in him—but I could not get a clear sense of what."

Hawk sucked in a breath, belying the depth of his pain. "Be careful, Mandy. You will be especially vulnerable now—watch even those you trust, for you do not know who the teacher is." At the look of worry in her eyes, he added. "I will live—." He flinched and took a deep breath, nearly arching from the spasm that tore through his body. "Someone has betrayed us…" He closed his eyes.

Mandy leaned over, close to his ear. "I will be careful." She accepted a blanket from someone in the crowd and placed it under his head. Meg worked to stop the bleeding, pressing one cloth hard to his shoulder wound, the other to the wound in his side.

Meg caught Mandy's eye. "You work hard to save a man you've only just met, even if you do know him from your dreams."

"So do you," Mandy challenged.

Meg shrugged. "Like he said, be careful Mandy."

Mandy looked up into her friend's concerned expression. "I will." Looking down at Hawk, she studied his face. "Do you want me to send for the teachers?"

"No." He clenched his teeth, opening his eyes and catching hers with a steely gaze. "It would be too dangerous for them. Besides," he reached up and tugged on one of her loose curls, "I have you."

Mandy caught herself just short of a full-blown panic. "I'm only an apprentice," she whispered. "There's much I do not know."

"You know enough." Hawk drew in a sharp breath, then mercifully, he passed out.

Cord shouldered his way, then, through the growing crowd with more cloth in his hands. "Sheriff Tucker is going to want a good explanation for this," he muttered in an undertone. "And when he finds out Hawk was hunting McKinney...."

Mandy caught his meaning, but the Doc appeared before she could reply.

Seeing Hawk's face, Mandy heard him mutter an oath of surprise. He quickly assessed Hawk's wounds. He put a finger in the shoulder wound, then the wound that passed through Hawk's side, moving it this way and that. "Lucky." She heard him mumble. "He'll be a mite sore, but the bullets didn't hit noth'n vital." He lifted the cloth and looked again. "Yep, damn lucky."

Mandy didn't know why, but she didn't like the fact he had put his finger in Hawk's wound like that. Still, she was relieved the bullet hadn't hit anything vital. She breathed in such a sigh of relief, it had him looking sharply at her. She ignored the questioning look in his eyes. "What about the one that hit his side? How do you know it didn't hit anything?"

"Passed clear on through, plenty of damage, but it'll mend. Important thing is, it went out the other side—and it missed his guts. Seen all kinds of damage done with the bullets hit the guts. Lucky," he muttered again, then dropped his voice to a near whisper. "Better we get him out of these clothes."

Mandy searched his face for an explanation, but he said no more.

To Tame a Wild Hawk

"You boys," he pointed out four good-sized men, "carry him to my office. Man's lost enough blood as it is. That's the biggest danger to him, right now, can't afford to lose much more."

When they reached the office, Doc Mallory barked out orders. Hot water, bandages, needles and thread. Laudanum, alcohol and clean cloth. It was longest hour of Mandy's life. She didn't want to examine why, this morning, she had almost hoped he would go, let her find another way to deal with McCandle. Now, she felt as though her life's breath would leave her if he were to die.

There was so much blood, the wound in his shoulder, deep. Doc had warned her of fever. And Hawk had said she couldn't endanger the teachers by sending for them.

He had proven to be a quick, deadly gunman, but that wasn't his true power.

Trickster coyote.

Doc Mallory, true to his word, immediately disposed of Hawk's clothes. She closed her eyes and felt the shock of the man in her dreams, the white Indian dressed in white man's clothes, now lying, shot, in the next room. She sensed the danger, clear to her core. His gun-hand was convenient for her revenge—but it wasn't the reason she wanted him to live. She sensed the whirling emotions lying close to her breast—felt the pounding of her heart deep in her chest.

At least it wasn't the only reason.

Chapter Four

Mandy slid down into her seat out in the waiting room. She looked down at the blood splattered on her bodice. Damp tendrils of hair escaped their confines and, now, clung to her neck and forehead. She leaned back in the cane chair in the tiny waiting room.

Four chairs sat against one wall, next to a desk that sat by the front door. Four more chairs sat across from her. The room, where the doctor did surgery, was off to her right. Next to the surgery room, a staircase led to rooms upstairs, where patients who were recovering were kept.

Mandy glanced up as the sheriff entered. She'd heard he'd just ridden in from the trail, where he'd been following some cattle rustlers for the last two days.

Sheriff Tucker was a man once bigger than life. Now, he was gray, years ahead of his time. Losing his wife seemed to take all the life out of him. Her heart clenched at the thought of all the pain he'd suffered. There was something odd about his wife's death—she wouldn't rest if McCandle had his hands in this too.

Lines of exhaustion etched deep tracks into his face. Dust lay in the crevices of his buckskin jacket. He moved with the precision of a man impatient to know why someone had shot up his town while he'd been absent.

He wasn't going to like this.

Lenore Wolfe

He stared down at her face for a long moment before raking a hand through his hair. "Hate to put you through anymore, Miss Kane. Need to hear your version of what happened." He nodded towards the sleeping man in the next room.

Mandy wanted to laugh. Sheriff Tucker, for the kind way he'd asked that, looked as though he wanted to throttle her.

Tucker had come to know her in the past two years, since McCandle had first started coming after her father's ranch. He knew she was trouble. Folks around town made innuendos about her being a witch. This infuriated the sheriff. She bit her lip. She wasn't about to go down without a fight, and she couldn't change. Poor Tucker. She'd made things hard on him. She hadn't meant to. But to get to McCandle—she'd had no choice but to side-step the sheriff.

Mandy had been thinking about Cord's warning throughout the surgery. She wasn't about to let the sheriff chase Hawk out of town. Not now. The *Grandmothers'* words kept ringing in her ears. Whatever happened, no matter her reservations about the marriage to take place, she knew that she would follow the path set before her. So she'd tell the truth—but only in part.

She slipped on the familiar mask of the young white woman in a town out west. "I came into Cord's Mercantile to get a few things I had forgotten. That awful man, Hawk shot...."

"Hawk?" he interrupted with raised eyebrows. His eyes quickly swung to the sleeping form in the next room and back to her. "Heard it was him, just didn't believe it. *Do you realize who the Hawk is?* He's the white-Indian who grew up with the Lakota!"

"Yes, of course I know who he is? Who, from around here, wouldn't?" she snapped. She rubbed her damp palms through the folds of her dress, centering herself, restoring calm to the rapid tempo of her heartbeat.

Not even paying attention to her temper, the sheriff sat down, heavily, on a cane back chair across from her, setting his Stetson on his knee. Wearily, he shook his head and muttered more to himself, "I thought he was dead or at least long gone from these parts."

Mandy swallowed, again, through the lump in her throat that wouldn't go down. "Is he wanted for something, sheriff?"

"No." He gave her a hard look. "No, I wish that were so." His eyes narrowed on her.

"Well." Mandy smiled, relief flooding her body, then she sobered. "That man he shot, he—grabbed me. He told Cord he was going to—was going to. . . . " She put her hands over her hot cheeks.

He raised an eyebrow in Meg's direction. "Is that what you'd say, Miss Anderson?"

Meg pushed herself away from the door jamb she'd been leaning against.

Mandy took a deep breath. She hadn't realized Meg was there. That rattled her. She never allowed herself to be so unaware of her surroundings. She caught the questioning look in Meg's crystal blue eyes.

At length, Meg answered the sheriff. "That's what happened, Sheriff. He was going to hurt Mandy—if you know what I mean. If the Hawk, there," she nodded toward the room where Hawk lay, "hadn't come in when he did. . . ." her voice trailed off.

Sheriff Tucker looked back at Mandy, concern evident in his eyes. "Did he harm you, Miss Kane?"

Mandy let out the breath, she hadn't been aware she'd been holding, and whispered a promise, to up above, she would let Meg know more of what the *Grandmothers'* had to say.

"No. Thanks to . . . Thanks to. . . ." Mandy nodded towards the bed where Hawk lay, a delayed reaction to everything causing her voice to shake.

Meg glanced at her, a worried frown on her face. "Cord told him to leave her alone," Meg told to the Sheriff. "But McKinney. . . ."

"McKinney!" Trucker's face showed more than a little surprise. *"The McKinney?"*

"Yes," Cord answered him from the doorway, where he was toweling his hands, *"the McKinney.* He stuck a gun to Mandy's head, said he was going to have some fun with her."

Tucker turned to him. "You heard what these ladies were telling me?"

Cord's brow furrowed. Throwing the towel aside, he scratched his jaw. "Most of it."

Tucker stood to face Cord, leaning his thigh against the desk where the doc greeted his patients. He dropped his hat on the desk, and folding his arms across his chest, he waited, finally glaring at Cord with impatience. "Well, do you have anything to add?"

Cord stood a moment, hands on hips, and met the sheriff's glare with a look of unconcern, a deep frown on his face. "Just that, if the Hawk hadn't come when he did—Hawk told him to let her go, and there was a lot of gun fire. When McKinney was dead, Hawk went outside, and there was a bunch waiting to jump him. They must have taken him by surprise—because he had to use his horse for a shield."

Mandy winced at his words. Out here a man's horse sometimes became his best friend. Some treated their horse better than they did themselves. They really couldn't afford to do less. A man's horse meant his life. Without it, he could well be dead. That still didn't stop some from abusing theirs.

"Did the Hawk recognize McKinney?"

"Yes," Mandy answered, then winced when she realized what she'd revealed. She was glad he hadn't been looking at her when she'd said it. She was sure her face had given her thoughts away.

"How did Hawk know McKinney?" Tucker rounded on her, hitting uncomfortably close to the truth.

Without glancing at Mandy, Cord answered evenly, "I guess a warrior like Hawk would make it his business to know."

"Yeah." Tucker's steely gaze moved over the Hawk, still as death, under some blankets on the surgery table in the next room. "I imagine so." He looked at Mandy. "You reckon that's what you'd say?"

Mandy glanced at Cord, then back at the Sheriff. "Seems right."

"Then, how come *I didn't recognize him* under all that trail dust—*and hair?*"

Mandy didn't back down. "Maybe Hawk had the bad luck to cross McKinney's path before?"

"I suppose." Tucker rubbed two days growth of stubble on his face. "But, I've seen McKinney before, and he didn't look noth'n like the man I saw outside, laid up in the pine box. His eyes narrowed on Mandy. "Heard a tale." He scratched the stubble on his face, once more. "Heard, wherever you see the Hawk, you see this one particular gunman." He watched Mandy's face closely.

This time she was ready—and she revealed nothing in the steady gaze she returned.

Tucker half smiled. "I don't cotton, much, to tales." He moved to the door. "If you think of anything else?" he eyed the three of them.

Mandy answered first, "Of course, Sheriff. You'll be the first to know."

To Tame a Wild Hawk

The sheriff picked up his Stetson, his eyes on her, studying her for another long, uncomfortable moment. Then, doffing his hat, he walked out the door, slamming it behind him and sending the doorbell jangling.

The three of them let out a collective breath.

"The man's too sharp." Cord sank onto the same cane-back chair the sheriff had occupied moments before. "I'd say he missed his calling. He should have been a lawyer."

Meg sat down beside Mandy, studying her face for a moment. "What are you up to?"

Mandy closed her eyes. When she opened them, she stood on a prairie.

A small child stood screaming, and a young boy stood to help her, but in the next instant a bullet struck her down. The boy's knees buckled, and he sank to the ground in a heap. Open mouthed, he stared at the man who held the gun. "Papa," he mouthed. Paralyzed, he watched him wrack another bullet into the chamber. His father lifted the rifle and took aim. He followed the direction his father pointed it in.

No!

Mandy fought for her equilibrium, slamming her way back into reality. She sucked in huge breaths of air, fighting to calm her racing heart.

"What, Mandy?" Meg demanded.

Tears slid unheeded down Mandy's face. "It is enough, yet there will be more. The price has already been too high."

"It was self-defense, Mandy," Meg reminded her.

Cord leaned forward, frowning hard at Mandy. "One of these days," he bit out, "the two of you are going to let me in on your little secret."

Meg gave him a completely innocent look, her brows raised in mock question. "What secret, Cord? I was simply saying, the sheriff would realize Hawk shot McKinney in self-defense. Do you believe differently?"

Mandy bit back a watery smile. Several times, Cord had been there when she'd had a vision. Several more times, he'd had witnessed unusual occurrences. Each time, Meg had acted as though she hadn't seen a thing, even when he'd demanded she admit that she had. Cord would have Meg's hide when he finally learned the truth. And somehow, Mandy knew . . . *he would learn the truth.*

Cord growled under his breath. "True." The look he pinned on Meg promised retribution. "But he'd been hunting McKinney for months. You know Tucker wouldn't have cottoned to that. He'd have run him out of town."

Meg glared at Cord, sitting forward in her chair. "He would have thought Hawk had done us all a favor," she said—as if they were not sitting there leading a double conversation.

Cord's eyes narrowed on Meg, reminding Mandy of an angry mountain lion. "Not Tucker! He's too much by-the-book for that."

Mandy watched Meg, waiting for her answer. As always, she watched these conversations between Meg and Cord with curiosity. She wondered how they could be so unaware of the chemistry between them. But, whenever, she broached the subject with Meg—well, let's just say, Meg denied it, with the same passion she was firing at Cord right now.

"He started it, did it for his own revenge, Cord," Meg retorted. "But he did end up saving us! He didn't have a choice in the end. It was self-defense!"

Mandy shook her head.

Cord's jaw throbbed, a sure indication of his anger. He leaned closer, putting them, nearly, nose-to-nose in the small office space. "Yeah," he stated evenly, "I, too, think Hawk could use a break. *I-kinda-like-the man!*"

Meg's chin rose a notch. Her crystal blue eyes lit with fire. "Yeah—well, I think he could *wind up being trouble*. But I guess we'll have to *wait and see*, won't we!" At that, she seemed to catch herself. She looked at Mandy and flushed.

Mandy nearly smiled. Did they even realize they had wound up switching sides in their argument? She raised both eyebrows at Meg in an, *I told you so*, manner.

Meg went for the, innocent, I didn't see that, look. Leaning back in her chair, she stared at the floor, feigning deep thought before looking at Mandy. "But I want to know what plan you've got rolling around in your head this time."

Mandy shook her head. *Oh, no, you don't,* her eyes told Meg, *nice try*. And Meg blushed. She stood to give her friend a moment, though she knew Cord would not do the same. Walking to the door of Hawk's room, she watched him for a moment. "I don't know how this will all work out. The only thing I know, for sure, is it's meant to be."

"Meant to be what?"

Mandy, her back still to her friends, smiled, knowing the reaction *that* question would get him. She waited for the next round, but only heard him mutter *"never mind"* under his breath. And she detected the word, *women*, which went unsaid.

Mandy turned back. "One day, it will all be clear. But for now, you will have to trust—I know what I'm doing."

Chapter Five

Mandy stood at the door of Doc's office. She needed to get started in helping Hawk to heal. More than that, she needed a moment alone. She needed to think. Visions pressed behind her eyes. Visions she did not want to see. Visions she did not want to think about. *Visions of Hawk. Visions of children beside him. His children—her children.*

Grandmothers, how can this be? What kind of future could we have? Hawk, having been raised by the Lakota and Cheyenne—I, having spent years with them. What will happen to us? Raising our children in a white man's world—in the way of the Lakota.

"Mandy?"

"Yes, Meg." She blinked hard to clear away the visions. Scrambling to pull her thoughts together, she hugged her childhood friend, wondering how to best answer her friend, yet keep her from realizing how troubled she felt. "I have told Doc I will help him," she stepped out on the boarded walk into the sunshine, her face away from Meg and Cord. "And you, Meg, already have to care for your grandmother, and you, Cord, your store."

"Mandy. . . ." Meg tried again. Then, let her off the hook. "You'll let me know if you need any help?"

Mandy smiled her relief. "I'll be fine," she reassured her. "Right now, I'm going to see to our patient. I'll be over to see you when I can."

Meg hugged her, and Mandy was grateful, knowing she had her friend's full support. Cord also hugged her and left for his store, and Mandy went back into the office, firmly closing the door behind her. She stood a moment, her gaze fixed on the door, fighting the visions. Finally, with a shake of her head, she began straightening the office, then set about to make Hawk more comfortable. She cleaned up all traces of the operation and set about tucking him in. Finally, she stood back, taking in his sleeping form.

The room shifted, and she stepped sideways to regain her balance. Blinking hard, she took in the walls around her. She stood in a room, where the outside walls were made of large logs. Panic invaded her senses. Danger lay all around her. Running to the door, she tried to pull it open, but it was locked. She banged on the door, yelling for someone to help. She turned with her back to the door, wildly looking for a way out. A boarded up window lay across the north wall. She ran up to it and tore at the boards, to no avail. She stared at her fingers, her nails busted, and her fingers bleeding. She swallowed hard—trying desperately to still the vortex of the tornado of fear, which whipped her about—fighting to center herself.

But she didn't know where the danger lay. She didn't know which way to turn, which way to run.

And the Grandmothers' voices seemed to be all around her, warning her to beware.

"Where are you, Mandy? Tell me what you see?" a voice commanded her.

Mandy's gaze flew to the Hawk's, widening in surprise to see his intense gaze on her.

She tore her gaze from his, staring at the room around her. She stood in Doc's clinic, in front of Hawk's bed. She shook her head, gathering her senses. "How long. . . . I mean. . . . *how are you awake?* I saw the doc give you the dose of laudanum, myself."

He started to move but seemed to think better of it. With a wince, he relaxed into his pillow. His lips pressed together for a moment, belying the depth of his pain. "He only did so for the sheriff's sake. He breathed through the discomfort. "He knew how I'd feel if he *really* gave me any of that. . . . " He scowled at the bottle of laudanum setting on the table beside his bed.

Mandy shifted. His cold expression towards a harmless medicine left her little doubt about why any man would want to run if he were truly riled—then, her mouth dropped open. You know the doc?" She shook her head.

Hawk tried, again, to sit and fell back, biting back a groan, his lips white around the edges. "Where were you, Amanda? You were in danger. I could feel it rolling off you. Where were you?"

She stood for a moment, not hearing him.

His deep voice pulled her back. "Mandy?"

To Tame a Wild Hawk

The room seemed, somehow, disjointed. Her body unraveled. Several things came together, in her mind, at once. She stood there, fighting his question, and, his uncanny ability to see right through her. "How long have you been awake?"

She gasped at him, realizing, a slow shock settling deep inside her. She could hide nothing from him. Where did that leave her?

"Come here, Amanda."

Her feet moved of their own accord. "Over here, where I can see you," he said, when she would have stopped.

She moved to stand near him. When she reached his side, his hand snaked out and grabbed her wrist, giving her a hard yank, setting her off balance, so she landed, hard, on his chest. He winced in pain, but his hand moved to hold her there, with gentle, yet unmovable, bands of muscle.

She was caught, and she didn't want to explore *that* idea too much.

"Where were you? His unusual green eyes mere inches from hers. His breath fanned her face.

She could feel her heartbeat, mingling with the beat of his. Her pulse raced. Her own heart was beating an erratic rhythm in her breast, and she was sure he could feel it—and that it told him everything.

"Tell me, Mandy?" he whispered.

She went weak. A delicious headiness stole over her, curling in the pit of her stomach. A soul deep need, she couldn't name, coursed through her veins.

"Tell me about the vision you were having?"

"Tell," she licked her lips, "you?"

That was her undoing, or maybe, it was his. He crushed her lips to his in a powerful kiss. Light exploded in Mandy's head. She could feel the heat from his body coursing through her own. With a sigh, she opened her mouth to him. He immediately plundered her soft mouth, tasting her, sipping at her sweet mouth as if it were nectar.

Fully possessing her.

His hands moved over her back. One stroked the sensitive flesh of the underside of her breast, and Mandy's defenses were stripped from her. She only knew of the intense feelings he was creating in her.

The sound of someone clearing their throat caused them to jump apart, and Mandy stood quickly.

Hawk groaned.

Mandy's bit her lip. She did not want to turn around and see who had caught them in such a compromising position.

"Bloody, hell," Hawk growled.

Mandy stared down at him, fractured. The Doc loved that English expression. He had everyone in town saying it. Yet that thought was lost as her face went up in flames, and it took every ounce of strength she had to turn and face Doc Mallory.

But he only chuckled. "Maybe I should have given you the laudanum after all," he directed at Hawk.

Mandy wished she could fade away, right there—even to faint—but she had never fainted in her life. Hawk hurt as he was—and her—oh, what could Doc be thinking?

She knew what he must think.

And what had gotten into her anyway, letting him kiss her that way?

"He's not a helpless boy, Mandy dear. That's why I didn't give him the laudanum. Do you remember the scars on his chest?"

Mandy only nodded, remembering the scars she'd seen during surgery. She let him talk. She needed the distraction. She did not tell him she'd seen those types of scars before.

"He has undergone the most painful ceremonies I've ever known. Those little bullet holes don't measure up to that."

Hawk scowled at him, and Mandy was amazed to watch the little man grin at him.

"When I met Hawk," he went on, "he was only eighteen years old. He'd spent the last twelve years of his life with the Lakota. A white man's disease had wiped out over half his tribe, including most of his family."

"I'm sure she's not interested in this, Mallory," Hawk had growled this at Doc, but he watched her, and his eyes promised he would know of the danger she had sensed.

To Tame a Wild Hawk

She looked away, unable to meet his gold-green gaze. She wanted to cover herself as if she were stripped naked and standing before him. He seemed to look right through her—know all her secrets.

Doc chuckled. "Sure she is, look at her. "Now let's see, where was I," he went on, "oh yeah, Hawk had decided to find out about his old world, but he was dressed as an Indian. Look at him. Except for those unusual eyes of his, little would give him away."

Hawk looked over, glared at Doc, but turned back, before she could escape, and continued to hold her captive, with eyes that seemed to see through to her soul. She stood, poised to escape as a small bird, caught in the mesmerizing, green-gold, gaze of a mountain cat, who crouched, watching, ready to devour her the instant she moved.

She did not.

"His momma was Spanish," Doc continued with his story. "His poppa, well, the only thing he's ever said about him was he was a big man with blond hair and unusual spring, green eyes. He's gotten something from each as you can see for yourself.

Then, Doc became serious, and he looked at the floor. "Anyway, when I found him, a bad bunch had gotten hold of him and taught him a whole new concept of pain. He was near death, and you'd have never recognized him.

Mandy vaguely wondered what kind of pain could surpass Lakota ceremonies, and bullet holes, and shuttered at the thought of him enduring it. Hawk gave her an imperceivable nod as if to say she would know, with promised retribution, if she did not tell him what he wanted to know.

"I took him in, taught him the white man's ways, helped him find his family." The old doc turned to Hawk, now, a deep sadness etched his face. "I heard you were after those men for what they did."

Mandy watched Hawk at the mention of this. Why was he after these men for what had happened on that plantation?

Hawk looked away, releasing Mandy. He turned his yellow-gold gaze on Doc.

The doc had his full attention now.

"Leave it alone, Mallory!"

Doc Mallory shook his head. "Don't be bitter, boy. It's over now. Let it go."

For one unguarded second, Mandy saw all the pain, living in his closely guarded heart, then the shutters went down. "Get out, *both of you.*"

"We're going, lad. You rest easy, now." Doc put a hand on Mandy's shoulder, breaking her out of her trance, guiding her to the door. He turned to shut it behind them. "Really. Rest now, Hawk. It's over."

Chapter Six

Blackness blanketed his mind like a cloak. A spindled hand of pain crawled its way along his body, like jagged glass embedded beneath the skin. Grabbing him by his arm, unseen claws moved to drag him down a deep, black hole. Hawk did not have to look, to know, the hole held a bottomless, darkness that threatened to swallow him and keep him there forever. He fought, calling on the steady drum beats of the Ancients, combining the beat with the heart of the earth with the steady beat of his own heart. He concentrated on that beat with all his might. If that beat were to stop, then so, too, would his life in this world be at end.

Black beasts rose in liquid fire. They sniffed the air as though catching a scent. He could only watch as they turned from him, heading for someone. He saw her in the same moment as the beast, her hair lifting, floating around her as though caught by a breeze. Her gray-green eyes locked with his. He sensed the beast, sensed the primal hunger. The claws of pain sank deep into his arm as he fought to tear free—fought to reach her. She stood fearless, watching the beast. In an instant, it was upon her. The beast headed down the dark hole of nothingness. Looking at the Hawk, it pulled her down after him. Her gaze remained steady, locked with his—as she sank from his sight.

"You should have got out," he raged. "It's too late. I can't save you. And it's too late for me. The white man's hell will claim me for all I have done."

He thrashed at the prison, which anchored him. The claws of pain entered his arm and threaded their way through him, layering him, like the bark on a tree, until it consumed him. This was not the way. This smelled of the danger he'd sensed for too long. This oozed of the evil he'd fought. He had taken his vengeance too far—and lost his soul.

Mandy woke in the still of the night with a jerk. Blinking hard, she peered through the fuzz of deep sleep, trying to orient herself. When she realized where she was, her gaze shot to Hawk, breathing a sigh of relief when he groaned. His groaning must have been what woke her.

He licked his lips, and she brought him a glass of water. She touched his forehead. He had developed a fever. With a sigh of disappointment, Mandy realized he was, more than just a little, hot to the touch. She sat for a moment chewing on her lip. Finally, it occurred to her, she was feeling sorry for herself. Disgusted, she busied herself, straightening his sheets. She picked up the glass for a refill. When he spoke, she nearly dropped it on him.

"Woman, what was the danger you sensed?" His voice sounded, surprisingly, strong.

"I uh. . . ." Mandy searched for an answer. "What is the danger you dreamed of?" she countered.

His eyebrow cocked. He tried to rise, failed, and fell back. "I believe they are intertwined." Almost as an afterthought, he peered at her. "I cannot work like this. Knowing you are in danger, and me—trapped in this bed."

"Go to sleep, Hawk," Mandy told him. "You're hot and in a lot of pain. We'll talk when you're better."

"I have to get out of here." He tried, again, to sit up.

Mandy pushed him back against the pillows. She felt the heat of him, the granite hard muscles, beneath her hands. She pulled away as if burned—trying to determine if the heat she felt had been his fever—or hers.

Mandy stood and mixed some herbs into his glass of water and pressed it to his lips. "Drink Hawk," she softly commanded. He drank. He leaned back, sinking deep into the pillows. Mandy walked to the highboy dresser. Setting down the glass, she reached for a fresh blanket.

"When I'm healed, I'm going to blister your backside for not telling me what I want to know."

Mandy gasped in shock at his crude remark. *That* had not come from the Hawk she knew him to be. Even if the Hawk she knew, she knew only from her dreams. When she finally gathered up the courage to turn around, it was to find him asleep.

"Of all the nerve," she muttered. "Toss out a challenge like that and fall asleep before I can yell at you." She covered him with the blanket. Picking up the pitcher, she blew out the lamp and went out for fresh water.

To Tame a Wild Hawk

Not seeing the grin on the, so-called, sleeping man she'd left behind in the dark.

Three days later, an exhausted Mandy poured herself a cup of hot, steaming coffee in the little kitchen off the corner of the house. It was even too early for the rosters to be up, she thought, fighting to keep her eyes open. Her eyelids felt as though they were filled with gritty sand, which spiraled endlessly in the heat of the sun.

She, and the doc, had battled with Hawk's nightmares, and his fever, for three days now. They took turns, day and night, to keep Hawk's fever down; yet, they appeared no closer to helping Hawk win against the fever that threatened to take his life.

Every bone in her body felt weighted down with fatigue. She had no idea what was keeping her on her feet.

She was staring at the wall when Meg walked in a few minutes later.

"You look exhausted, Mandy. Why do you not allow someone to give you a break?"

Mandy turned and smiled wearily at her best friend.

Meagan studied her for what seemed to be an interminable moment. "So how are things going?" she prodded.

Mandy let out a sigh of frustration. "He seems determined to die."

Meg frowned at her. "Why on earth would he want to do that?"

"I have no idea." A deep sadness took Mandy over for a moment. She shook her head to break out of her thoughts. "You want a cup of coffee?" She started to rise.

"You sit. I'll get it."

Meagan crossed the room and got a cup out of the whitewashed, board cupboard. She poured herself some of the hot brew and sat down in a creaky wooden chair.

"He's full of nightmares, Meg." Mandy wanted to bury her head in her hands. She wanted to cry. She did neither.

Meg's eyes narrowed on her. "It sounds as though you care quite a bit, Mandy."

Mandy surprised herself by shrugging.

"This is the man you've been telling Ashley, for years now, is your future, your fiancé." It wasn't a question. "I thought you made all that up. I should have made the connection between him and your dreams."

Mandy looked at her friend and sighed. "I did make that up." She pulled a face and picked up her cup. "And I didn't." She let the memories of many dreams float lazily through her mind, like white puffy clouds on a beautiful, warm day. "I have had these dreams for several years now, since I lived with the Lakota. The teachers taught me much about dreaming and our many spirit helpers—and most especially, about the *Grandmothers*. I knew the dreams meant something. I knew this was supposed to be the man I'd, someday, marry." Mandy let her cup fall back in the saucer with a clatter, which seemed to rouse her out of her deep thoughts. She shrugged again. "But these dreams seemed contradicted, lately, when everything that's been happening has indicated I would marry McCandle. I was afraid to believe, and, even more, afraid to reach out and take hold of my destiny. Now I know the things I saw in my dream were meant to be. We *will* fight McCandle." She sobered. "But not without much death."

"So this *Hawk* is your destiny," Meg whispered, a knowing look in her eyes, a small, knowing, smile touching her lips.

Mandy winced at the question. The white Indian had chosen to dress as a gunman to hunt his enemy. That was the way of the path. It gave him the opportunity to hunt his enemy in a white man's world, without bringing more bloodshed on the Lakota.

Meagan sipped at her tea for a moment. Finally, she lifted her head and looked Mandy directly in the eye. "You know, after what we witnessed in the store, he's likely done some terrible things?"

Mandy stood and set her cup and saucer in the porcelain sink. "Yes, I know." She looked at her friend. "There is meaning behind everything we do. For Hawk, this means somewhere in his life, he was thrust into a bad situation and played the hand he was dealt."

"Hmmm, and how did you get so wise?" Meg gently teased.

"I've been listening."

A worry frown worked its way across Meg's face. "Mandy, you have to admit, it has all moved rather quickly. . . . "

"He is to be my husband."

Meagan's mouth dropped open, and Mandy reached up and gently closed it.

To Tame a Wild Hawk

Meg shook her head. "I know." she almost whispered, looking down at her hands. "And I suspected you were going to say that, again, even though you didn't put it in those *exact* words before. But in Cord's store, he was a gunslinger. And you know, and I know, he's played that part before—been dressed in those clothes before. Aren't you afraid of what that means?" Meg's cracked glass, blue eyes were intent with earnest. "It means you are to marry a white Indian with a hidden agenda," she went on, "masquerading as a gunslinger. And from what I saw," she emphasized her point by leaning in towards Mandy, "he's good at it." She stood and moved closer to Mandy. "Is this really supposed to be any better than marrying McCandle? Tell me if I am wrong. Because, I fail to see how trading in the one killer, for another, is supposed to make your predicament better."

"I know, Meg." Mandy took friend's hand in hers. "But I have loved this man all my life."

Meagan's mouth dropped open for the second time.

"We have been together in other lifetimes," Mandy went on. "And together, we will defeat McCandle in this lifetime, too, from the path he has been on for far too long. This time we must win, once and for all. This cannot be allowed to go around, again, for another lifetime. And here, he has been allowed to reign as a powerful cattle baron, terrorizing families, for much too long."

Meg frowned. "I'm always amazed at how well you remember the lives you have lived before this one." She looked deflated and happy at the same time. "I hope I will feel, what you feel, one day, even for a little while. To love a man for many lifetimes. . . ." She shook her head in wonder.

It was Mandy's turn to frown. "You're not going to marry that man your father arranged for you, are you Meg?"

"Will I have a choice? When I'm penniless and begging in the streets?"

"I would *never* let that happen to you! Don't you dare *marry that monster.*"

Meg smiled at Mandy. "You're so brave, Mandy. I've always admired how very brave you are."

"So are you," Mandy scolded. "You just don't realize it." She stood and hugged her friend. "Promise me you won't do anything rash," Mandy begged her friend. "Besides, you are meant for a different destiny." She wrinkled her nose, smiling.

Meg frowned at her, then shook her head as though she didn't even *want* to try to figure that one out. "I promise." She walked to the door of the kitchen. She turned back. "Is there anything I can help you with?"

"I just have to get his fever down," Mandy told her, washing their cups and putting them up to dry. "Besides, you already have enough, caring for your grandmother."

Meg smiled, crossing to hug her friend, once more. "I'll be back to visit, again, soon. I've an idea this is going to get interesting. And I don't want to miss the party."

Mandy went back in to check Hawk. His fever seemed lower, and she sighed in relief.

He talked a lot in his sleep, in Lakota and in Cheyenne. Most of which, she understood. She shook her head. He had loved his Cheyenne family, deeply. He also rambled on, on several occasions, about deadly white man's diseases.

At times, she wept for him. At times, she wept *with* him, especially, when he relived the deaths of the woman and the boy. At the moment, he was mumbling something about a man who kept leading him around in circles, killing the people he loved.

Mandy frowned. She thought about McCandle.

Be careful child. There is great danger ahead of you both.

When next Hawk woke, it was full daylight. All the curtains, as well as the windows, were open. A fresh summer breeze tugged playfully at the frilly, lace material, filling the room with the scent of wildflowers. The sun shone brightly, promising a warm summer day.

He looked around and found her writing away in some leather-backed journal in her lap. He lay there, watching her, for several minutes before she lost her concentration enough to feel his gaze on her, and her hand trembled.

Her aquamarine ones lifted and locked with his. Her heart hammered in her breast. How could he do this to her? With just one smoldering look, he set her blood on fire.

"I see you're still here."

Mandy swallowed.

"I thought you were fighting those dreams of yours that told you, you and I would be together?" he gently teased.

To Tame a Wild Hawk

Mandy looked down and toyed with the soft, silk ribbon bookmark on her journal.

He changed the subject. "How long have I been here?"

She could have kissed him. "Five days."

Hawk started. "What?"

"You had a ragging fever." She looked away. "But it was the nightmares you were locked into that scared us the most." She swallowed hard at the anger she saw in his eyes. "Hawk, it looked as though you battled yourself to live."

"I remember telling you to leave."

"And I told you. When you were well enough, you could toss. . . . " She went red. "Well, never mind."

"So you want to find out what is between us." It wasn't a question.

"Wh-at?"

With some effort, Hawk sat up.

"Don't, you'll tear your stitches," Mandy dumped her journal in her haste to stop him. He grabbed her hand—and yanked. Too late, she realized she had fallen in his trap.

Hawk pinned her with one hand and ran the other freely up her back. "Are you sure you want to stick around?" His hand stopped to cup her bottom before moving to settle on the small of her back. With only a grunt on his part, he pulled her full on top of him and, blankets and all, wrapped his legs around her skirts. "Is this what you want, Mandy love."

She gasped, and he cocked an eyebrow at her. His gaze dropped, meaningfully, to her mouth. Mandy stared at him. She wasn't fooled. Despite his levity, something still covered him in darkness. What had happened to him to make the dark shadows that shrouded him?

Unbidden, the dreams returned.

Hawk stood at a creek, a small boy at his side. She went to him as if she belonged.

He is your destiny, child.

But how can this be, Grandmothers? He is so angry. He's nearly lost.

Trust, my child, you will walk the journey together.

A sound, which was part growl, part groan, erupted from his throat. Mandy's hands shot through his hair, and she laid her cheek next to his.

When she leaned back to look into his eyes, the heat she saw there jolted her backwards—but he held her fast. Mandy's thoughts spiraled into a thousand pieces. Heat ripped through her.

Suddenly, he shoved her off the bed, sending her stumbling. Her hand shot to her mouth in shock, a sob caught in her throat. She shook her head. Only then, realizing her hair lay in wild waves about her.

He stared at her, mutely, trying to gain control of the violent beating of his heart—to bring his breathing under control. She was beautiful, standing there with her hair spilled around her, like spun silk.

No woman had ever sent him out of control. He had always been the master. Now, looking at her, he sensed the same ragging feelings he'd sensed before, watching her with his hated enemies arm around her waist. Rage tore through his gut, leaving him weak. It's too late, damn you, he raged inside, staring, unseeing, towards the north. It's too late for him. Too late for her.

Too late for them.

Right then, he wanted to kill McKinney more for touching her than killing the woman and child. He wanted her. And that made him angry. It made him crazy. Destiny be hanged. Having touched her, he knew, the wanting, the need, would never go away. He'd sensed the danger. And just like the first time he'd kissed her, he knew—he wanted her. He wanted everything a future with her represented.

"I've never behaved this way before." She whispered this.

"I know." His liquid, golden gaze eyes penetrated hers. "But if you stay, you'll do it again. Do you understand, Mandy?" His voice shook with emotion. "If you stay, this will only be the beginning of what I will do to you. I will make you beg me to touch you."

Mandy stood completely still. Half of her screamed to run—the other half already begged for him to touch her again.

"Come here, Mandy." It was a command.

Mandy turned and ran.

Mandy stood in front of Doc's office, with her face to the sun. She breathed the warm, fresh air, deep into her lungs, cleansing them from the stale air of the hospital bed. She frowned, suddenly, her small slice of peace gone, now, shattered, at the unwelcome sight heading her way.

To Tame a Wild Hawk

Ashley McCandle strode straight towards her with, what looked to be, murderous intent. He grabbed her arm. Opening the Doc's office door with his free hand, he yanked her through it, slamming it behind them. He stood, with a bruising grip on her arm, not moving.

Mandy stood, quietly, hoping he would calm down and very, very happy, they had managed to move Hawk to a room upstairs that morning.

Finally, he turned to her, but he had not gained control of his rage. He released her arm—but rounded on her. "Mandy what the hell do you think you're doing, taking care of that man?" he hissed through clenched teeth.

Mandy pressed her fingers to her temples. McCandle was the most arrogant man she'd ever known, but even she was amazed that he'd barged into Doc's house like this, uninvited. "I'm sure you've heard all over town what happened," she answered.

"I went out to the ranch again," Ashley closed in on her as he spoke; his voice lowering with every word he enunciated, until it became a menacing growl, "only to have those God forsaken men of yours tell me you'd be gone for a few days. I hit Ned for having the nerve to try and throw me off your land, and that boy, Timmy...."

"Tommy," Mandy corrected.

Ashley sneered. "He's gonna get himself killed, if he don't learn his place."

Mandy gasped. "Oh, Ashley!"

His rage altered, somewhat, at her reaction. "Your damn men refused to tell me where you were?"

Mandy lifted her chin with anger. "That's because, it's *none of your business.*"

"It *is* my business," he grabbed her by the back of her hair and forced her to look at him, "where my future wife is concerned. Now, *why-are-you-here?*"

She fought back the tears, smarting her eyes, from the searing pain he was causing. "You are not now, nor will you ever be, my husband!" She gritted her teeth as he twisted his grip on her hair, all the more tighter. "I have told you for nearly three years now, *I already have a fiancé.*"

"Lies." McCandle lowered his face even closer to hers. "That's all those ever were, just lies to throw me off track. Do you think I didn't know that?"

Meg slipped in the office door and came around Ashley. "I came to warn you, *about him,*" she gestured at McCandle. She wrinkled her nose. "I'm sorry I got here, too late."

Ashley turned his ugly snarl on Mandy's best friend. Still holding Mandy close to his chest, he turned and hissed into her face, "I want you to stop seeing this little tart."

Mandy stared at Meg, hoping she would keep silent, but her hope was short lived.

Meg's brows shot up. "Who? Me?" She moved closer to where McCandle had hold of Mandy. "Why, McCandle. You wouldn't be afraid of little ole me, now, would you?"

McCandle's face turned red with hate. He yanked his hand from Mandy's hair and stepped in front of Meg. "One of these days," his lips curled in a feral, snarl as he leaned in toward Meg, "your mouth is *gonna get you killed.*"

Meg leaned closer to Ashley's face. "Why, I'll say, McCandle, is that a threat?"

Mandy pulled her friend around, close to her. "Stop it," she whispered. Meg squeezed her hand and turned back to McCandle. "By the way, did you have anything to do with McKinney being in town?"

Mandy gasped.

If the Christian demon had a face, McCandle's face looked demonic. Meg and Mandy knew, he wasn't a man accustomed to answering questions. "I've heard enough." He turned and grabbed Mandy's wrist. "You're coming with me. I will not tolerate you staying here and tending to that man."

Meg grabbed at Mandy. *"No, McCandle!"*

"She has no choice." McCandle's, once handsome, face twisted in hate. "Not if she wants to save that precious ranch of hers."

Mandy took hold of the crystal hanging around her neck and centered. Her body hummed with the power of the *Grandmothers*.

McCandle let go of her wrist, then appeared surprised he had done so. He looked at her, an odd expression on his face.

"I don't need *you* to save my ranch," Mandy spoke quietly. "I need to save my ranch *from you*. Thank you, but I have everything worked out fine without your generous offer."

McCandle stared, confused, at his hand, but her last words seemed to bolster him back up. "That's right. . . ." He didn't seem to notice Meg pulling Mandy farther from his reach. "It *was* generous of me." He straightened his suit. "You couldn't do it without me, Mandy. You *need me* to save that ranch of yours."

To Tame a Wild Hawk

Mandy glared at him. "I won't come crawling to you."

McCandle's green gaze narrowed on her.

Mandy steeled herself. As before, contact with him had left her weak. She sensed the dark cloud that shrouded him, but she could not find the source. She saw only the dark, cloaked man, who had been seen hanging around Ashley, a lot, of late.

"And just what are you gonna do, Miss Kane?" He raised both brows and drawled on, "Are you going to hire that gunslinger in there? I wouldn't do that if I were you. Not if you wish him *to live.*" He strode forth, pushing Meg aside as easily as if he'd swatted at a fly. Reaching her, he ran a finger down her flushed face. *"I'll see him in hell first."*

Cold shock flooded Mandy's body. McCandle's unusual, green eyes held the vacancy of a mad man. She didn't doubt him for a minute. The powers he held, he wielded without control, a madman with power, growing stronger each day. With his father out of town, there was no one else to stop him. His father was a mad man, too, to be sure. But he was nowhere *near* as insane as his son.

McCandle straightened the cuff on his sleeve. His gaze lifted, and he stared intently at Mandy for a moment, then turning his head, ever so slightly, he looked directly out the window. Mandy followed his gaze to the man in a long, dark, well-tailored suit, standing out on the boarded walk. For some, unexplained, reason, she shivered. When she gained her senses, she realized McCandle was staring at her. "Who's that man, Ashley?"

He grinned, and Mandy felt a chill crawl over her skin.

He turned away. "It begins," he flung back over his shoulder. Walking out, he slammed the door.

Mandy shivered and felt Meg put an arm around her. "He's insane." A worry frown marred her face. Mandy turned to look at Meg but did not see her friend.

Be careful child. You are all in grave danger. He has the power of your enemies. His power will challenge all you are, and all that is the Hawk.

Mandy shivered, again.

Chapter Seven

When she peeked into Hawk's room later, he was asleep. She retrieved her journal and sat down, but she couldn't find the words to write. Hawk lay sleeping peacefully. She saw herself laying there with him. He was warning her, and, right now, she should be back at her ranch. She'd even gone out and had her rig hitched up.

But she couldn't go.

Over, and over, she told herself he was her only hope. She warred with the *Grandmothers'* words, which said he was her destiny. Yet when she looked up, now, to find his golden-green eyes watching her, when she found her breath lodged in her throat every time he touched her, she knew—she'd crossed a path, and there *was no* going back.

"Come here, Mandy."

She stood on shaky legs and made her way before him.

He took her hand and turned it over. With slow, sensual movements, he rubbed the pad of his thumb over the sensitive flesh of her palm.

She swayed.

"I want you to tell me why you came back when you fight the destiny between us? And I want you to tell me of your dreams."

Mandy sidestepped the mention of the dreams and focused on his first question. "I don't know," she whispered. "I tried, but I could not go."

Hawk let his head fall back and sighed. "You have no idea the man that I am. I need to be clear. When this is over, I have to go." He leaned forward and kissed the palm of her hand, then sighed again, lying back against the pillows, once more. "I cannot see how even the *Grandmothers* could know why."

Mandy stared at him for a long moment. She took a long, shuddering breath. "I do not know why you do to me what you do." She shrugged. "And I do not understand my visions. I do not know why you did, what you did, in the store, or why you must leave me, once this is done. I do not know why, if that is so, I don't, just, go ahead and marry McCandle," her voice rose with growing intensity. "But I do know *this*, I need you to help me. *I must not lose my land*. I cannot let McCandle win. He murdered my father, and he has to pay." She narrowed her eyes in agitation. "I will do everything I can to get you to stay," she added, "but if I can't, I will avenge my father my own way, even if I have to marry that vile man and kill him in his sleep."

Hearing this, Hawk half sat up, wincing from the pain it cost him. *"The hell you will."* He could not think why she would say this when she knew their path. He did not care that this new thought contradicted everything he'd just told her about having to leave. His grip on her hand tightened.

Everything about her caused him to challenge everything he thought he knew. He'd think one thing—and do another. She was making him crazy with want. She was all he thought about, night and day.

"If you don't help me, that's *one* of the only *two* plans I have left."

No. She couldn't know why he must leave. And she would hate him when she knew. But in spite of that, *this was their path. Their destiny*—and there was no other way. They would have to find a way to work through it. Why did she fight him? "He killed your pa!" He could not believe she'd even suggest it.

"Yes."

Stubbornness made him ask, "And you'd let him touch you? The way *I touched you?*"

Mandy closed her eyes—and lied, "If I have to."

"Open your eyes, Mandy," he commanded. "Look me in the eyes when you say that."

Mandy sighed in defeat.

To Tame a Wild Hawk

"Why do you fight us?" Hawk's voice was gentle now. "There is more to us than killing McCandle. There is more than either of us know at this moment. You will have to decide something one day." He touched her cheek. "But we will win."

Mandy pulled back, glaring at him. "If you are suggesting, by your use of the word *us*, we let him get away with killing my father and hand over the very ranch he murdered my father for," she pulled farther out of his reach in anger, "I will *never* agree. *Never!*"

Hawk frowned. He'd never suggested such a thing. What was she really afraid of? But that wasn't the thing that held his attention at the moment. It was the idea of Mandy—and Ashley. "Then, you would let him touch you?" He still needed to hear her answer, in spite of himself. He couldn't get past the idea she would let McCandle touch her.

"If that was the only way I had left to me. . . ." she whispered.

"Say it.'

"Then, yes!" she nearly yelled. "I would do whatever it takes."

"You're still not saying it, Mandy," he whispered through clenched teeth.

Mandy sighed. Tears stung her eyes. "It's not in me to give up, Hawk. I cannot walk away and accept what he did."

"No," Hawk went still as a mountain lion, "I can see you cannot."

Hawk slept through the evening meal and right through the night. But Doc was happy to see it. "It's a healing, restful, sleep," he assured Mandy.

She stared out the window. The look in Hawk's golden eyes should have warned her off, but she had ignored the warning. Why did she do that? Was she so afraid of her feelings for him, she would deliberately provoke him that way?

Doc came into the room and seeing her, his wise old face split into a grin. "You got more than you bargained for. Didn't you, Mandy girl?"

Mandy turned and looked at him sadly. "From the first moment I saw him, even when I was held in the grip of that murdering McKinney, I. . . . "

"Don't give up on him, Mandy girl." Doc took her hand. "He needs you. He just don't know it yet. He needs your goodness. But more than that, he needs your love."

Mandy's head shot up in shock, her free hand going to her throat.

Doc turned away, picking up his bag. "I have to go see to the Brown's little girl. Poor little mite," he shook his head, "been sick all her six years. I'll probably be back late. They always have me for dinner." He pulled open the door. "Fight for him, Mandy. He won't know what he's thrown away—till it's too late."

Mandy didn't hear the door shut. She was still thinking on one thing. Love. She had loved the man in her visions. She had loved him in past lives—and she loved him still. She loved a man, who masqueraded as a gunfighter. And from the way he used that weapon, she knew, Meg was right—he was more than dressing the part.

No! She couldn't have fallen in love with a man who held a secret that might keep them apart forever. A gunman. A man, who, even if he stayed now, would be on the next stage out when his job was done. Yet all the sense in the world would not change what her heart wanted. She wanted Hawk. She had known him, forever—been in love with him, forever. She looked down at her trembling hands in realization. It was hopeless. She was in love with a man as changing, and unpredictable, as a storm—and would be gone with the next wind—taking her heart with him.

Blinding, morning sunlight filled the room as Mandy tied the drapes back with their thick rope ties. Hawk sat up, wincing from his sore shoulder. "What time is it?"

"Almost time for lunch." She tried to avoid looking at him—and failed. She swallowed hard when her traitorous eyes followed the dark, curly hair covering a massive chiseled chest, then dropped lower still to see only a thin sheet hiding what was beneath. Her cheeks flamed when she realized the direction of her thoughts and flew wide when they clashed with his golden ones.

His eyes were smoky, but his lips were turned upward in a sardonic grin. One eyebrow arched in wicked amusement. "Don't stop now."

Mandy's own eyes went black with anger. "You, sir, are no gentleman, even if you dress the part in that suit and put on a show."

"I quite agree." He grinned unabashed. "I'm a heathen, with a soul as black as the darkest night." Suddenly, his eyes became stormy. "And speaking of—come here, Amanda," he commanded softly.

She shook her head, almost violently, sending her dark hair flying. "Oh, no! No, I did so before and. . . ." she flushed, unable to finish.

To Tame a Wild Hawk

Dark eyebrows collided, giving him the look of his namesake. "Then, I shall come to you." He reached to draw back the covers as he spoke.

Mandy got a glimpse of dark curls and jumped forward. "All right! I . . . just lay back down, you'll open your wounds."

When she reached his side, her gaze collided with his. She was drawn down, deep into their golden depths—spiraling down—drowning in their green-gold pools. Her breath caught, and she reached out to steady herself.

A warm hand, with the strength of steel and the gentleness of a soft kiss, grasped hers, pulled her slowly into his embrace. When his lips were mere inches from hers, he asked in a husky voice, "What were your visions of?"

Mandy took a deep breath and tried to still her thundering heart. Unfair. Hawk didn't follow any of the rules. He might be dangerous to his enemy, but if she had any of the senses her papa bestowed her with, she'd run as far, and as fast, as she could—for he was far more dangerous to her.

"I-I think you know," she whispered.

He arched his hawk-like brows at her. "I do, but I want to hear you say it."

"No," Mandy pulled back. "A man with your manners does not deserve confessions." She swallowed hard, realizing what she'd just revealed.

Hawk *pounced* on that one. "Confessions?" He grinned as if he were a man with a juicy morsel, his hot gaze searching for the rest.

Mandy groaned and scrambled out of his grasp. She helped him as he struggled to put some pillows behind him, careful to stay out of his reach. Biting her lip, she prayed for the right words. Finally, she spoke, her voice barely above a whisper, "This town is owned by McCandle, Hawk. I have nowhere else to turn. By your own words, you will follow the path set before us, but when it's done, you will leave me, alone. I will have no choice. My ranch hands are good, but they're not fools. And there's not a man outside my ranch who would even *consider* going up against McCandle without the backing of a good gunman and the power to follow him." If you turn away from me, I will take the only path left to me. I will not let him win!"

She saw the barely leashed fury simmering in his golden gaze and the ridged planes in his body.

"Just because you have the upper hand on me—does not mean you own me. Remember, by your own words, you will leave me." Her eyes narrowed. She turned away. Then, said over her shoulder, "Now, my ranch hands will be waiting when you're ready."

Hawk correctly read the warning, neatly veiled, beneath her words. He chose to ignore it, irritating her further. "Why are your hands not afraid of McCandle?"

"They've been with my papa for years. They think of me as their daughter."

Hawk nodded. After a moment, he asked, "Would that be Jason McCandle?"

"Yes. You know him?"

Hawk's nod was curt. "All right, I'll go by your rules," he grinned, "under one condition."

Wide-eyed, Mandy nodded. "Wh-what condition?"

"That you never ask me why I was after McCandle," he bit out. Mandy's eyes narrowed on him. She bit her lip, wondering at this new development. She wanted to ask him already. How could she agree to such an ultimatum? Yet how could she not? Hawk wanted revenge as bad as she did, that much was obvious. It's why he'd come here after McKinney. But why? She would agree—for now, but the burning need for answers was too much a part of her, not to be sated.

"All right," she nodded, "I agree to your terms."

Hawk grinned. "Like hell you do." He pierced her to the spot with his golden gaze. "It will drive you insane. But know this, Mandy. This is the one thing your busy little mind will leave alone. The only reason I brought it up is because, sooner or later, you're going to want to ask, why. And I want it clear. Don't even try to get those particular answers, Mandy. Do not be hurting for my past, and do not try to understand that side of me. It would only get you hurt." His gaze narrowed. "Understood?"

"Yes," she answered in a breathy whisper.

"No. You do not. But you will.

Chapter Eight

Spurs a jangling, a tall, dark stranger stopped at the bar and set his Winchester on the bar top. "Whiskey," was all he said, and he did not raise his head or acknowledge the bartender when he said it

The bartender opened his mouth to object to the rifle, but when his eyes met the steely ones of the stranger, the words stuck in his throat. He poured the drink instead. "That'll be two bits, mister," he managed to get out.

The stranger slapped a coin on the bar top, then tossed back his whiskey. His lips pulled back. "Seen a man named Hawk, here abouts?" he asked after a moment.

"Friend of yours?" the bartender countered. People around here didn't cotton to questions, especially, McCandle."

The strangers gray eyes narrowed to steely slits.

The bartender swallowed. This man didn't abide by anyone's rules. "He's laid up at the doc's on down the street."

The stranger's face remained emotionless, but if it was possible, his eyes got deadlier. "Laid up?"

The bartender felt sorry for McCandle. Hawk, on his own, was a formidable enemy. But up against these two, he didn't stand a chance. "Did I say laid up?" He made to clean up an imaginary spot. "He's up and around now."

The stranger reached up and tipped the brim of his hat. "Much obliged." He picked up his Winchester and strode out the door, spurs ringing out in deadly quiet.

"Well, I'll be damned."

A cowboy sneered at him, picking up his own whiskey. "You might be when McCandle gets wind of this."

The barkeeper gave him a hard look. "Get out of my sight." He tossed down his towel. "I've got someone to go see."

When Mandy answered the door in mid-afternoon, it was to meet the deadliest man she'd seen, yet, in the west, standing on her front step. Her heart leaped into her throat when she realized, his presence could only mean one thing.

He was after Hawk.

She tried to stop him. But he pushed by her.

"Hawk!" she yelled.

He looked in the first room. Finding nothing, he went bounding up the stairs, Mandy right behind him. He located Hawk's room in the next moment, his huge, imposing frame in the door, blocking her way.

At least he wasn't shooting. Finally, he moved inside, and she was able to slip by.

Hawk let his colt slip back in his holster with a scowl.

"One-up on you, old man," the stranger said.

Hawk growled, then grinned. "Actually, thanks to Mandy's warning, I was one-up on you," he retorted.

Mandy looked at Hawk, then the stranger. They'd lost their minds.

"Mandy," Hawk gestured at the man, "this is Jake."

That's all Hawk told her, just Jake. It was Mandy's turn to scowl.

Hawk cocked one of those damnable eyebrows at her. "And this is Mandy," he said with meaning.

Jake's gaze was intent on Hawk. He surveyed Mandy with new interest. "Ma'am," he tipped his hat.

To Tame a Wild Hawk

"Who the hell *are you?*" Mandy shot at him. "And what do you think you're doing, barging in here like that?"

Hawk grinned.

Jake frowned, his eyes narrowing on her.

Mandy swallowed. "I mean, you don't go barging into Doc's without even waiting to be invited in." Then, she turned. "Gentlemen, I'll get you some coffee."

When she'd left, Jake turned to Hawk. "So where'd you find her?"

Hawk ignored the question. He'd never really explained the *Grandmothers* to Jake. Some, but not all. Besides, there was a better topic. "She wants me to help her to save her ranch—from a man named McCandle."

Jake's eyes narrowed to mere slits, at this. "Are you going to?"

Hawk nodded. "Yep. Cause he's our man."

Jake's gunmetal eyes went killer cold. "In that case, I want in."

"I thought you might say that." Hawk moved carefully to the door. "Mandy, we'll be requiring something a little stronger than coffee," he said down the hall.

"Now you're talk'n." Jake smiled.

And Hawk knew—Jake rarely smiled.

Chapter Nine

Deep mist enshrouded him, making it hard to see her. Frantic, Hawk reached for her again. And again, he missed. He sensed him. His enemy. He lay close, now. Hawk had to reach her before it was too late. Mandy rose from the mist. Hawk wanted to shout his relief—until he realized how it was she rose. Powerful talons wrapped their way around her waist. One, slowly curled around her neck. The tip of one talon bit into her. Hawk sprang forward, but it was too late. A talon sank deep into her side.

Hawk sat up in a sweat. A nightmare. That's all it was—a damn nightmare. He sat all the way up, welcoming the searing pain that ripped through his side. He had not been able to save one beautiful young woman who lived on a plantation. He had not been able to save the boy. He sensed the same danger with Mandy. The dream warned him. He had not reached her in time. He wanted to strike out at something. He had not reached her in time!

Hawk heard her voice but did not answer at first. He could still feel the dream, when he looked up.

She was standing there with sexy, sleep-lidded eyes, having been awakened from a deep sleep. Her dark hair tumbled loosely about her in a cloud. The filmy, white nightgown, she wore, added much to the imagination. Right now, Hawk's was working overtime. He pried his tongue of the roof of his mouth. Silently, he cursed himself for continually losing his tight rein of control around this bewitching woman.

He realized Mandy's sleep-drugged, mind wasn't allowing her the usual protections she would have exercised if she'd been fully awake. He should shake her out of it, wake her fully and send her out, but he couldn't bring himself to do so. He saw only the gleam in her beautiful eyes as he held out his hand.

Her body moved forward as though in a trance. In the low flicker of the lantern light, she placed her small hand in the larger one he now held out, palm up.

Slowly, he drew her down beside him and laid her on her back, looming up over her as he rested on his good side. With slow, tantalizing patience, he lowered his lips to hers. He had waited all his life for this one, defining, moment. With ringing clarity, he knew he'd come home.

His mind waged war with his heart, which had been, for so long, encased in glacial retreat. He was walking on dangerously thin ice, but his heart wasn't listening. He only knew this woman, and her enchanting beauty, intrigued him—invited him to walk where he'd never dared walk, never even knew he wanted to walk, before now.

She made him long for things he'd never dared to believe could be his, until the moment he'd laid eyes on her. His hands moved over her soft curves, the filmy material of her gown hiding nothing. He found her softness his exquisite torture. But Mandy was a lady, and the Tississata's believed a maiden should always be cherished. He wouldn't cheapen her, or what they shared, for one night in paradise, especially not in a hospital bed.

With a low groan he pulled away, leaving them both bereft.

At first, she tried to pull him back to her, but he pinned her hands. "Mandy, get up!"

Mandy shook her head. Gradually, the fog lifted, and she saw his golden eyes piercing her as if he were the hawk itself, holding her prey. With dawning realization, she sat up, horrified. She closed her eyes. It was obvious what Hawk thought.

"Do not." He shook her gently. "Do not ever be ashamed of how we feel when we come together." He hooked a finger under her chin, forcing her to look at him. "I have not had too many good things come into my life, Mandy. For once, it's going to be right. Not with me shot up. And not where we are." He pushed the hair back from her face. "I do not *ever* want to see you have regrets."

To Tame a Wild Hawk

Mandy's eyes filled with tears. In this beautiful man, with one bad reputation, hid a heart wanting to love. Beneath those cold eyes hid a lonely man, needing love in return. She was falling for a man, the territories knew as White Indian. She was falling in love with a man, who led a double life as a man who had the heart of a warrior, yet sought vengeance in the white man's world, in the spirit of the west, as a fast gun.

She moved off the bed and backed away from him. But it was too late.

For every woman, there is that one man who could get a woman to go anywhere he wanted her to go, do anything he wanted her to do—reach into her soul and turn her whole world on its ear—challenge everything, she thought she believed.

If she believed that man didn't exist. She hasn't met him, yet. She might try to deny the truth of it. But if she met him, that one man, she was lucky if he stood behind her. Not so lucky if he came to crush her. And a woman might only learn the truth of it—when he walked out of her life.

Hawk was that man. He was her destiny. And he, alone, could raise her up.

Or break her.

Mandy placed the coffee on the old silver tray, smiling as she listened to the man snarling in the next room. He really didn't adapt well to being trapped in a bed until he was healed. It had been over a week since Hawk had been shot. There was no doubt in her mind, there would be no more keeping him down.

It was time to go to the ranch.

Maybe there, she could talk him into letting himself rest a while. She smiled at the thought.

She doubted it.

She placed his breakfast on the tray and shut down the cook stove, hanging the checkered hot pads back on their hook. Taking him home seemed so final, so intimate. Mandy swallowed, hard. Dear Goddess, please don't let her be making a mistake. Yet how could anything that felt so right, be wrong. Besides, the *Grandmothers* had spoken of Hawk as her destiny. And they were right, for how could she beat her papa's killers without him? She had tried. For several months, now, she had been stealing their cattle, like they had stolen from the neighboring ranches around them. She had tried robbing their payroll stage, mysteriously giving the money back to the ranchers, where it belonged.

Nothing had, even remotely, put a dent in McCandle.

There were still her nightly escapades. She shook her head. It had been weeks, and she still had not achieved what she'd set out to do. Soon, she vowed. Soon—maybe things would turn her way.

Goddess, please do not let anything happen to Hawk. She nearly dropped the tray at the thought and set it back on the table. What if Hawk got killed because she'd involved him? She couldn't bear it. She swallowed hard at the thought. It felt as though her lungs had caved in. Maybe she should have found a way to deal with McCandle on her own. The more she thought on this, the more she realized how selfish it was for her to have ever involved him in the first place. She would never be able to bear it if anything happened to him because of her. Why had it never occurred to her that she could lose him?

The way she'd lost her papa.

"Papa," she whispered.

Her throat caught. She couldn't lose Hawk to McCandles, too. She picked up her tray, her thoughts locked on a new mission.

Hawk scowled menacingly at her when she entered her room with the tray a moment later, but his glare altered at the sight of her own sour expression. He grabbed at his gun-belt hanging on the bed post. "What is it? What's wrong?"

Mandy set the tray by the bed and wiped her damp palms on the apron. "Hawk, I've been thinking . . ."

Hawk grumbled and let his Colt drop back into its holster. "More like worrying. Why do women always worry?"

Mandy ignored his sarcasm. She knew it was hard for a man like Hawk to stay down. When men like Hawk were held down for long, they usually wound up acting like an ugly, old grizzly bear coming out of hibernation—mean and grouchy.

She fought for her breath, and the courage, to continue. She knew Hawk was going to fight her on this. "Hawk, I do not think I should enlist your help after all."

To Tame a Wild Hawk

Hawk's unusual gold-green eyes narrowed on her, making her want to fidget.

"Do not look at me like that." She moved to the dresser to thwart his gaze.

"I think you try to sabotage us because of your fears," he stated so quietly she nearly did not hear him.

"Hawk!"

"You are not going to get rid of me now, Mandy. Our circles are intertwined. Do you understand? I will decide if, and when, I go."

Mandy did not like the way he had put that. "You're the most infuriating man I have ever met," she pouted.

Hawk grinned at her, his anger gone. "And you are beautiful when you are mad, Mandy. You're eyes get all snappy and glowing."

"Of all the. . . . " Mandy grabbed a pillow off the hope chest and heaved it at him.

Hawk caught it easily, laughing and wincing from the pain it caused.

Mandy was spellbound. For a moment she stood, mesmerized by the transformation in Hawk's face when he laughed. She wished she could make him laugh more often.

"You really are reprehensible," she told him, but the anger was gone from her too.

Hawk scowled, once more, his fun gone, now that his little spitfire was no longer crackling. Mandy was his fire—all heat. "I'm a heathen, remember. Not a gentleman."

"The Lakota treat their women well, Hawk. So that doesn't hold water with me."

Hawk's eyes hardened. Mandy saw herself like a rabbit, poised to take flight—the Hawk moving in with dangerous, deadly talons. Now what had she done? One minute he was boyish laughter—the next impassive menace. There was much she didn't understand about this man.

Like almost everything.

What had happened to make him so cold at times? "Tell me about the Lakota. How did you come to be with them, Mandy?"

Mandy tried to look away. Her eyes wouldn't obey. She stayed there, locked with his glowing ones, as if his by his command. And only when he was ready—would he release her.

Mandy shook her head and whispered, "It was a long time ago."

"Not good enough, Mandy. How old were you when you were taken?"

Mandy ignored the question. "It will have to be, Hawk. It's all I've got to offer."

"Woman, sometimes I want to, what to the white men say, paddle your back-side."

Mandy lifted her chin. "You do. . . . " her voice trailed off when she realized what she was saying. Hawk swung up out of his bed, and Mandy jumped. "I'm sorry." Not sounding the least bit repentant. "I do not take kindly to your threatening to paddle me."

Hawk kept coming. At the last second, Mandy decided to run for it, but his hand snaked out, and it was too late. The rabbit was snared—in her own trap.

"Let go of me!"

Hawk arched one damnable eyebrow.

"Okay," she conceded, "so you would dare. But if you do . . . as the Goddess is my witness, I will not forget it. And I will get even. . . ."

Relax." Hawk pulled her close. "I'm not going to harm that pretty little backside of yours." He stopped and suddenly yanked her forward. "But if you ever endanger yourself . . . " He let his meaning sink in.

Mandy let out a breath, somewhat mollified. "Then, why did you say it?"

Hawk shrugged. "To see those eyes of yours spark."

"Oh you—arrogant pig of a man."

Hawk yanked her to his chest. "Take that back, Mandy!" Hawk bit out, his face mere inches from hers.

Mandy's face was mutinous. Some things she *had* picked up from the white-man's world, *very well*. A woman running a ranch was one of them. The other was letting her temper have free reign at the most inopportune times. And at those times, it got her in a whole lot of trouble.

This was one of them.

To Tame a Wild Hawk

Hawk turned and headed for the bed, with Mandy in tow.

Mandy tried to pull back. "What are you doing?"

"You're in the habit of losing your temper and saying whatever comes to your mind when you do so. I'm going to teach you some manners.

She dug in her heels, now, in full panic. "How?" She'd been counting on Hawk to act like a warrior—not a gunman.

"Maybe I'll show you a better use for all that fire," he threatened.

Hawk, the Lakota never spanked their children either!" she shrieked, mistaking his meaning. *This wasn't the warrior she had in mind.*

Who was she kidding? She hadn't been doing much thinking at all.

Hawk only sat on the bed, pulling her down *over* his lap. He ran his hands slowly up her back. She felt the heat from the fire already licking its way through her body, ready to consume everything in its path. Desperately, she looked around for an escape. The things Hawk did to her with one smoldering look—and with his hands . . .

"Say, you're sorry, Mandy."

"I am sorry," Mandy whispered. "I do not know what came over me. I have never been so rude to anyone before." She threw up a hand. "Well, except for McCandle, of course." She sighed. And the sheriff. Well, and at times, with Cord. And all the time with papa . . . But *I am* sorry, Hawk," she whispered the last.

He sat her up and kissed her softly. "Now," he kissed her again, "tell me about your time with the Lakota."

Chapter Ten

A bellow of fury blasted from outside the window, causing Mandy and Hawk to jump apart. They were down on the first floor and had been, as usual now, arguing. They had, in fact, also wound up kissing, which had also become a pattern, forgetting that—most of the first floor was visible from the street.

A moment later, the front door swung inward, slamming against the wall. McCandle stormed across the room and stood, taking in Mandy's swollen lips and the blush steadily rising in her face. He did not move, his cold, green eyes just taking her in, his face impassive. Finally, he walked slowly around them. "This...." he indicated Hawk with a dismissive sweep of his hand. "You really want me to believe *this* is your mystery man. That this is the man, you've been telling me for the past three years, you've been waiting for," if ice held a tone, McCandle's voice held the inflection of ice, all the more chilling for the calm, clipped way he delivered each word, stopping in front of Mandy, clearly ignoring the cold, wintery quietness that had swept over Hawk, "when you know you're just wasting time. You *will* marry me. Why do you play these silly games?"

McCandle was either very brave, or a fool.

Mandy's eyes flew wide and dropped to the hand Hawk had taken in a bone-crushing grip when he had heard McCandle's words. As if in a trance, her eyes traveled up and collided with Hawk's violent ones. Not understanding the anger she saw directed her way, in the golden depths of his gaze, she mutely shook her head. "You were in my visions. . . ." she stammered to Hawk.

"*Your visions!*" McCandle interrupted, sneering the words. "Witch, if you expect me to believe *this* is the man you have claimed, all *this time*, is coming home to marry you," McCandle said, his voice laden with sarcasm, "well, my little beauty, play your games with some other fool. We both know, when you're done playing, where you'll be. So," he waved at Hawk with another dismissive sweep of his hand, "stop wasting this man's time. Tell him you're done playing and *get your sweet little ass home, where you belong.*"

Mandy was mute with rage. Before she could think it through, or get two words out, Ashley turned his attention on Hawk.

"So tell me." He looked straight at Hawk. "You're not *really thinking* of going along with her insane little plan and marrying her, are you?" He clucked his tongue. "No, I'm sure you're a wise man and see through the little witch's games. Wise of you. You wouldn't want her to *get you killed*," he growled the last in deep, low tones.

Mandy gasped.

Hawk's eyes traveled, once again, to McCandle's hair, then back down to McCandle's unusual, spring-green eyes, with such hatred the blond man, unwittingly, winced. Hawk pulled Mandy firmly to his side. He did not speak, his intent clear.

McCandle took a step back, his jaw pumping in fury, his hand on his gun-belt.

Hawk turned Mandy's hand, palm up, and stroked it. "You have threatened her, haven't you?"

Mandy stared at his face. There was no trace of violence there, now. So why did the hairs stand up on the back of her neck? With the feel of slow motion, she looked over at McCandle. He looked as if he were strangling. Whether from fear, or anger, she couldn't be sure.

McCandle looked beside himself. "*Who the hell do you think you are*, coming into *this* town, *my town*, claiming *my* future wife as your own?" His tone was quiet.

Too, quiet.

Hawk grinned, his grip tightening. Mandy knew what it felt to be prey— to be captured, so predatory was his smile in all its violence.

To Tame a Wild Hawk

"I am Hawk. And I've come," he kissed Mandy's fingers, "to claim," he looked up and into McCandle eyes, his own gaze mesmerizing with what Mandy had only seen in a cougar's eyes—right before it ripped its prey to pieces, "what's mine."

Mandy could only stare at Hawk.

McCandle gave a start at the double innuendo. He stood there for a long moment, as though he were trying to comprehend what he'd just heard.

Without another word, he turned and stalked out.

Mandy stared after him, until Hawk, himself, blocked her view. He was so close she had to tilt her head back, to look up. "I can explain," she offered.

"Please do."

"There was *no* fiancé," she got out quickly, "just my visions. I lied. I was desperate. He had me backed against a wall, and he was insisting I marry him. I had to do *something*."

"So you told him you already have a fiancé, and he believed you," Hawk's tone held obvious skepticism. He was, again, stroking the palm of her hand.

Meg had a cousin who likes to travel. She told him to send me little trinkets from all over, with short little cards attached that said things like I can't wait to be with you again." She licked her lips and looked away. "Of course, they weren't signed.

"Of course," Hawk drawled. "And why all the secrecy?" His voice was so calm, Mandy's heart picked up another notch. She gave him a nervous little laugh, misunderstanding his meaning. "I just added a little mystery, you know, to drive him crazy."

"No. I meant, why not tell me this sooner?"

Her eyes met his. "It hasn't come up?" she tried. She knew he wasn't going to like the next part, and she wished he'd let go of her hand. "I would tell him, he would soon see," she bit her lip and whispered, "and then, it would be—too late."

The irony of what she had done undid him. He didn't know whether to laugh or shout. She couldn't have planned it better if she'd tried.

McCandle would not take this lightly.

Could not take this lightly.

He had spent too much time trying to lure him here. McCandle had invested years, in his revenge against him. All this time, Hawk had thought it was *Jason* McCandle—but Jason had, obviously, had a son soon after he had massacred all those people on the wagon train. Hawk could hardly reconcile this twist of fate. Why come after him? The Hawk? Did not McCandle already have it all? He had the ranch. He had Jason.

Now, after all this time, and all of the young, McCandle's careful planning, he had brought Hawk to town, only to learn that Hawk knew the woman he, himself, had planned to marry. Too find out, the woman he planned to marry, the woman who had been putting him, off all this time, with her mystery man, had been putting him off—for the Hawk.

The brother he wanted to kill.

McCandle had a grudge, and it was a grudge that had already cost untold lives.

Mandy was unwittingly fueling the fire.

Hawk stared down at Mandy. After a long moment, he gave her a tight smile. "Between you and me, Mandy love," he cupped her face in his hands, "we've just declared war."

Several hours later, Mandy stared at the patterns on the rug, which lay over the wood-slat floor, remembering those words. She turned and went the other direction in her agitation. Before she had gone three steps, she turned back, almost violently, and headed the other direction.

"I can't believe he's going along with this," Mandy mumbled, again, looking up to where her best friend had been watching her pace for the past hour. "Meg, whatever possessed us to start this mysterious fiancé farce?" She made a face as she stumbled over the word, and then, nearly tripped over the carpet.

Just desserts.

"You started it." Meg was only too happy to remind her. "And if you don't quit pacing, you're going to wear out the carpet. Besides, you're giving me a headache."

"Damn," Mandy gave into uncharacteristic swearing. "Damn. Damn. Damn."

To Tame a Wild Hawk

A deep-throated growl from the doorway caused both women to jump. "That is the second time I've caught you swearing. Once more," he strode forth and took hold of her arm, "and I'll take soap to your mouth."

Maybe her swearing was more characteristic than she realized. *"You wouldn't dare!"* Mandy tried to yank her arm free.

"Oh, I think he would." Meg laughed when Mandy glared at her. She added, "And I don't think I'd mind *anything that man wanted to do to me.*"

Mandy rolled her eyes, knowing her friend was baiting her. "Thanks to *that man*, I no longer have a *mysterious fiancé*. I, now, have a *real one!* McCandle thinks *he* is my mysterious fiancé." She poked him in the chest. Forgetting, in her anger, she was the one responsible for McCandle's misconception. "You're both the same. You come *waltzing* into town and say you're going to marry me, and I'm just supposed to fall at your feet," her voice rose steadily with each word. "You crook your finger, and I'm supposed to follow you anywhere."

Too late, she saw the thunderous look in his golden-green gaze, and she tried to bolt. Damn the man was fast. She was going to have to get better at seeing *that particular* expression in time, or she was in deep trouble.

Hell! She was already in deep trouble.

In that instant, she was hauled against his brick-like chest. "By your own admission, you are now, *my* woman." His voice was husky.

Of all the nerve. He looked—victorious.

"Now you did it," Meagan chimed in.

Unusual green eyes turned and glowered at her.

"I was just leaving," she laughed, jumping to gather her things. "I think it's time for the rest of the town to hear the good news, now you're up and about, don't you?" She didn't wait for a reply, just bolted out the door, her musical laughter floating back to them.

"No, Meg!" Mandy yelled, trying to break free of Hawk. "Meagan wait!" This time, Mandy did beat on his chest. "Now, look what you've done, you brute."

Hawk held her in his tight embrace until she stood quietly, her eyes cast down. He hooked a finger under her chin, tilting her face up. Mandy closed her eyes. "You're not a coward, Mandy."

She couldn't detect any anger in his voice. Gathering her courage, she peeked at him. Golden eyes glowered back at her. Mandy squeezed her eyes shut again. "Yes, I am," she whispered.

She heard him chuckle. "No, you are not."

Mandy shivered at the sound of his voice. "With you, I am."

She felt Hawk's deep laugh against her breast, felt him kiss her eyelids. Her pulse leaped through her veins.

"Hawk?" She peeked at him. "McCandle was angrier than I have ever seen him. He will do everything in his power to kill you."

Hawk caught a stray curl and rubbed it between his fingers. "Men have tried before."

She looked at him, honesty slipping through her lips. "I could not bear it if anything happened to you," she looked down, "I mean—because of me."

He raised her chin in his hand. "Would you cry for me, Mandy?" She could not hold the intensity she saw in depths of his golden-green eyes.

She could not bear to meet the pain in his gaze.

"That is not funny, Hawk!"

"Would you?" he demanded.

This time, she did not look away. The heartrending tenderness in his gaze made her knees buckle. His right arm tightened around her as if they were steel bands.

"Yes," she whispered.

"Hmmm, nice," he caressed her face with his free hand.

"Nice?"

"Yeah," he answered. "It's just nice to know someone would be there, who cared enough to cry."

She swallowed a sob in her throat. "You have lost everyone, haven't you, Hawk?"

He pressed his forehead against hers. "Not everyone. I have friends who are closer to me than blood." At this reminder, he wondered when Kid would show. He brushed a hand against her cheek. "You have lost everyone, too." He pulled away from her, leaving Mandy feeling hurt. "Well, at least you solved our little problem."

To Tame a Wild Hawk

She struggled to mask her disappointment. "What problem was that?"

"Now, you'll have a good reason for having me in the house."

"I was going to put you in the bunkhouse," she answered, sweetly.

"Not on your life." He walked out the door.

Mandy nodded, not trusting herself to speak.

It was hours later when he strolled back in.

Mandy looked up, an unguarded expression flickering through her eyes. "Hawk?"

Something deep, and warm, within him shifted, and he knew, his life had been forever changed by this beautiful, enchanting woman. "It's me, little one," he answered softly, wanting for some, undefinable, reason to reassure her. To let her know he wasn't about to abandon her, now he was finally with her.

Mandy stared at him. Her thoughts spun. Her emotions whirled. She fought to regain control of herself, not liking the emotional vulnerability that she'd always been able to push aside—until he walked into her life. "You're beautiful," she whispered.

Hawk strode towards her. "Mandy, are you okay? You're very pale."

Mandy continued to stare at him. "I thought you left." She gave a little shrug.

Hawk pulled her into the safety of his arms, his throat tightening, convulsively. "I won't leave you, little one, I promise," he said in the language of his people. So there was a soft, vulnerable woman beneath all the bravado. Somehow, that only made it more difficult for Hawk to hang onto what senses he had left. Her vulnerability, was his vulnerability to her. The last of his defenses were stripped away.

But somehow, he'd have to protect her—from himself.

He leaned back, tilting her face up and stroking her dark-auburn hair. "We'll find a way Mandy, I promise you. We'll beat McCandle. We're in this together, all the way."

She tried to turn away, but Hawk held her firmly. "Don't, Mandy. Don't hide your tears from me."

Mandy looked up at him, her breath quickening as his lips kissed, first the path of her tears, then softly kissed her mouth. "You're lips are soft, as if they were the first flowers of spring," he whispered against her mouth. "They make a man want to breathe, deep, their fragrant scent," he kissed her again, "to kiss away the dew," and again, "to taste their succulent sweetness."

Mandy groaned as a fiery path burned its way through her body. She leaned into him, making it easier for him to deepen the kiss. Her hands moved over his shoulders, then up to lace themselves in his hair.

He broke free from her lips and kissed her face, then her eyes, then down her neck. "Mandy," he breathed. "Sweet, sweet, Mandy, I want you."

"As I want you," she whispered back.

Doc chuckled from the doorway. "Then, I guess it's a good thing you two young, folks are getting married." He grinned, then sobered. "Sorry, Mandy," he added, seeing her blush. "Didn't mean to embarrass you," but he continued to grin, unabashed, at the couple.

Hawk glowered at him. "What the hell do you want?"

Doc's grin widened at Hawk's discomfiture. "I just heard the news, and now, I'm here to admonish you two for not telling me first. In fact, I was the last to hear it."

Mandy flushed deeper. "Doc Mallory. . . . "

"Sorry, Doc," Hawk broke in. "We, sort of, surprised ourselves, and Meg happened to be here. The rest is self-explanatory."

"Yes," Doc agreed, still grinning. "I can see that. Meg has a great love for rubbing things in McCandle's face."

"You got here just in time, though. We're sort of celebrating." Hawk glowered at Doc's amusement as he reached into his pocket, producing a small satin covered, box. "It was my mothers."

Mandy stared at it. Her hands shaking, she fumbled to open it, and Hawk's larger ones covered hers. She looked up into his eyes as he helped her open it. Inside was the most exquisite ring she'd ever seen. "Oh Hawk," she breathed. "It's beautiful."

Hawk lifted the ring from its nest and took her left hand into his, slipping it slowly onto her ring finger. He let out a relieved breath when he saw how well it fit her.

Watching her face as she stared at the ring, he marveled at the light shining there. His heart jumped in his chest. Then, he scowled. If half the people, he knew, could see him now, mooning over her as if he were a love sick schoolboy. . . . "

To Tame a Wild Hawk

He looked down at Mandy's face, then at the still grinning doctor.

"Don't even think about running now, lad," the old man teased him.

Hawk glowered at him, "Wouldn't dream of it."

Mandy looked up at him, smiling. "He has promised to stick with me, no matter what it takes," she told Doc.

Doc chuckled. "Well, Hawk, I reckon it will take a lifetime."

Hawk felt the blow of those words. "Yeah—I reckon it will," he answered.

Mandy had felt the blow of those words, too. Her heart skipped a beat. He would be here . . . until the threat of McCandle was over, but what then? She half watched as Hawk crossed the room and began to pack his saddlebags, mumbling an answer when he told her they needed to pick up more supplies.

"We'll leave first thing in the morning, Mandy." He finished and looked up. "Mandy?"

"What?" she murmured. Then, "Oh yeah—that will be fine."

Doc smiled at them. "Well, I guess I will see you two young people at dinner." He stretched his back and headed for the door.

Hawk nodded at him as he crossed the room to stand in front of Mandy. "What's wrong, second thoughts already?" He cocked a dark brow. "And here we are, just engaged."

Mandy shook her head, trying to throw off the shadows. "No, just. . . . " She smiled. "It's been a long day."

Hawk lifted her chin with his finger. "What did I tell you about lying to me?"

Mandy avoided his eyes, shivering at his touch.

"Mandy, I'm not a good choice for a husband. Hell, I'm not even a bad one. I am the worse one you could make. His gaze went to the window, taking on a far-away look. "And when I have to go, you will still be stuck with me. I do not even know when I'll be able to come back," e said this more to himself.

Mandy frowned. He had never said anything about coming back before. Was he forced to leave? Did it have something to do with his mysterious identity as a gun hand?

Hawk looked at her, seemed to correctly read her thoughts, and looked away. For a second, she thought she saw pain flicker through his beautiful, golden eyes. In the next instant it was gone, making her think she'd imagined it.

"You're a crazy woman for getting into a marriage with me." Hawk picked up the saddlebags but stared at them as if he could not comprehend what they were. "A woman like you does not go around marrying a man like me, with the type of past I have. No matter our destiny. No matter the lifetimes we've shared. *It will damage you.*"

"No—you won't, Mandy whispered, putting the correct meaning to his words.

A shadow passed over his face. "Mandy, you do not know what you are saying."

Mandy touched his brow. "Yes, I do, Hawk," she answered softly.

"Let it go, Mandy," he growled.

Mandy dropped her head for a second, letting her hand fall to her side. Then straightened, resolutely. "We'd better wash for dinner."

Hawk's nod was curt. "I want to make an early night of it. I want you to come with me to pick up those supplies."

Mandy blinked. "I just got supplies."

"I have other things in mind," his tone brooked no argument.

Mandy's delicate brows shot up. "Fine," she bit off.

Hawk's golden gaze rooted her to the spot. "If you do exactly what I say, when I say, you might stay alive. Do you understand? It might well mean your life."

Eyes blazing, Mandy swept out of the room.

Hawk hot on her trail.

Chapter Eleven

Mandy followed Hawk down the sidewalk. "What did you mean by war?" Mandy had lost track of how many times she'd asked him that same question in the last hour. Hawk did the same thing he'd done each time she'd asked. He simply didn't answer her, only ushered her along. He'd updated the provisions she'd sent out to the ranch, adding a wagon load of supplies of his own. She looked at all the provisions he had laid in the wagon. "What are you planning?" she asked him again. He had enough supplies to wage two wars. But, once again, he only pulled her along, this time into Cord's Mercantile.

Her heart hammered, Cord. Well, Cord would lecture her. And Hawk, she threw up her hands. With Hawk, who knew?

He steered her to the front of the store, giving Cord an intense look until Cord stopped what he was doing and looked up.

"Morning, Mr. Hawk."

"Just, Hawk."

Cord glanced at Mandy. "Hawk," he repeated. "Everything you ordered to your satisfaction?"

"They were fine," Hawk reassured him, "but I need you to order a dress. A very *special* dress." He took hold of Mandy's hand. "It's for our wedding."

Mandy stared at him.

"A wedding dress?" Cord stammered, looking from Hawk to Mandy, and back again.

"I'm going to need it to be ready within the month," Hawk clarified.

Mandy felt her heart drop, through her soles. The wedding. That's what this is all about. This is all a show for Ashley—to flush him out.

Cord's face waxed bloodless. He looked at Mandy. "Does this means your father . . .?"

"I assure you," Hawk growled," there is *no* mistake."

"My father knew all about my fiancé," Mandy reassured him, getting into the role.

Cord stared at her, dumb-founded. "Mandy, have you talked to your father's attorney yet? You better let him know your—um—mysterious fiancé has *finally* shown up."

Mandy watched as Hawk's eyes narrowed on Cord. Yep, he had taken exception to the word *finally*. She bit her lip, shaking her head. She hoped Hawk wouldn't pay attention to the mention of her seeing Perry.

It was a short wish.

Hawk looked at her—and frowned. "We'll do that next, then. Now, about the dress?"

"Dash it!" Mandy muttered.

That damnable eyebrow shot up. "My dear?"

She bit down, hard, on her tongue to keep from retorting.

Cord left for the backroom to grab the catalogs. When he returned, he handed them to Hawk. He looked—relieved. Mandy frowned at him, wondering at this new development. But she didn't have time to wonder long.

Hawk set the catalogs down at a table with a beautiful flowered cloth thrown over it. He was looking at her, expectantly. She looked down at the first catalog. When she looked at Hawk, she found he was already examining the dress. She'd have never thought he'd be so attentive to such a thing.

It melted her heart.

The two of them poured through the books for the next hour, until she came across the perfect dress and paused to look at it more closely. "It's beautiful," she breathed.

To Tame a Wild Hawk

"We'll take this one," Hawk told Cord.

Cord was busy sweeping—and whistling. Again, Mandy frowned at him. Why did he suddenly seem so—happy? He came right over. He smiled when he saw the dress. "An excellent choice."

"How long will it take?" Hawk was already pulling out some bills.

"Three or four weeks," Cord answered, looking over at Mandy, who was staring at him like he'd grown two heads. "What?"

She tilted her head to one side. "I don't know." She frowned." Why are you so happy all of a sudden?"

"Can't I be happy for you?" Cord retorted.

Mandy's gaze narrowed on him. Something was up, and she wouldn't rest until she figured out what it was.

"Is there anyone who can do alterations?" Hawk asked Mandy.

Mandy frowned at him, now, puzzled about why he worried over such details. "Actually, Meg is very good at sewing." She could just see the *Grandmothers* smiling.

"I also need to see your wedding bands," Hawk informed Cord.

"You might want to order those, too," Cord replied. He finished writing down the size of dress, measured and wrote out all the details for ordering the rings as Hawk watched over his every move. "Will there be anything else?"

"That will do." Hawk paid him and led his speechless fiancée to the door.

"Wasn't that going a bit far?" Mandy demanded outside the door.

"What?" Hawk asked, innocently.

"The ring. The *alterations.*" She pulled a face. *"The dress. . . . "* Mandy clarified.

"Not at all." Hawks took her arm and lead her down the walk. "Where is this attorney's office?"

She pointed at the office. "Couldn't we come back and see him another day?"

Hawk's eyes narrowed on her face. "No," he said simply and led her across the street to the door that said *Perry, Attorney at Law*.

A happy young attorney, with a pointed nose and watery eyes, greeted them at the door and ushered them towards two high-backed chairs setting in front of his mahogany desk. When they were seated, he sat down and steepled his fingers, looking at Mandy. "I think you've been avoiding me." He adjusted his spectacles and unlocked a drawer, taking out a sheaf of papers. His hands shook, slightly, when he thumbed through them. "You have an idea of what your father put in his will, don't you?"

Mandy winced. Hawk's eyes narrowed on her, again, and she steeled herself not to squirm. His golden gaze dropped to Perry's trembling hands.

Perry took a deep breath, gathered his courage, and continued, "You know your father didn't believe in your mysterious fiancé. I'm glad to see he was mistaken."

Mandy merely nodded and waited for him to continue.

"He didn't want you to run *The Northern Rose* on your own."

"Yeah," Mandy frowned, "so what did he do?"

"Now, don't go getting crazy on me, Mandy. It's not a problem, now that your mysterious fiancé has *finally* shown up," Perry stammered.

Mandy's gaze shot to Hawk's face. His eyes had narrowed, dangerously, on Perry's face. She swallowed and turned back to the attorney. "What did he do?"

Perry cleared his throat, having realized that he had, inadvertently, drawn the entirely wrong kind of attention from Hawk and straightened his papers, clearing his throat, again. "He gave you three months to marry this *mysterious* fiancé. Unfortunately, you wouldn't see me and over half of that time is up."

Mandy face turned molten. *"He did what?"*

"Why do you think I so desperately wanted to talk to you?" Perry stood up. "Did you think if you ignored me, it would all go away?" he yelled back, then immediately backed off at the warning in Hawk's eyes. He shifted. Swallowing hard, he sat back down.

"Or what?" she bit out between clenched teeth.

Perry swallowed, plainly taken back. He glanced at Hawk. "Or what?" he repeated, still watching Hawk's face. He looked as if he was mentally counting the seconds until his death. The look on his face was almost enough to cause Mandy to laugh out loud. Whether in amusement, or crazy rage, she couldn't tell.

"What if I didn't produce my mysterious fiancé?" she enunciated with mounting anger.

To Tame a Wild Hawk

"Oh, that." Perry licked his lips and cleared his throat, never taking his eyes off the deadly gunfighter. "Well, as I said, it's not a problem anymore."

"Perry!" Mandy warned, jumping up and leaning over the desk at him.

Hawk sat forward, and Perry looked hard put not to jump up and run. "He arranged for you to marry, Cord," he stammered.

Mandy went still as death.

Hawk frowned.

"And if I'd refused?"

"Mandy, it doesn't matter, now that you're marrying the Hawk, here. The rest is irrelevant."

"If I had refused?" Mandy repeated through clenched teeth.

Perry swallowed. He clearly did not want to reveal what her father put in his will.

"Perry!"

He glanced at Hawk. "He arranged for the ranch to be sold—to the McCandles'," he nearly whispered.

Mandy's knees buckled. Hawk stood in a flash, guiding her down into her chair. "Goddess, how could he? They murdered him! He knew what they were. How could he hand over the thing they were willing to murder him for?"

Perry's voice gentled. "He knew. But none of that was as important to him as making sure you didn't try to take McCandles on by yourself."

She swallowed, hard, at the tears that stung the backs of her eyes. How could this be happening? "But to give it to them?" She shook her head in shock. "Why marry Cord? He's a store manager. How could he possibly stand up against McCandles?"

This time, it was Hawk who answered her. "He wasn't always a store manager."

She frowned, waiting for him to continue.

"I thought I recognized him." He looked at Mandy. "He used to pack a gun," he told her gently. "Was good at it, from everything I've heard. A bad bunch murdered his wife when he was in his early twenties?" He looked at Perry for confirmation.

Perry only nodded, and Hawk continued, "He went crazy, killed the entire bunch. When it was over, he put up his Colts for good. The mercantile was a good way to make sure people didn't uncover his past. It was one of the last places people would expect to find a man, good with a gun."

"Why didn't I know this? And why would he take them down for me?"

"Because, he came here for a fresh start," Perry answered. "He didn't want anyone to know. Your father must have either guessed, or Cord told him."

Hawk touched her face. "But he would have taken down his Colts down for you, love." His eyes were so gentle, Mandy wanted to cry.

"But he's not that old. How could a man have lived two lifetimes already?" She splayed her hands in confusion. "And to give himself away—for me." Tears filled her eyes at the realization of what he'd been willing to do for her. And with it, the realization of what he'd nearly given up . . . and why he'd been happy when he'd heard their news.

He was in love with Meg--and honor-bound—to her.

Hawk took her gloved hand into his own rough one, gently squeezing it.

She shook her head. "We've always been great friends. He watched me grow up. He's like a brother I never had," her voice continued to rise. "But to be his wife—how could you papa?" She turned her face away and whispered. "I never really knew Cord at all."

"Or you, pa," she whispered to herself.

Hawk pulled her out of the chair. "Come on Mandy," he tucked her firmly to his side, "we're going to get you home."

"Home?" she murmured, looking lost.

"So you'll marry soon?" Perry persisted. "Time's up, October, 28th."

Barely a month away.

"We'll let you know the date." Hawk maneuvered Mandy towards the door. "But we won't be waiting long."

Perry grinned, clearly relieved.

Hawk opened the door. At the last second, just before Hawk could guide her outside, Mandy turned back to Perry. "What would have happened if I had married Cord, and then divorced him after the wedding?"

To Tame a Wild Hawk

Perry's lips thinned in a straight line. It was clear he didn't want to answer. Finally, he said, his voice so quiet Mandy nearly couldn't hear him, "You would still forfeit the ranch."

Mandy's gaze was riveted on Hawk's face. He managed to get her out the door before she tried to hit him. "What the hell are you doing?" she raged at him. "It's a fake! It's all a fake. How could you go on pretending?" She gave a laugh that bordered on hysterical. "You heard him. . . ." She swallowed a sob and whispered, "You said yourself. No matter what, when this is done, you'll go. I can't marry you and have you take off after we've taken down McCandle! It will violate my father's will. *I have to marry Cord—or lose everything.*" She glared at him in wild anger—and hurt. "If I marry you, you will just run off and leave me alone."

"Like bloody hell!" Hawk roared.

Mandy jumped, brows raised, and glared at him. "If I marry you, you will just run off and leave me alone," she repeated, tears coursing down her cheeks.

He caught her chin and forced her to look at him. "You will not now, nor ever, entertain the notion of marrying Cord!" he ordered.

"Hawk, you heard Perry. If I marry you, you'll have to go when we're done fighting McCandles, and then, the same thing will happen all over again with some other cattle lord looking for an easy ranch to add to his collection and seeing a woman, on her own, as easy prey. McCandles, or the next cattle baron, they're all the same. I don't have a choice!"

His gaze swept over her face. He reached up and ran a finger down her cheek. "When I walked away, you were supposed to marry someone decent, someone you could love and be happy—have babies." He gnashed his teeth. "I'm not going to walk away—have the light go out of my life, so you can marry someone who's led the same lie as me."

"I wasn't given a choice. . . ." Light of his life? Her heart thumped. What was he saying?

"You could marry me—for good?" Hawk growled.

Just to save her. No! She shook her head.

Hawk's eyes went cold. He grabbed her hand, hauling her down the boarded walk towards their wagon, which was, by now, loaded down with supplies.

He lifted her up and roughly thrust her on the seat.

Neither Hawk, nor Mandy, spoke for a moment as he stared into her aqua eyes. Finally, Mandy couldn't take it. "I won't have you marry me—to save me from my father's will," she blurted out.

The anger went out of Hawk's eyes, and she let out the breath she'd been holding. He looked at her, a deep tenderness lighting those gold-green eyes now. "Oh, I can name several reasons I'd marry you. But it wouldn't be just to save your beautiful backside."

His husky tone, and the meaning behind his words, stirred an answering fire deep within her. But he's not marrying you because he loves you, her mind whispered. Her heart answered with a wavering beat—he wanted her, but that wasn't enough. Biting her lip, she looked away. She swallowed the despair rising in her throat and closed her eyes to the warning. Her heart ached with pain.

Maybe someday he'd love her? But what if he didn't? Could she live with him, loving him, knowing he'd never return her love? That would be the worst kind of hell.

At least with Cord, there wouldn't be any surprises. She would never love him like this, and he would always care for her as though she were a sister—and be forever pining away for Mandy's best friend—and the life they never had. Bile choked her. She didn't have a choice. She could never marry a man, knowing he thought of her as though she were a sister. She could never take away the man Meg was in love with—no matter her father's will. So if she wanted to save her ranch—she would have to marry the Hawk.

And damn the consequences.

She looked at him—and knew he waited to hear her say it. . . . "Yes," she said simply.

He yanked her back off the wagon seat and whirled her around in his arms, giving her a gentle kiss right there on the street. Several people stopped and openly stared. A couple of the gentler women waved their fans over their face and looked as though they'd faint from the impropriety of it—but Mandy didn't care.

What was one more story to set their tongues a wagging about her.

Hawk gently placed her back on the wagon seat. He gave a nod to the ranch hand.

She looked at Pete as he sat down beside her. Tommy jumped up into the back and settled himself amongst the supplies. Old Charlie rode up beside the

To Tame a Wild Hawk

wagon on his horse. She glanced at them both in surprise, then back down at Hawk in panic, "What about you?"

He mounted a livery horse. "I'll be there, Mandy." He rode over next to the wagon seat, and right in front of the whole town, who by now had gathered to quite a crowd, he kissed her, again. "I promise. Now, go home."

He rode off.

Chapter Twelve

Mandy paced the window, willing his return, willing the very shapes of him and his horse to emerge. As if by will alone, he would come. He would be there. For two days, she had waited—waited, and waited. Yet still, he had not shown. Where in Goddesses' name was he? He'd sworn to be here! She fought her heavy eyelids. She hadn't slept, hadn't eaten. Couldn't concentrate. He had to come! He was her only hope.

Her only weapon.

What if he'd changed his mind? What if the mysterious fiancé, thing, had done him in? If he didn't show, it would be a terrible blow after the little scene she'd put on for the McCandles. Winning was all that mattered. She'd sworn revenge. She would have it. She could let nothing else stand in her way.

If he didn't show, she could never marry Cord—to save her ranch—and stand between him—and Meg.

No. She could let nothing stand her way.

Absolutely nothing!

Then, why?

Why did her body scream every time he touched her, every time he kissed her? She was mad. She had to be. . . . How else could a man have such a devastating effect on her body? How could he play her—as if by magic?

How could he make her forget her vows of revenge?

Never again, she swore! She would be the master. McCandle had caused too much harm to let him get away.

Besides, she didn't have a choice. She couldn't marry Cord. And anything else put her at McCandle's mercy.

She ignored the voices of the *Grandmothers*, telling her Hawk was her destiny. She concentrated only on taking McCandle down. The alternative was too unsettling. She didn't want to think about how cleanly Hawk had climbed into her veins, sang in her blood.

No! She would never go back on her word to her papa. She balled her fists and hit the frame of the window. He would show! He had to show.

In total exhaustion, she flung herself into her rocking chair. Not once, had she considered fatigue now ruled her thoughts. "Where is he?" she yelled at the ceiling. Her head rolled back, her eyelids too heavy to be denied, one moment longer. Her last coherent thought willed the sound of a single horse's hooves, pounding the ground beneath them.

He would come. *He had to.*

Sleep claimed her, and with it, once more, the dream.

A dense fog shrouded her head, the same dense fog that overtook her every time she closed her eyes. The fear. She ran, but there was no end to the fog. No matter which way she went, it enveloped her, threatened to suffocate her. She wanted to scream. She opened her mouth, but no sound came out. He was coming for her father. Her papa. No, papa! Blindly, she fought the fog, thrashing at it, trying in vain to claw her way through it. "No, papa!" she mouthed. Terror clawed at her heart. "Goddess, help him. No!"

Hands of steel lifted her and held her to a massive wall of granite. In sheer terror, she fought with all her will and might, but it only subdued her.

"Amanda!" a voice pierced the fog. "It's me, Hawk. Wake up, Mandy. It's only a dream. Wake-up."

Slowly, Mandy floated up out of the fog. Raising her head, her eyes opened and clashed with the gold ones of the man holding her tight."

"Woman," his tone was gentle, "what were you dreaming? You fought me as though McCandle himself was on your tail."

"He is." She was half surprised to hear her voice working. "He's most definitely on my tail, every day, and with every nightmare, until I kill the tormentor," she nearly yelled. She pressed at his chest with both hands. "Put me down!"

"Not until you tell me about the dream."

To Tame a Wild Hawk

"There's nothing to tell, just fog, endless fog and no way out. I can feel my papa's danger. But no words would come out to warn him." She, again, pushed against him. *"Now, put me down!"*

"Mandy!" He released her legs. Letting her slide down the length of him but kept her firmly trapped in his arms. "Where is your washbasin?" He pointedly looked around the room. "You need some of this heat taken out of you."

"Do you think me so daft as to tell you!" she practically spat the words.

"Have it your way," his answer was smooth. He settled her over his shoulder.

She screeched at him in sunrise. *"Put me down this minute!"*

His only answer was to walk from the room, searching for the washbasin. He walked from room to room, heedless of the pounding she was giving his back.

"Put me down," she screamed. *"Hawk, I mean it!"*

Finding the basin, he lowered her and held her easily in one arm as he reached for the pitcher of cool water with his free hand. "I wouldn't add anything more, were I you woman, if you'd have me go easy on you." Seeing the look in her eyes, he eyed the washtub full of water she hadn't taken out. It was cold, now. It would do, nicely.

Mandy was too enraged to see reason. "You green eyed. . . ." She gasped when she hit the water, clothes and all. She should have relented, then. But she only saw red. She thought sure she could rip him apart with her bare hands.

She came up, throwing water at him as fast as she could and knew a great satisfaction to see him nearly as drenched as she. She would have run, then. Really, she would have. If he had not looked down at her, just then, and the cold fury in his eyes struck such terror in her heart, she was rooted to the spot for several seconds. When her brain finally had the sense to scream, run, she turned to do just that, knowing the same terror as in her dreams of feeling as though she were going in slow motion. And when she felt a steel hand maniacal her arm, she knew, she had tried too little, too late.

He picked her up, with one fluid motion and headed straight to the first bedroom he'd spotted on the way in. On reaching it, he flung her on the bed. Then, turned and slammed the door shut with a booted foot.

Mandy's face drained of all blood, leaving it a sick white. She knew fear, now, which matched none other—not even when McKinney had held her a helpless prisoner. She watched as he came slowly forward as though stalking his prey, a menacing glitter in his eyes, so cold was his fury. When he reached the bed, she made a mad dash for the other side, felt her foot grasped, her body being pulled slowly towards him. Too late, she tried for reason, "Hawk. I didn't mean it," she screeched.

"You should have thought of that before," he growled. "Tell me, Mandy, do you always allow such free rein to your temper?"

"Papa told me the same. I have tried, but—I didn't mean it, Hawk. Truly I didn't."

He picked her up, easily, and set her face down over his lap. She struggled and screeched but to no avail. When she would have cursed him again, she felt him softly caress her buttocks—and was swamped with a whole different type of heat.

"Did you really think I would hurt you?" he bit out.

She couldn't have moved.

One hand held her firmly at the small of her back, and his free hand was doing delicious things, which made her feel she'd gone mad—considering where she was and what he'd been threatening to do. Warmth swirled through her, paying no heed to her anger—or embarrassment.

His voice was husky when he next spoke, "I warn you, Mandy. Don't ever try that again or what you feel from my hands will not be pleasant."

Her voice was a hiss. "Nobody could ever accuse you of being a gentleman, no matter the years you spent in the South."

She could feel every ridged line beneath her body and knew firsthand, he struggled with his anger. "You test a man sorely, Mandy."

She lay silent, waiting.

Finally, he sat her up. Taking in her pouting mouth, he tried to restrain himself—and lost. With a growl, he threaded his fingers through her hair, now loose from their struggles. "Every time I see your hair bound, I will free it," he whispered this, a breath from her lips. "Like your spirit, I will have it be free, my woman."

She shivered at his possessive words. An almost violent need stole through her blood. With a start, she realized how true his words had been. She closed her eyes and shuddered with the force of it. Yes, she was his, as truly as though he'd made it so. She was his, and she'd never belong to another. Anger, as well as pain from this revelation, made her challenge him. "It is only this farce I started. I am not truly your woman!"

His eyes pierced hers, seeming to steal deep into her soul, to know her thoughts. She wanted to look away, but her eyes, of their own violation, were held captive by this, seemingly, hypnotic effect he held over her. "Did you not pay heed to the *Grandmothers?* You are my woman," he stated simply. "I will make it so."

At times, she thought, he was completely Indian in his male arrogance. He commanded it. It was him, a part of him, this confidence. This complete knowledge of who he was. What he wanted. He would not pretend otherwise.

She was startled to realize she would not have him pretend otherwise. It was part of what struck such fear in his enemy's hearts. It undermined them. That, and how deadly fast he was—how swift his retribution.

Like someone else she knew, she thought vaguely.

She shook her head, violently. No! Where did that come from? He was nothing like Jason McCandle. Nothing!

Hawk, seeing her shake her head, and misinterpreting its meaning, stood suddenly, leaving Mandy bereft.

When she realized what he thought, she stood and grabbed his arm. "No, Hawk. I wasn't telling you, no. I was just thinking something, and I reacted to those thoughts."

Hawk turned back to her, his hand reaching up and caressing her cheek. "Tell me of them," he commanded quietly.

She looked confused, then answered. "I was thinking how much like Jason McCandle you are."

He sucked in his breath.

"I know." She gave a shaky laugh. "Now you know why I was shaking my head. I couldn't believe I had thought it. You are nothing like him. Only...."

"Only, what?" he demanded.

"How swift you are with your retribution, like him...." she answered and frowned. "And...."

He gave her a slight shake to prod her.

"It's just, now that I think about it, you're very much like him. Yet you're as different as night and day. Isn't it funny? Him so light, you so dark, yet him being the evil one, while you're," she lifted her eyes and gazed at him with all the soft, melting emotions she felt, shining in her eyes, "anything but. . . . " she almost whispered.

She sighed and turned away while Hawk watched her intently. "To be fair, Jason is not the evil one. Though, he rules this town as though he were a king. It's his son who is evil. I just wish I could be certain Jason had nothing to do with my father's death. I wish I could be certain it was only his son."

Hawk took hold of her arm and pulled her gently to his chest. She went, not even questioning it until much later. It felt too good.

So right.

His hand softly stroked her, up and down her back. He caressed her, soothing her. After a time, he gently raised her chin, lowering his mouth to cover hers in a tender kiss. No sooner their mouths meeting, and the fire sparking to full blown flames, then the wind, seeming to flare up and fan those flames into a raging fire.

He knew he possessed her in that single kiss. Yet her spirit would not be conquered. That is what he loved about her, her spirit. She would not give her heart easily, and once given, it would be his forever. Not given, then easily taken away. No, indeed, they would grow old together. Their love would grow stronger as each year came and went. But first, she would have to recognize this love, for she had a strong mind and was proud.

He felt her body shake with the power of his kiss. A need so deep it took his breath, stole through him, and she brought her arms around his neck. She reached inside his soul, firing flames, which seemingly wrapped her body inside his. She belonged to him and to him alone. He would kill any man who tried to touch her this way.

She wrapped her arms tighter around his neck, matching him kiss for kiss, arching her body towards his, melding them as one.

He lifted her, settling them both on the bed. A voice in the back of his mind telling him he wanted more than this one night. His heart ignoring his logical mind, too deeply entrenched with its own needs, and desires, to pay him heed. It told him, only, that she was his, now—and forever. He didn't question this. He knew it to be so.

Mandy wrapped her legs around him. Never had she experienced anything like this. So great were these feelings, they shook her to her core. Her body trembled with her need.

To Tame a Wild Hawk

It took her several seconds to realize someone was banging on the door. And even when she comprehended it, she tried hard to ignore it, so great did she want Hawk to continue this assault on her body of such exquisite torture. However, the loud banging was anything but exquisite.

In fact, *it was downright annoying.*

Hawk rose up with a deep scowl that, once again, reminded her she was glad she was not his enemy. "What the hell?" he demanded. He pulled away and marched out the door, no doubt bent on doing someone great harm.

Mandy would have laughed, if she had not been afraid for whoever knocked. She jumped up and raced after him, reaching him as he yanked the door open, a deadly look in his eyes. His body tensed to pounce.

And he came face-to-face with Ashley.

She thought she would laugh out-loud when she saw the look on Ashley's face. He looked from her lips, still swollen from Hawk's kisses, to Mandy's wet clothes, then Hawks, before traveling up to Hawk's menacing scowl. Ashley bellowed his rage. "I'll kill you, by God. I'll slit you like a fish, from head to toe," he raged.

It wasn't funny. Truly, it wasn't. And much later, they would talk to every man on the ranch, to work out how McCandle had stolen onto the ranch, endangering everyone, but right here, right now, it was fortuitous. If only Hawk hadn't had the unbelievable manners to stand there—and smile, now that he saw who it was, as if he were actually happy to see him. It was a smile so smug, and well, sated, you would think something more than kissing had been going on in the next room.

And when Mandy looked at Ashley, he was dark purple. He sputtered, and for once, in all the time she'd known him, he was without words to say.

Mandy bit down, hard, on her lip but could stop the smile that stole through. She lost, a giggle escaped. Then, the tears came as she dissolved into laughter. And when she would have stopped, she could not, for the look on Ashley's face was a rare treasure. A gift, long in coming, for all the years he'd stolen the laughter from her life.

That she would never, again, see him like this, was well known to her. That she would pay a dear price for this, she knew with no doubt. But she'd enjoy the gift while it lasted.

"I demand to know what's going on here," Ashley bellowed when he found his voice.

Mandy wiped the tears from her eyes and, smiling sweetly, said, "Why, nothing, Ashley. We . . . we," she deliberately stuttered, "why, we were just talking."

Hawk called on all his will to keep a neutral expression, but he would have to remember how well she had played this little performance.

Ashley glared at her, then Hawk, before rounding on her, "You belong to me Mandy, and it matters not what games you play. You will be *my wife*. I'll see you dead before you marry this—man," he sneered up at Hawk. "So you'd better hear me, Mandy. Marry me—or watch the buzzards pick his bones, then your own."

Mandy had sobered during this attack. She'd never thought he would go so far, or be this blatant with his attacks. The man was either a fool, or he knew, no one, here in this valley, had the power to stop him.

And Mandy knew, Ashley was no fool.

"Then, you'd better kill us, quickly," Hawk growled, "because we *will* marry—and soon."

Mandy gasped. Hawk had just challenged him.

Jake rounded the corner of the ranch house. Seeing him, McCandle backed up, but only a step. "You had better watch your back, Hawk," he hissed. "For the instant you let your guard down, I'll be there. You can count on it."

Hawk held his hand out to Mandy. She placed her smaller one in his without hesitation. He pierced Ashley with a menacing glare. "I'll be waiting," he answered, his voice low and cold.

Ashley winced from the violence he saw in Hawk's eyes. But he turned his back on him and went down the steps. He mounted his horse, eyeing Jake, who now had his Colt trained on him, before looking at Hawk again. "You may be fast, but you'll lose. Simply because you care too much, and you have honor." He grinned, his handsome face now ugly with his hate. "I would have shot you in the back, just now."

Hawk grinned at him. Genuine amusement glittered in his eyes. "I know. That's what makes this so much fun."

By this time, half the ranch had spotted the commotion. Tommy ran up to Jake and handed him his rifle. Nick had another trained on Ashley from the barn.

To Tame a Wild Hawk

Ashley's face twisted in rage. If he saw the hands had surrounded him, he paid them no mind. "You're so damn sure of yourself, aren't you?" His ugly smile appeared again. "But you're right about the fun. I *will* enjoy myself, immensely, when I slowly gut you. And I'll take great pleasure in listening to your every scream. You will beg me to let you die." He laughed. "And I will grant you your wish." He whirled his horse and left, Jake's rifle trained on his back, until he was out of sight.

Hawk hugged Mandy to him. She shivered and hugged him back. "He's dangerous, Hawk."

Hawk leaned back, looking at her. "A worthy opponent," he smiled.

"This isn't a game, Hawk. He'll kill you if he gets the chance," Mandy yelled, hitting his chest with her fists.

He grabbed both her tiny fists in one of his. "It is to me," he answered. "I know this land Mandy, and I know what I'm doing."

"He was raised in this area, too," she reminded him.

"But he never took the time to know the land," Hawk told her.

"And what difference will that make when he shoots you in the back," she railed at him. "He's right, you're just so damn sure of yourself."

"I heard that," he growled.

She hugged him tightly to her. "Be careful."

He smoothed her hair and kissed her forehead, and eyes, then, her nose and gently brushed her lips. "I'm not taking any chances."

He picked her up and carried her in the house and gently set her on her feet. He looked down at his wet clothes, then hers. "I'm going to change and go out to talk to your men. I want you to get out of those wet clothes and get some sleep." He turned her towards the hall. "I told you I'd come. Why did you wait for me? It's obvious you haven't slept in sometime," he frowned at her.

"I was afraid you'd changed your mind." She turned and made her way down the hall. Hawk watched her walk away. Shaking his head, he went to change.

Chapter thirteen

Lydia was no lady to be mocked. She'd been the housekeeper for Mandy's father ever since Mandy could remember. For propriety sake, she'd been dubbed, Aunt Lydia. There had been more than one rumor, over the years, of a hidden love affair between her and Mandy's father, but no one ever said this to either of them.

And no one doubted, Lydia was, indeed, a lady.

Dark, exotic eyes of the older, beautiful woman, glared at Hawk with an intensity that belied her tiny, five-foot frame. She was standing in the doorway of her kitchen, starring at Hawk, who was sitting at the kitchen table as though he owned the place.

Her feathers were ruffled like a Spanish hen.

Mandy grinned. "Aunt Lydia, this is my long, awaited *mysterious* fiancé, finally arrived." She sensed, rather than saw, Hawk tense at the table.

Lydia puffed up as though she were a chicken protecting her chicks.

Mandy stifled a giggle.

"All of this time." Lydia wagged a finger at him, "and you have not shown your face. Why show up, now?"

"Would I let *my love* marry McCandle?" He grinned at her.

"No, of course not." Aunt Lydia flushed at his smile.

Mandy rolled her eyes, dramatically. Was there any woman immune to his charms?

Aunt Lydia turned, her dark eyes boring into Mandy. "I never believed that story about you're *mysterious* fiancé. Where did you meet him?"

Biting back another grin, Mandy fought to sound plausible. "You remember, when I went visiting Sarah over three years ago." She breathed a sigh of relief when she saw her Aunt Lydia frown. After all, it was during that time she'd started telling Ashley she was engaged. Her father simply refused to believe it, and so, it appeared, had Aunt Lydia.

Huffing, and grumbling under her breath, Aunt Lydia shooed Hawk from the kitchen with her tiny manicured hands. "Go on now—I've got supper to put on."

Giving her his most charming smile, Hawk rolled easily to his feet. His lithe-like grace did not escape her Aunt Lydia, if the admiration in her eyes was anything to go by. Mandy groaned. Aunt Lydia was already half won over.

Hawk charmed her Aunt Lydia all day, and by the time they sat down to dinner that night, anyone could see Hawk had completely won her over.

When Lydia looked away, Hawk winked at Mandy and grinned.

"Doesn't it bother you he's a gun-fighter?" she blurted out.

Hawk glared at her.

"Of course not child," Aunt Lydia hastily assured her, smiling at Hawk. "He's just what we need around here. He is, after all, an able-bodied man, capable of saving the ranch. And it's plain you two love each other."

It was Hawk's turn to scowl, and Mandy's turn to grin at him.

"What would you think if I took Mandy into town to go shopping?"

Aunt Lydia turned and bestowed him with a beautiful smile. "Why, I think that is a lovely idea."

She beamed. "Since her father died, she's had little to bring her joy. It would be wonderful for her." Her eyes we're soft. "Thank you, Hawk."

Mandy rolled her eyes.

Chapter fourteen

They had a visitor that afternoon. A very handsome young man, Hawk introduced as Kid. Mandy could tell he was about half Lakota, which must be how he knew Hawk. They exchanged a warm, warrior's greeting, telling her they knew each other well and appeared close, like brothers.

Kid's sharp gaze told her, in spite his youth, he was dangerous. He didn't miss anything, and he didn't miss the way Hawk kept looking over at Mandy. So when Hawk introduced Mandy, Kid's eyebrows shot up in question, and Mandy groaned. Jake folded his arms, clearly enjoying himself.

Hawk scowled.

But Kid just stood there waiting. Hawk snarled at Jake, and Jake raised one brow at him in amusement. Hawk glared at the Kid. "Okay Kid, have it your way. You want an explanation. . . ." He put his arm around Mandy. "I've decided to marry."

Kid's brows shot up in perfect imitation of Hawk. "You're," he grinned, "kidding right?"

Hawk folded his arms as though to challenge Kid to dispute him in this.

Kid started to laugh. "You're not kidding." From the depth of his bowels he rocked back and forth on his heels, his head thrown back, and he shouted his laughter to the sun till tears ran from his eyes, and he had to hold his sides.

Hawk growled, every bit as menacingly as any cougar Mandy had ever heard. She jumped at the sound and retreated several steps, shivering at the menace in his eyes.

Kid saw it and only laughed harder. "I'm sorry," he said between big guffaws. "But this," his laughter filled the air, "is too perfect."

Mandy stared at him as though he'd gone mad. The look on Hawk's face would freeze most men to their toes—and Kid only laughed harder. The man was either a fool, or he had nothing to fear from Hawk.

No. He was a fool.

Kid swung Mandy into a big hug. "Do I get to kiss the bride?" Then, he kissed her before Hawk could say, no. Or perhaps, because he knew he'd say, no.

Hawk growled, again, and Mandy jumped back.

"Ahhh. . . . She'd beautiful," Kid said. "And man can she kiss."

Mandy groaned. A fool. No doubt about it.

Hawk literally snarled. "Touch her again, and I'll break every bone in your fool neck."

Kid laughed with delight. "I do believe you've got it bad, old man."

Mandy stared at Hawk with a new interest. How odd. Surely he couldn't be jealous? She smiled to herself, the thought warming her to her toes.

At Kid's last remark, Hawk realized how much he was giving away and pulled up short. He was making an ass of himself.

Kid sobered. "I got your message. I came as fast as I could."

Hawk grunted.

"You're preparing for war, I see."

"Yes," Hawk told him and clapped him on the shoulder. "Come, I'll introduce you to the hands, and we'll tell you all about it."

"Oh, no!" Mandy exclaimed when the three of them appeared ready to walk away and leave her standing there. "You don't get to dismiss me. This is my war—okay—our war," she amended, because—that look was back in Hawk's eyes. "But you're not going to just dismiss me as some unimportant piece of fluff." She wagged her finger at him.

To Tame a Wild Hawk

"Then, come on," Hawk invited, stepping off the porch.

Mandy stood there a second—not trusting what she'd just heard. That was too easy, she thought after a moment, and took off after them.

Chapter Fifteen

Moving with the stealth of a cat, Mandy moved silently across McCandle's yard. With practiced ease, she slipped behind a tree and dashed across the darkened grass. She'd been doing this for a long time—but never with Hawk around. He'd have her hide if he caught her.

Slipping a knife from her pocket, she picked the lock open on the verandah door. She closed the door quietly behind her and started her weekly search of Ashley's desk. She had been searching this room, periodically, for more than a month—to no avail.

She just had to find the combination to his safe. *Grandmothers* help me sense where to look.

Hearing a noise, she slipped behind the curtain that had become her hiding place whenever he'd come into his office. Once more, she kept the vigil that tried the very ends of her patience, until Ashley finally went to bed.

What kind of business had a man up in the middle of the night so many times?

Two hours later, he finally left, and Mandy breathed a deep sigh of relief and total frustration. She resumed her search for another half-hour, then silently made her way back out of the house and across the yard.

Maybe next time.

When she arrived home, almost an hour later, she quietly walked her horse toward the barn and prayed she wouldn't be caught. She unsaddled her horse with trembling hands and brushed her down, settling her in for the night. Then, she slipped up to her room on trembling legs. She scowled. She'd never been afraid before. And it wasn't Ashley McCandle who made her afraid, now.

It was Hawk.

This nightly routine was getting old, and every time she went, the stakes got higher, the risk greater. But now, with Hawk, the risk was simply *too* great. She could only hope she'd find what she was looking for soon—or catch Ashley opening the safe—because, she was bound to be caught by one of them. And somehow, she thought it better to be caught by Ashley.

She lay beneath the covers and tried to calm the rapid beating of her heart. If he didn't do what she wanted soon, she had little doubt she'd be caught.

She was amazed she hadn't been already.

How she'd managed it, night after night, both frightened and exhilarated her. Well, it was true—she had help—someone on the inside. Sneaking in wasn't hard. His hands all turned in before dark for an early morning. Sitting in the same room with him, some nights, tried her to the limits. But doing so, on so many nights. . . . Sooner or later, he would have noticed the lock on the Verandah was unlocked some mornings—if she hadn't met Star Flower on her third night there. The beautiful, young Indian maiden had been covering her tracks ever since. But sooner, or later, he would become aware, he was no longer alone in the room—and then, Goddess help her.

Chapter Sixteen

Mandy had been locked down on the ranch for two weeks when she finally had enough. No, they still hadn't made that trip to town. The problem was, Hawk had her men watching her, to make sure she didn't leave the ranch without him. She chewed this over for a couple of hours before deciding, she'd just have to hope she got lucky.

She walked to the barn, acting nonchalant, considering the rage Hawk would be in if he caught up with her. She managed to get her horse saddled without incident, but was mildly surprised when, after waiting for Chuck to walk on the other side of the barn, she was able to lead her horse straight down the lane. Once she was out of hearing distance, she got on her horse and rode fast.

The problem was—Chuck had been the one on watch when Ashley had succeeded in sneaking onto the ranch.

She knew a twinge of conscience when she thought of the set down Chuck would receive if she didn't beat Hawk home, but the joy of being free, after two stifling weeks, was too wonderful to fret long.

An hour later, she reached town and headed straight for the livery. She walked her sorrel mare to the rear of the stable, unsaddled her and started brushing her down. Ben always teased her about currying her own horse, but she insisted on doing it herself.

When she arrived at Meg's house, a few minutes later, her friend hugged her. "Where's Hawk?" Meg looked around her. Not seeing him there, she guessed, correctly, what Mandy had done, pulled her friend in and shut the door. "Mandy tell me you didn't come alone."

"The men were all busy." Mandy laughed. "I wasn't about to pull one off work, when I can handle a gun as well, or better, as any of them."

"Mandy, Ashley has been in a rage. The whole town is talking about it. He's acting crazy." Her shoulders dropped. "Well, you're going to do what you want, despite what I say, but do be careful."

Mandy frowned. "I will. But I've always been able to sense him before. It's that smell of evil, you know. You can't mistake it, once you've got a good sniff."

Meg wrinkled her nose and linked arms with Mandy. "Come on, we'll have tea. You can tell me everything that's happened."

Mandy sat down in a comfortable chair in the parlor and told her all about Kid. By the time she finished, tears were rolling down Meg's face."

"Well, I can't stay long. I don't dare risk Hawk beating me home. But it sure has been fun. When this is over, you and I are going to go shopping and eat at fancy hotels. We're going to do all the things we used to do before McCandle got in the way," she said with meaning. Just saying it reminded her of all that McCandle had cost them.

"Take care of yourself." Meg handed her a pastry to take along. "Don't sneak in without Hawk, again."

"I'll be fine." Mandy tucked her colt in her skirt pocket.

When she reached the stable, she, again, didn't wait for the livery boy but started saddling Chance herself. "I know this was a short visit, but it can't be helped. I'll give you a little extra grain when we get home," she told her.

She did not get the slightest sniff of evil, and when it came, she did not sense it coming.

"Oh, but you're not going *anywhere*," came a snarl from behind her.

She jumped, pivoted around, and came face-to-face to Ashley. She went for her Colt but no sooner cleared it from the folds of her skirts before he slapped it from her hand. "Damn you, Ashley," she hissed. And damn the propriety that had kept her from wearing the holster where she'd have had an easier reach.

He grabbed her by the hair, forcing his fingers through her bun and tearing it out. She could never seem to keep her hair up lately, she thought wildly.

To Tame a Wild Hawk

He yanked her to him and covered her mouth in a brutal kiss. Mandy was stunned for a second, then gagged and struggled violently. She clawed his face and yanked at his hair, tearing hunks of it from his head, but he paid her no heed. He was mad with his rage she realized, just as Meg had warned, and didn't notice the blood running down his face.

"Tell me, Mandy, have you slept with him," he hissed, twisting her arm.

Mandy paled and shook her head, unnerved.

He stroked her face with his free hand. "I believe you. And I also believe, if I take your maidenhood, you will marry me."

"No, I will never marry you!" she screeched in fear. *"Never. Do you hear me? Why won't you listen?"*

He sneered. "We'll see, Mandy, love." He drug her over and flung her in the hay, nearly crushing her when his body followed, landing heavily on top of her. He pinned her hands above her head and ripped her bodice down, his hands returning to squeeze her breast, painfully.

"I'll kill you," she screamed at him.

Why wouldn't anybody come? Surely, half the town could hear her. We're they so afraid, they'd let him rape her? She opened her mouth to give a full blown scream and received a stunning blow for her efforts. She knew little else from that moment on, her mind too hazy from the blow. Then, all went black.

Mandy had no idea how much time had passed when she felt cool air, and realized she wasn't being crushed anymore—but she couldn't seem to focus.

She wondered she was conscious at all. But she could feel the *Grandmothers,* there, with her.

Center on the Goddess, child, they warned her. You will need to focus more than ever, now. His power grows strong.

Grandmothers, how could this happen? How could I have let this happen?

He has blocked you from detecting McCandle.

He . . . you mean the man in the dark suit?

Yes, child. There is much danger around you. More than ever before. His power grows strong.

Gentle hands lifted and carried her. A voice spoke softly in her ear. Hawk, she thought drowsily. It had sounded like Hawk. But, no, it couldn't be him. He didn't even know she'd left the ranch.

A while later, she woke in Doc's office. She tried to lift her head, but the pain . . . she groaned and laid back. "Hold still Mandy, and it won't hurt so much," a voice spoke next to her ear. Gentle hands moved over her, soothed her.

She licked her lips. "Hawk?" she whispered.

"Yes, love, I'm here."

She took a deep, raged breath and whispered, "How did you know where to find me?"

"The *Grandmothers* warned me you were in danger," he whispered by her ear.

"You can hear them?"

"No. I just knew. And. . .then, I knew who warned me."

"Ashley—he. . . ."

"Shhh, love, it's over," Hawk told her, softly. "And for now, he's hurting *too bad* to give us much trouble for a few weeks," he finished with a growl.

She licked her lips. "Did he? Did he. . . .?" she couldn't say it.

He took her hand in both of his. "No, love, I got there in time to stop him." Rage filled him at how close a call it'd been.

"You didn't kill him?" she hissed. "Good."

Hawk frowned at her. "I thought you'd be angry that I didn't. In fact, I would have, but Ben and several other men pulled me off him. Funny thing, since I know every, single one of them wanted to kill him, too."

"Probably, instinct," she whispered. She licked her lips. "I want him, myself. Do you understand? He's mine. He will die by my hand," she choked out, struggling to sit.

"All right, Mandy," he whispered near her ear, pressing her back. "We'll talk more when you're well."

"I mean it, Hawk," she mouthed, her eyes drifting shut.

Hawk's eyes glittered with dangerous menace. He was consumed with rage. Never had he known such fear. He'd thought her lost to him.

To Tame a Wild Hawk

"Easy, boy," Hawk felt the doc's hand on his shoulder. "That kind of anger will make you careless, and you can't afford to make mistakes."

"I just made one. And Mandy paid the price," he raged in a voice threaded with deep emotion. "What if I can't protect her?" he bit out through clenched teeth.

"You can, better than anyone I know," Doc told him. There was a long moment of silence before Doc thoughtfully added, "Who better than you? It makes sense, doesn't it, him being so dangerous, and you, the only one who can take him down?"

Hawk swung and locked eyes with the old man's. Did he know something?

Doc shrugged. "You got to get over this hate. It'll eat you up."

Hawk stared at Mandy. He'd never told the Doc, never told anyone, except Jake—and Kid. "I wish I could forget?" he mumbled.

"Why are you fighting this particular battle?" Doc shot at him.

Hawk's gaze narrowed on him. "Maybe, in the beginning, I thought I had been handed my revenge on a silver platter—but things change."

"What things?"

"Her," Hawk answered, still watching her. "I want her for my wife, in fact, not in some farce of a game. I want the life it offers. I'm tired of roaming, never belonging," he looked away, "the loneliness."

"I'm glad to hear it." The old doc grinned. "Get this behind you, and I wish you much happiness."

"Thanks," Hawk said, finally smiling. Now, to convince her.

She was dreaming. She knew it, but she didn't want it to stop.

A peaceful smile touched Mandy's lips. She dreamed of warm, strong hands that drew her near and wrapped her in the blissful cocoon. Nothing could touch her here.

Here, she felt safe.

She fought the light, shining brightly on her face, threatening to wake her—and make her face reality. She wanted to snuggle in his arms, even if it was only a dream. But warm sunshine, streaming in the open window, forced her to total consciousness. Up, and up, she drifted, until dark lashes lifted and revealed the handsome white Indian lying beside her.

Lenore Wolfe

With a start she realized, it wasn't a dream. She was, in fact, wrapped in Hawk's possessive embrace. His large, muscular leg lay over her and firmly pinned her to the bed. His arm draped around her, holding her cheek close to his massive chest. From the even rise and fall of his chest, she guessed him to be asleep.

The instant she shifted, that changed.

His beautiful, golden eyes opened, his full, sensual lips turning up at the corners as he mumbled a husky, "Morning."

Mandy licked her lips and tried to swallow past the dry lump in her throat. Her voice, when she spoke, was a whisper. "Hawk?" she got out. "You shouldn't be here. Do you realize how this looks?"

His husky voice, when he answered, sent tremors down her spine. "I wasn't about to let you out of my sight, again."

"You said yourself, Ashley's too laid up to bother us for a while," she pointed out, trying to dislodge his arm.

His arm only tightened. "He can still give orders," Hawk told her. "Besides, the only one here is Doc."

With a sigh, she gave herself up to the overwhelming need to be right where she was, snuggled in his protective embrace. It had been so long since she felt safe. The need to hold him—and be held by him—felt so powerful, it frightened her with its intensity.

She realized, with a start, how much she loved this wild, untamed man. That nothing in her life would ever be the same, again, and with frightening clarity, she knew, she never wanted to know what living without him, now that he'd woven his way into her heart, would do to her. Without him, never again would she know happiness, at least, not without a shadow darkening it.

So intense was her love for him, it wracked her soul and caused tears to spring to her eyes. Her love for him filled her heart to overflowing, till she felt her heart would burst with joy. She listened to the steady rhythm of Hawk's breathing as he drifted back off to sleep. She wondered how easy it was to hold each other now, so peacefully, when every other time they'd gotten within arms-reach of each other, it led to volatile passions, kisses, war, anger and even more violent kisses. But now, here they lay, entwined, with all these intense feelings inside her, yet she felt content to just—be.

Her eyelids grew heavy, and she succumbed to a peaceful sleep with the same blissful smile touching her lips, as before.

To Tame a Wild Hawk

It was late *the next* morning when Mandy finally awoke. Hawk had slept, with his head in his arms, at the foot of the bed, had been, in fact, dreaming of Mandy's kisses—and sunshine. She stirred, and he lifted his head, now fully awake, looking quickly to her.

"You're awake." She smiled. "You look like hell."

"So do you," he answered with a teasing grin.

She groaned. "I'll bet I do."

He came forward and took her hand into both of his. "I otta tan your backside for what you did."

She looked into his eyes. "Would it help to say, I'm sorry?"

"If you ever place yourself in danger like that, again, you can expect swift retribution."

Mandy lowered her eyes. "It *was* really foolish, wasn't it?" *And if he knew about her weekly escapades to Ashley's house . . . in every effort to get inside his safe. . . .* "But I honestly thought I could take care of myself. I could always sense him. But I did not now," she whispered. "I cannot believe I did not sense him."

Hawk's gaze narrowed on her. "Do you know why that is?"

She looked up at him. He wasn't going to like this. "It is the man in the suit."

A muscle jumped in his jaw, and he looked away.

"The *Grandmothers* tell me he grows stronger."

Hawk looked at her with such tenderness, it made her heart jump. "Then, we will just have to be more careful, more so, now, than ever, because I'm never losing you to the *likes of him.*" He pushed a hand through his hair in frustration. "Mandy, it's time we got married." He told her bluntly, then wanted to kick himself for being such a clod. He should have asked her, not told her. But he was just so afraid she'd say, no. Well, he'd come this far, there could be no help for it, now.

"Just like that. You say it, and it's done. Is that it?"

"Ashley has upped-the-anti and, besides, you've only a few days left to marry—or forfeit your ranch."

Mandy was crushed. She knew they were going to get married. He'd made that clear. The *Grandmothers* had made that clear. Heck, *her dreams had made that clear.* But she'd hoped he'd *want* to marry her, not to fix her father's will, not to stop McCandles, not even for destiny—but for her. "And what happens when it's over? Do we divorce?" Mandy asked, holding her breath.

"Heed me, well, *my woman*. You will always be mine," he growled. "You marry me—*there will be no divorce*. I will never let you go." With that, he strode from the room.

Well, she thought with a smile, it was a start.

When, next, Mandy woke, it was to find Hawk next to her, again, his lips nuzzling her neck, a wild raging fire tearing through her breast. Where, before, she'd felt a warm tingling, now, was replaced by an all-consuming heat. She felt hot—and when she turned and met Hawk's lips—her last coherent thought was that, he felt hot, too.

A knock on the door had Hawk springing from the bed, and Mandy snatching up the covers, a hot flush staining her cheeks. Meagan opened the door an instant later, sweeping into the room with a beautiful wedding gown in her arms.

"It's ready?" Hawk questioned with an ease that had Mandy glowering.

How could he be so calm, while she, herself, lay shaking to the point she had to hide her hands and bite down on her trembling lips?

"With a few alterations, as soon as Mandy tries it on, it will be," Meg answered, with a lighthearted giggle. "Oh, Mandy, how I envy you—snapping up a man like Hawk."

Mandy frowned. What had gotten into her friend? "What's going on?" she demanded.

Hawk's dark eyes held her aquamarine ones. How could he touch her so from across the room? She was quickly reminded of moments before that, to her irritation, and his delight, had her blushing again.

"I know it's every bride's dream to wear a beautiful gown to her wedding," he told her softly. His words caressing her like a kiss.

"Oh dear," Meg murmured, finally noticing Mandy's well kissed lips.

Mandy turned a baleful glare on her friend. *"Not one word,"* she warned.

Meg only laughed. "I can't wait to see Ashley's face."

"Not until after the wedding!" Hawk reminded her sharply.

To Tame a Wild Hawk

Meg blinked. "Well, of course." Her answer was smug smile. "But then, I shall march right over, the instant you're on your way home, and relay the happy news."

Listening to them, dawning crashed over Mandy's head. He intended to marry her—*now*—*today*. "There's not going to be a wedding!" she growled, sending two pairs of eyes in her direction. "Not today!" she quickly amended, seeing Hawk's fierce, dark look.

"Explain yourself!"

Hawk, I simply can't go to my wedding with a giant bruise on the side of my head."

Hawk's eyes glittered. He swallowed his disappointment at her obvious lack of enthusiasm.

"The bruise is on the side of your head, Mandy. Your face is virtually unmarked." He fetched a mirror off the highboy and held it front of her for her to see.

She sat up and bent her knees, looking in the mirror.

"I swear he'll pay for what he's done to you," he said, misreading the pain in her eyes.

"He already has, from what everyone has told me," she told him, softly. But her eyes had been betraying her anguish, and fear, at having no more barriers to put up against him. She could not let the McCandles win.

Maybe Hawk would love her—someday.

"That's only the beginning of what I have planned for him," Hawk growled, dragging her thoughts back to the present.

Meagan sat on the other side of the bed and examined her head. "Why, if he had hit your face as hard, as he hit your head, he'd have broken your jaw," she breathed, her crystal-blue eyes wide with shock. "The whole side of your head is purple."

Mandy's own eyes flew to Hawk's, and saw a menacing steal run through him unlike anything she'd witnessed before. But then, she hadn't been very alert when he'd pulled Ashley off her. She changed the subject before he decided to have another go at Ashley. "Hawk, I can't do this today . . ."

"Be there at three." He slammed out of the room.

"Arrogant, insufferable brute," she flung after him, hitting the bed with her fists, "always telling me what to do!"

"I heard that Mandy," he growled from the hall.

Meagan shook her head with reproach, peeking out into the hallway to make sure Hawk had actually gone this time. "Mandy, you should have seen him when you were unconscious," she told her, when she was sure he was gone. "He was quite out of his mind. He only wants to protect you from Ashley." Meg's eyes narrowed on her friend in total seriousness. "He really cares for you. Let him love you, let him help you and protect you, as only a husband would."

Mandy snorted, unladylike. "And how long will he care, Meg? How long before he gets restless and moves on? I will not fool myself into thinking this is a real wedding. It's a bargain—nothing more. A farce I started with my anger. I get a husband's protection, and Ashley off my back, on at least the marriage part." She looked down at the coverlet, she was picking at with her nail, and took a deep breath so her voice wouldn't betray her pain. "I'll probably never know what Hawk's getting out of this. He's after his own revenge, but he won't tell me what it is."

Meagan frowned. "He knew Ashley—before meeting you?"

Mandy nodded. "Knew him—and hates him more than I do, if you can believe that." She ran her fingers through her hair and turned away. "I've seen how he looked at Ashley, when he didn't think anyone was watching him. He hates him with a bitterness that can only bode ill for all of us." She glanced at Meg, was surprised to see her friend's frown deepen until it furrowed her brow.

Meg's eyes suddenly brightened, and she smiled. "Maybe so, but I saw Hawk hover over your bed, frantic with worry. He cares deeply for you, no matter his thoughts of revenge for Ashley." She brushed imaginary wrinkles from Mandy's wedding gown. "And you love him, despite your own vows of revenge against McCandles. So you see. Your love, and your mutual goals, will see you through."

Mandy fell back against her pillows—and groaned.

Meg looked at her and frowned. "Besides, aren't you forgetting something? Isn't that the destiny the *Grandmothers* have told you about?" She smiled when Mandy buried her face. "You would like to pretend otherwise because it scares you so much. But the *Grandmothers* have told you, he is. And you, yourself, have dreamed of him for many years." She shook her head when Mandy would have argued. "No, Mandy, you have *dreamed of this*—for years. You know this is your path—as you say." She laid her hand on Mandy's arm. "You're just scared. And it's understandable. He affects you deeply, anyone can see that . . . but the *Grandmothers* were right—*he is your destiny*. So stop fighting it!" She grinned.

Mandy buried her face in the covers and resigned herself to her fate.

Chapter Seventeen

Beads glittered off Mandy's dress and veil, matching the tears glistening in her eyes. She stared at her reflection in the old mirror, held in place by gnarled, curled hands of carved oak. It was her wedding day. Brides were supposed to be happy on their wedding day, she thought with despair. What kind of bargain had she made? What kind of happiness could she ever find in such a bargain, forever loving him, and he never returning her love. Eventually, getting restless, maybe even taking up with town whores. "Not *bloody* likely!" she growled aloud, making Meg jump. She'd likely kill him first.

She stared at her reflection in the mirror. Her gown was exquisite. It clung, tightly, to her waist, thrusting up, and enhancing, her bosom. The v-shape, making her small waist, appear tiny. The gown was covered with yards of lace, Meg's lace, she thought with a smile. Meg had a passion for lace.

She gave Meagan a hug, causing her friend to frown with worry. Meg had piled her hair high on her head. Hundreds of tiny ringlets spilled softly down, and a beautiful lace veil, lay in folds, over her hair and shoulders.

"You're a beautiful bride," Meg whispered with tears in her eyes.

Mandy smiled through her own tears.

Doc cleared his throat at the door, and both women turned and smiled at him. He grinned at Mandy. "My dear, you are, indeed, a vision."

Mandy crossed the room and hugged him. "Thank you for agreeing to give me away," she whispered in his ear, afraid to speak out-loud for fear her voice would betray her.

"An honor, Mandy dear, I assure you. You make an old man proud." He tucked her hand in his arm and led her down the stairs.

Hawk was not disappointed when, minutes later, she was escorted to the front room

He was stunned.

He drank her in, with a possessive gleam in his gold-green eyes. Mandy felt the familiar warmth steal through her, leaving her limp and weak as a kitten.

If she stared into his eyes, she could feel his hands. She shook her head at her volatile emotions and darted a worried look at the others in the room, wondering if her thoughts had been as transparent to them—as they appeared to be to Hawk. The fire in his eyes told her—he could read her mind.

He was magnificent—standing there, waiting for her to reach his side. And soon after she did, their lives became irrevocably woven together. Mandy likened it to a silvery, invisible thread, joining their hearts. And she knew the *Grandmothers* smiled.

She felt rebellious, right now, with their sure vision of her path. A path with the Hawk . . . their lives entwined. Her heart pounded—fanciful thoughts. But her mind soon followed down the path her heart had taken, with what would have been—could have been—had she not insisted this marriage be—in name only.

She had done so, only an hour ago, and he had only looked at her, an unreadable gleam in his eyes. He hadn't argued, hadn't said one word.

She had wanted to cry.

"Second thoughts already?" his whisper caressed her face.

Meg hugged her, then, and ran off to take care of their hotel.

Mandy frowned as she watched her friend disappear. Meg was clearly enjoying this—too much. She shook her head at Hawk. "No, the marriage has its merits," she answered, trying for a neutral tone.

He let that jab slide, grinning. "I wasn't talking about the marriage—exactly."

To Tame a Wild Hawk

Startled, she looked up and was captured, completely off guard, by the intense look in his gold eyes. He'd read her mind, again, drat the man, or was her body giving her away?

She should look away—really she should—but suddenly, she couldn't remember why.

"Give over Mandy," he whispered. His gaze refusing to release her from the fine thread he was weaving around her. She was caressed by it—captured by it. And each time, the web grew stronger. "You want this marriage in every way, every bit as much as I, admit it, Mandy," his low voice fanned the flames.

Mandy opened her mouth, then shut it. She fought for control, lost, and opened her mouth, again, but the words of denial wouldn't come.

His hand touched the side of her face, his thumb sliding possessively over her lips, stroking her bottom lip again, and again, until she thought she would faint with pleasure.

She'd made a fatal mistake with her heart, thinking she could control this. She should have listened to the danger signs—to all the warnings, and now, it was too late. There was no holding back—*any part of her*, at least, not anything strong enough to hold back this tide of love—and desire. Even though, *the love part* lay only on her side.

She'd been a fool

And her heart was going to pay the price, but she couldn't stop, now.

Hawk's intense, green-gold eyes searched her face, knew the exact instant she surrendered, and only by iron will did he wait to hear the words.

Words avowing her *complete* surrender.

She nodded.

He shook his head. "Say it," he softly commanded. "Tell me what you want."

Mandy's tongue darted out to moisten her lips and heard Hawk groan. She swallowed, her eyes closing for a moment with her body's reaction to that simple sound. The fires were rapidly burning out of control. "You." She looked into his golden gaze. "I *want* you."

Hawk picked her up and walked straight out of Doc's house and across the street to the hotel, where he'd rented a room for the night.

Mandy wouldn't think until much later, how they must have scandalized the town. He set her down at the door, pausing only long enough to unlock it.

"You were *very* sure of yourself," she whispered with heat but not from anger.

"Sure of us," he corrected, swinging her back up into his strong arms. Carrying her across the threshold, he kicked the door shut behind him, setting her down only long enough to lock it. He turned—pulling her to him.

Her eyes locked with his, once again, as he cupped her chin, his lips lowering to claim hers. Their tongues melded, and mated, darting out to meet each other, only to withdraw again. He ran his tongue over her lips and teeth, tasting all of her, sucking her tongue in a way that buckled her knees, causing her to twine her hands through his hair, meeting him thrust for thrust, not even noticing when he lifted her and placed her on the bed.

Within moments, he pulled off her gown and laid it carefully over a chair. He unfastened her corset and slipped her out of her chemise—all the while kissing her, touching her, reveling in the feel of her—until she was finally free of every stitch of cloth, and he could touch her without restraint.

His hand molded her breast, then his mouth covered it with kisses—breathing lightly on it, raining it with kisses, again—and only, when she started to writhe beneath him, finally taking it into his mouth.

Mandy gasped at the intensity of it and moaned his name out loud.

He slipped out of his jacket and shirt, then pressed her breasts to his bare chest, causing them both to groan with the pleasure. Pulling back, he resumed his tender administrations to first one breast, then, the other, till she begged for something she couldn't name.

His hand caressed her thighs, his fingers touching, lightly, over the softness of her inner thigh—touching, touching—exquisite fire, which finally came to rest in the softness of her curls between the apex of her thighs, causing her to buck and cry out.

Yet still, did he tease her unmercifully, kissing her, touching her, watching her desire build, until she was gasping and crying out with pleasure.

He quickly removed the rest of his clothes before resuming the sweet assault on her body, which had her crying his name and weeping. If he died now, he'd die happy, with the sound of his name on her lips. Knowing he'd brought her this pleasure. And in which, it was his name she screamed and when she moaned, she moaned for him, wanting only him. It touched something soft, deep within him. And if she had opened her eyes, right then, she would have been shocked to see the tears that shimmered in his golden eyes.

He moved over her, moving her legs around him as he pressed, slowly, inside her—stopping briefly at the barrier before pushing through—taking her cry deep within him, kissing her, soothing her. He felt her accept him, then move with him. She began to thrash, and he felt her tremble and cry out from the intense feelings washing over her—waves, which crashed over her as she clung to him with her startled moans.

Mandy felt the building waves, upon waves, of pleasure and knew something would burst if he didn't stop—almost thinking to fight him with mounting fear of what was happening to her—yet before she could gain enough coherent thought to begin to fight—the tide broke over her, making her body spasm with the most intense pleasure she had ever known. Muscles inside her pulsed with the force of the pleasure, holding her in throws of passion, making her scream from its intensity. Her climax brought him over the edge of control, causing him to seek his own release as he pulsed violently inside her, exalting with her from the force of their combined pleasure, pushing deep inside her before collapsing on top her. He rolled them both to one side while still inside her, gathering her in his fierce embrace, overwhelmed by what had just happened.

Tears shimmered in Mandy's eyes with the power of her emotions. Never, could she have conceived anything like what had just taken place.

This was the meaning of becoming one.

Her heart overflowed and surged in her chest, and she squeezed him tightly to her. Unable to hold back the power of her love, she held onto him with everything in her heart.

He rained kisses over her face, caressing her, touching her, cherishing her. He tasted her tears, understanding them for what they were. For the intensity of what had passed between them, shook him just as deep.

When she moved her hips towards him in unspoken desire, his response was immediate, and with the slow leisure of savoring the beauty and delight, of such unequaled joy, he made love to her, again.

Chapter Eighteen

Lydia had a whole celebration feast planned when Mandy and Hawk arrived home, late the next day. Smiling in apology, Mandy glanced, a bit shy, at Hawk and he grumbled, but after they ate he laughingly joined the festivities and asked her to dance. His gold-green eyes stared into hers as they swayed back and forth in each other's arms. Looking into her wide, shinning eyes, he tried not to put a name to the emotions he saw there.

It was a couple of hours later, when the hush from the guests, and the pounding of the ground of many horses, brought an end to the joyous occasion.

Hawk cursed himself ten kinds of a fool. He'd left his gun in the house, not wanting to spoil the celebration with the reminder of the ever-present danger of their neighbor.

She was making him soft, and it was going to get them all killed.

A beaten, and bruised, Ashley, and a dozen of his men, rode right through the crowd. They ran their horses into the tables, laden down with food, roping everything they could and pulling things over, shooting their guns in the air. Ashley rode right up to Hawk, who refused to move, even when the horse came to a shuddering stop, ramming into him, snorting wildly and throwing its head. Ashley's evil smile twisted his once handsome features. "So you think you've won, Hawk?" He leered, crudely, at Mandy.

Hawk gave him a cold, measured look.

Mandy grasped Hawk's arm, scared stiff Ashley would shoot him, heedless of his being unarmed.

"Why don't you get down?" Hawk quietly invited.

Ashley grinned. "What? And do the noble thing, taking off my gun-belt and making this an even fight?" He waved a finger at Hawk like a naughty boy, clucking his tongue. "Shame on you, Hawk. You should know me better, by now."

"No stomach for a fair fight?" Hawk softly taunted.

Ashley grinned, again, his face ugly. "Sell out, Hawk. I give you one week. Then, I'll kill you and bed Mandy. I'll even think of you every time I take her."

Hawk took a menacing dive at Ashley, surprising him with the speed of his attack, knocking him from his horse. He came up, dragging Ashley with him, an ominous blade glittering at his throat as he held him in a vice-like grip.

"Where'd—where'd that come from?" Ashley sputtered.

I never go completely unarmed," Hawk hissed. "You would do well to remember that in the future. Now, tell your men to leave."

When Ashley didn't immediately comply, Hawk pricked his neck, drawing a thin line of blood. Ashley turned purple, afraid to breathe. The slightest movement could be fatal. "Leave!" he yelped.

"But boss," one man started to argue.

"Now!" Ashley whispered as the tip entered his flesh. They turned and rode out but stopped outside the ranch, still waiting within sight, as a warning.

Hawk watched for a moment. Then, easing the tip out of Ashley's neck, he told him, "If you step foot on this ranch again, I'll kill you. If I see you within a mile of Mandy—I'll kill you." He tossed Ashley face first in the dirt. "And if you ever provoke me again, like you did tonight . . . "

"Yeah, yeah, I know," Ashley sputtered, "you'll kill me." He stood up and slapped his Stetson on his leg to knock off most of the dust, then ground it back down on his head and remounted his horse.

Then, were understood," Hawk said, unemotionally.

To Tame a Wild Hawk

Cold rage glittered in Ashley's eyes as he raked Mandy, but he wasn't a stupid man. He didn't have to look around to know, by now he had better than a dozen rifles trained on him. And he didn't have to look in their faces to know—he wouldn't catch them unawares a second time.

He reined back, causing his mount to rear and turned hate filled eyes on Hawk. "Enjoy her while you can. Because, there will come a day, soon, when I will bed your wife. But now, I'll make sure you live long enough to watch—and listen to her scream my name." He turned his horse and sawing at the reins, he spurred him into a dead run—as Hawk reached for the nearest rifle.

He yanked one from Ned's grasp, taking deadly aim at Ashley's back, only to have Mandy yank the barrel down as he squeezed the trigger.

He glared at her with barely leashed fury.

"If you do this, you'll be no better than he is. He told you that himself, not so long ago, remember?"

Hawk's jaw clenched, but Mandy gathered her courage and met his fury, head on. She felt several men back away, and she couldn't blame them. She knew the exact moment when the cold rage left him. She saw it in his eyes, knew the second he returned to her—when she felt it in the release of the deadly grip he had on the rifle beneath his hands.

After a long moment, he gently took her hands from the gun and extended it back to Ned—who reluctantly came forward to claim it—watching Hawk's eyes as he did so. But his fury was gone. Hawk gathered Mandy to him—and after hugging her tight—he picked her up, and ignoring the collective gasps of the guests—he carried his wife to bed.

Kid and Jake grinned, wickedly, and set up watch. They were still grinning when they encouraged the neighbors to continue on with their celebration.

"You enjoy shocking people," Mandy laughed, her arms locked behind Hawk's neck.

He carried her upstairs and though the door. Crossing the room, he set her gently on the bed. "I'm sorry your evening was ruined," he told her, his voice husky.

"Oh, I disagree. Not every girl gets to have her hero save her on her wedding celebration." She pulled him down to her. "And without getting a single man killed." Hawk kissed her deeply, then nuzzled her neck and nibbled at her earlobes.

"Oh, Hawk," she shivered, "you make me feel so good. I never knew I could feel this way. I can't imagine never feeling this again." She sobered when she realized what she'd said. For, someday, she would have to learn to live without him. He'd be here till they'd dealt with Ashley, she reminded herself. Then, he'd be gone like the wind. And who knew if, or when, he'd be back. Her dreams saw them together—and their children. They didn't say if he stuck around long enough to see them grow up, and he, himself, had said, when this was done—he had no choice—but to go.

"Such sad thoughts I see in those beautiful eyes of yours," Hawk murmured as he kissed her face, then pressed kisses in her hair. "Do my kisses make you unhappy, then?"

She pulled his lips to hers and kissed him back, wildly.

He chuckled. "I think it's safe to say, no." And he kissed her back, kneading her back, sliding his hands over her.

He made love to her, slowly, inch by tantalizing inch, making her scream with wild abandon. And only, when she crashed over the edge of wild oblivion, did he give over the control, growling his release into her sweet body.

Mandy blushed, furiously, when she woke the next morning to find him watching her.

He chuckled, "You're beautiful, *mitawin*, my woman—my wife."

She blushed deeper. "So are you."

He scowled. "Men are not beautiful."

"Well, if a man could be," she told him, "you would be. I believe the Lakota would say, your face is pleasing to me."

He laughed. "Everything about you pleases me, darlin'"

"Hawk," she asked innocently, "what is your stake in this fight?"

Hawk's eyes narrowed, dangerously. Mandy gulped and giggled, despite the look of pure menace in his eyes. "I was teasing. I figured you married me, so I could ask."

"You figured, wrong."

"I see," Mandy looked away. "Shall we go eat? Half the house must be waiting for us by now."

To Tame a Wild Hawk

"Sure," Hawk murmured, "but first." He climbed on top of her and started seducing her—all over again.

It was sometime later, before Mandy managed to get washed, dressed and down the stairs without being ravished. Hawk had left ahead of her to check on the men.

She blushed, furiously, again, when she saw everyone downstairs, waiting.

Kid grinned at her. "You look beautiful."

Jake jabbed him, hard, in the ribs.

"Dag-nabit, easy on the ribs," Kid complained.

"Better that than that pretty face of yours," Jake threatened.

"Well, hell man, why didn't you just say so."

"I thought I just did," Jake growled.

"Not before you cracked two of my ribs," Kid grumbled.

"What was that?"

"Noth'n." Kid grinned.

"Is Hawk around?" Mandy asked them.

"He was out checking his horse. He'll be in shortly," Jake answered.

"I never got to kiss the bride," Kid stepped up to her.

"You do, and I'll break your fool neck," Hawk growled from the doorway. He walked up and put a possessive arm around her. "I seem to remember, you took that kiss, before."

Jake's eyebrow shot up. "That's right. In that case. . ."

"Don't even think . . ."

But Jake was already doing more than thinking. He pulled her firmly into his solid embrace and kissed her hard.

Hawk growled, and Jake stepped back. For the first time since Mandy had known him, he grinned.

Hawk's fist slammed, hard, into his jaw. Jake's head snapped around, and he staggered. Something to behold. Mandy knew, a lesser man would have been knocked down. But Jake touched his jaw and grinned at Hawk.

"You got it bad, old friend."

Hawk scowled.

Jake picked up his hat and set it on his head. He tipped it at Mandy. "Ma'am, *it was a pleasure.*" And chuckling, he strode out of the house.

Kid stared after him. "Well, I'll be hanged."

Mandy looked at Hawk. The look he gave her was wholly possessive.

"I think I'm going to kill the next man who touches you."

She smiled at him. She couldn't know how beautiful she looked standing there.

"They'd hang you," she told him, teasingly. "Then, I'd have to live my life without you, where all the Jakes and Kids in the world would be free to kiss me."

Hawk scowled and grabbed her by the shoulders. "The only lips you'll know on yours, will be mine." He kissed her deeply. He kissed her possessively. "The only man to ever touch your exquisite body, will be me," he growled. "For you are my woman," he touched her cheek gently. "My wife." He picked her up and kissing her senseless, he carried her back up the stairs.

Chapter Nineteen

"Let me go, you lily-liver'd pole cat," a young woman screeched at the man trying in vain to hold her arm. She turned back to the man who held her full attention, with a wide swing of her knife—that had everyone backing up with some haste. "Why I'll cut you up and use you for bear bate, you fish-eyed, yellow-bellied snake." Having slipped the grasp of those who fought to hold her back, she again leaped for his throat.

Hawk and Mandy made their way inside one of the town's bigger saloons. Jake had headed that way, with Kid, when they first entered town. Mandy knew he'd seen them. With the slightest tilt of his head, he acknowledged he'd seen them, Mandy felt Hawk's return communication, more than she saw it. She was impressed by the easy way they knew what each other was up to. She supposed, they'd learned that during the war.

They hadn't said so, but she'd gleaned little bits of information from them, from things they'd discussed around the ranch. They had fought together during the Civil War. And from the sounds of it, they'd fought together, ever since—at one thing or another.

The four of them had come to town for that promised outing, which had never happened, but Hawk had not forgotten. He'd surprised Mandy with it, only that morning. She'd been delighted. Hawk and Mandy were to enjoy themselves, Kid and Jake to guard, and make sure they did just that.

They'd had lunch, had done some shopping and were heading towards the Cord's Mercantile when the crowd, and the commotion, had drawn them down the boarded walk, having been told *who* the woman was yelling at and curious about *the woman herself*, yelling at the top of her lungs.

"I'll kill you for the lie'n, theiv'n murderer you are, McCandle," she was screaming, now. "There ain't no place far enough, no ground deep enough, to hide you from me, you dung-covered swine. You're gonna rue the day you stole my papa's land and kilt him. I'm gonna cut you up and feed your eyes to the buzzards."

By this time, Mandy was trying to hide her mirth behind a gloved hand as she watched two men trying to get a hold of the young woman. Already, one man was sporting a black eye and bleeding profusely from his nose. The other had a busted lip, and his hand was cut open. They were desperately trying to wrestle a six inch blade out of her hands—and fast getting nowhere.

Ashley was backed against one wall and quite pale. For once in his life, he was speechless. He watched, open mouthed, while his men fought to get the woman under control, to no avail.

Mandy caught a flash of movement out of the corner of her eye, just before Kid sprung over a short wall, grabbing the young woman from behind, around her middle.

Hawk groaned and, taking Mandy's elbow, moved them to where he could better cover Kid. She didn't have to see, to know, Jake had done the same.

"All right, hell cat, give me the knife," Kid told the girl. "Little girls shouldn't play with knives," which earned him a grunt when she slammed her elbow into his ribs. He managed to disarm her with a quick downward yank on her arm, causing her to turn on him in full fury. She hit him square in the nose and kicked him in the shin with the point of her boot, to which, he threw her over his shoulder and exited the saloon in all possible haste, considering she was beating him unmercifully on the back.

"I want that little witch thrown in jail," Ashley bellowed, finding his voice.

"That won't be necessary." Mandy smiled sweetly as Sheriff Tucker came up beside her. "She works for me. I'll pay for any damage she's done here."

Ashley rounded on her in rage. "You saw her! She was trying *to kill me.*"

Hawk chuckled. "Come now, McCandle, that little thing." He grinned. "Surely, you wouldn't want us thinking you could be taken by such a small slip of a woman?" He grunted when he felt Mandy's elbow in his side. "I thought not," he added, when he saw Ashley relent. He took Mandy by the elbow, so she couldn't elbow him again, nodding at Jake to take care of things, and led her outside.

Kid had managed to get the she-cat in the wagon, to Hawk's amusement and Mandy's amazement, but when the girl flew at Kid for the third time, Mandy was done. "Enough!"

The girl looked up in surprise, Mandy noted her beautiful, yellow, cat-colored eyes. The she-cat, and hell-cat, Kid had graced her with was very apt.

"If you're an enemy of Ashley," Mandy told her, "you're amongst friends. I need you out at *The Northern Rose*. That, lily liver'd pole cat, as you called him, is out to take it."

"Really!" The girl smiled, and Kid was visibly shaken. Mandy rolled her eyes.

"Well, then," she thrust out a gloved hand. "You've got yourself a hand."

"Hired hand?" Kid bellowed. *"You're going to make her a hired-hand?"*

"Sure thing." The girl turned her beautiful smile on Kid. "By the way, I'm Katherine, but everyone calls me Kat, and I'm a top notch cow hand, crack shot and could skin the hide off a live grizzly."

"Not on your life!" Kid started. . . .

"You've got yourself a job," Mandy interrupted.

Kid looked at Hawk. Hawk shrugged and grinned back at Kid.

Kat smiled, then, frowned. "If you're after McCandle, then why didn't you let me save you the trouble in there—and skin him?"

"Because, wild-cat," Kid growled, "you would have hung on the next sun rise."

"Yeah, well," a deep sadness flashed through Kat's eyes, "that wouldn't have been so bad. He'd be dead, like I promised pa, and I would have avenged my family. Besides," she shrugged, "I'm alone now, so you see my dy'n wouldn't have been so bad."

"No, I don't see," Kid bit out through clenched teeth. "It's seems to me, you've been given a second chance. You should live it the fullest."

"Besides," Mandy broke in gently, "we're going to get McCandle. All of us—together. McCandle, and his hands, will be the ones who go down. It doesn't seem right, us going down with him, now does it?"

Lenore Wolfe

Kat cocked her head, her intense, golden gaze studying Mandy for a moment. "Do you really think it's possible? I mean bringing him down, really making him suffer?"

"Yes, I do!" Mandy answered confidently. "Not only possible, but it's in the bag." Her aqua eyes narrowed. "I swear it."

Good," Kat said brightly. "I can see you want him as bad as me. So you and I are going *to get him*—then, I'll skin him."

Mandy laughed, and Hawk grinned. Kid just rolled his eyes.

The wagon always seemed to take forever to Mandy. The sun's unmerciful, intensity made her wish she could unbutton a couple of the buttons of the stifling material from around her neck, which was beginning to feel as if it were choking the life out of her.

Surreptitiously, she studied Hawk on the seat beside her. Every time the wagon hit a bump, and their legs brushed together, Mandy felt an all new heat through the fabric of her dress, she was sure had nothing to do with the sun.

She thought about all the changes in her life, in such a short time, and sighed. At least, she had hope. For the first time, since papa died, there was real hope. Mandy glanced back at Kid and Kat, who were not getting on so well, from the look of things.

"I'm gonna scratch your eyes out," Kat bellowed from the rear of the wagon.

"Why, you little hell-cat, I swear, I'm gonna tan your backside," Kid yelled back.

Turning, so he could be heard above they're screeching and fighting, Hawk asked Kid, "Are you sure you wouldn't rather ride that horse of yours?"

"Like I said," Kid shot back, "I don't trust her not to scratch up the boards. I'm gonna stay with the little kitten till she's tame, and—ouch!"

"You had that coming, Kid." Mandy laughed.

"Dang Kat, but you punch a hell of a wallop," Kid exclaimed in amazement.

Kat crossed her arms and glared mutinously at him.

To Tame a Wild Hawk

Grinning, Hawk turned back to the horses. "Gid-up there." He slapped the reins. "I do believe Kid has met his match," he confided to Mandy at a near whisper.

Mandy agreed, smiling back at him.

The hands spilled out of the bunk-house when the wagon rolled up. The wagon no sooner rolled to a stop, and young Tommy was there. He grabbed hold of the team and helped Mandy down.

"How'd things go, Hawk?" old man, Charlie limped forward. "Any trouble?"

"Only when we found the wild-cat, here, trying to skin McCandle."

Kat peered at Charlie and appeared to take to him instantly, if the smile she bestowed on him, and the hand she thrust out, were any indication.

He gave her a hardy handshake. "Glad to have you aboard . . . "

"Kat," she supplied.

He gave her a toothless smile. "I'm Charlie. If you need anything, let me know."

"Thank you."

I'm Nick, the foreman."

Howdy," Kat answered, touching the brim of her hat.

Hi, I'm Tommy."

Good to know you, Tommy." Kat smiled at him.

Tommy looked dazed.

Kid had, had enough. He glared at them all and stomped off.

Hawk was laughing, by then. Mandy forgot all about Kid, and Kat, at the sight of it. She stared, first in amazement, then as a soft vortex of emotions flowed through her veins, she caught herself wanting to see his laughter for the rest of her years.

Early the next morning, Hawk found Charlie and Kat braiding leather to repair some bridles, and Charlie telling Kat every tall tale his old, cow-poke's, forgetful, mind could lay claim to.

Kat was laughing, a full, happy laugh. Her laughter husky—and extremely sexy—if the look on Kid's face was anything to judge by.

Hawk spotted him, several yards away, watching Kat with an intensity that told Hawk, serious trouble lay ahead. He had never seen the Kid serious about anything. He took everything with a smile, even charm, including his fighting. Kid obviously had it bad Hawk thought, shaking his head.

He was going to enjoy watching this.

That is, if he could keep Kid from killing every man Kat turned that smile on, including old Charlie.

Hawk came to a stop in front of Charlie. "It's time for the round-up."

Charlie looked up at him. "Yeah, that's what Ned said last night."

Kat took the rope from him as he stood up. "You go on ahead, I'll finish it."

"This will be the first year I've not been hankerin to get out on it," Charlie continued, stretching the creaks out of his old bones.

Hawk nodded. "Watch your backs." His gaze included Kat.

"And you, yours," she shot back. "We're gonna need you alive."

"We're all going to stay alive," Hawk answered. "We'll spend the day making preparations, cause we'll be heading out at first light."

Chapter Twenty

Waves of heat shimmered down on the prairie grass, late the next afternoon. They'd begun the fall round-up. It was hot, dirty work. More so, with the warm fall they were having. And having to keep looking over their shoulders wasn't helping.

Mandy untied her bandana and mopped the back of her damp neck with it. "Hawk, I've been wondering."

Hawk swallowed a groan and tried not to look at her. Her face was damp in the sweltering sun, and all he could think about was kissing her. He leaned over, studying the tracks beside him. "What?"

"Everyone knows you as Lakota. Yet you talked about your Cheyenne family when you were so sick."

Dismounting, Hawk studied the tracks closer. "The warrior who found me was Cheyenne." He frowned. There were horse tracks crossing the cattle tracks—and they were on Mandy's land. "He died at the hands of the Crow when I was ten. He didn't have a brother, so my mother chose to go back to her people. When I became of age, I became a Lakota warrior." He looked up at her and clenched his jaw. Why did just looking at her make him want to haul her off her horse and find a nice shaded tree to lay her down? Blister it—he turned away.

Mandy stared at the muscles rippling down his back. Even the thicker shirt he had on could not hide them. She pulled her mind from that hot trail of thought. Looking around, she tried to center her thoughts somewhere else, anywhere else.

She knew the Cheyenne and Lakota were like brothers. They often spent summers together, and intertribal marriage wasn't uncommon.

She peered out across the plains. "Do you think we'll have any trouble?"

"Yes," he answered, flatly.

She looked back at him in surprise.

Hawk remounted his dun, colored horse. "They'll be here—and we'll be waiting."

"How can you be so sure?"

"Cause I'd never miss an opportunity like this one."

Mandy shivered. The fighting would begin soon. Who knew how it would end.

"I'm sending you home tomorrow." Hawk's gaze bore into her, his eyes, unblinking—his face, impassive.

"What?!" Mandy twisted in the saddle to see him better. "No, *you're not*. I work the round-up in the spring. I help the hands bring in cattle all summer long, and I work the fall round-up. I have, every year, since I've been here. And I'm not going to stop because of you."

Hawk only looked at her. His face so dispassionate it scared her. "You're going home." He turned his back and rode away

Leaving Mandy no choice but to catch up.

That evening, they sat around the camp-fire eating supper. The fire crackled, blue hues deep in the orange and red. They'd headed for a grove of timber to camp for the night. The smell of pine filled the air as they swapped stories over a rattlesnake Charlie killed that day.

"Twern't nothin," Charlie mussed. "Why back in fifty-five, I stumbled on the most confounded thing you ever saw. Why it had three heads and lay at least nine feet long. I wheeled my horse and lit out of there like my ass was on fire. When I looked back, the dad-blasted thing was right behind us. Poor Keeter, he done run his fastest, but that snake was keeping up." He sat back and lit his pipe.

"Well!" Tommy sat up, his eyes wide.

To Tame a Wild Hawk

Charlie grinned, clearly pleased. "Why, I shot off two of his heads. Now he's an ordinary rattler like the rest.

Tommy turned red. "What'd ya go'n do that for? Why, plenty around here would pay pure gold to see a snake like that."

There were plenty of guffs and ribbing around the fire for several minutes.

"Hell. If you think that's something," Jake's voice broke in, "back in South America, they've got a snake called an anaconda, who gets up to thirty feet long and bigger around than Jed, there's, arm."

Tommy came up onto his knees, clearly excited. "Really? Is it poisonous?"

Jake breathed a deep sigh, every eye on him. The quiet punctuated the night, except for the occasional noises from the cows. "Nope," Jake answered.

"Oh," Tommy sat back, clearly disappointed.

"They wrap themselves around a man, their coils covering him from head to toe. Then, they squeeze the life out of him and eat him, swallow him whole."

Tommy's eyes got as big as saucers, his mouth forming an "O". He opened his mouth to speak, but nothing came out.

"What'd ya go'n tell a fool story like that fer?" Charlie grated out. "Why look at the boy? Just how dumb do you think he is? Imagine telling a story like that!"

Mandy glanced at Hawk. He smothered a grin. She tried—but couldn't help it—she laughed out-loud

Charlie glared at her.

Jake's face split into a rare grin. "Easy, old timer."

Charlie tossed down his cup and grabbed his rifle. "I'll take the next watch." He walked off mumbling something about some people, and their tall tales.

Hawk lost the battle and grinned openly, and Mandy giggled.

Jake grinned back. "Guess next time, I'll know better than to steal his thunder."

They slept on the ground with nothing between them, and it, but a soogan quilt and rose by four in the morning. Eating sowbelly and biscuits, they chased it down with hot coffee, thick as sludge. Each of them picked out a horse from the cavvy, which Ned chased into a crude, makeshift corral. Hawk gave them the orders for the day, and they were mounted and riding, long before the sun burned the sky.

They fanned out in large circles, coming back towards the middle with the cattle, and doing it all over again. Near noon, they all rode toward the chuck wagon.

Mandy felt hot, tired and dusty, but she couldn't dwell on it with these guys around her. She'd never had so much fun at a roundup.

"Oh bury me not, on the lone prairie," Kid sang off key.

Mandy winced.

"Kid, I'm gonna string you up," Jake growled.

"And I'll skin him for ya," Kat added.

"What?" Kid eyed them innocently. "We're supposed to sing to the cows. It keeps them calm."

"The only thing your singing is doing is making them want to get the hell out of Dodge."

"We're not in Dodge," Kid grumbled.

Hawk rode up beside Mandy and cupped her cheek. "How are you doing?

She leaned into his palm. "I'm fine." When they'd got up this morning, he had said no more about sending her home. She'd waited all morning, expecting him to send her packing at any moment. And she was tense from it.

"Why do you insist on coming out here?" he growled. "It's hard work."

"I can handle hard work, Hawk," Mandy glared at him, pulling away.

He leaned over and kissed her anger away. "I know you can. So you can put away your claws. You work harder than most men. But you shouldn't."

"Will you two knock it off," Jake growled, dismounting at the chuck wagon.

Charlie chuckled at Jake. "You need a woman."

"Damn it, old timer. The last thing I need is a woman."

To Tame a Wild Hawk

Charlie was undaunted. "Sure ya do. It keeps a man from acting like a grizzly bear."

Jake scowled at Charlie. "Where's the grub?" he snarled at the cook.

Kid started singing, and Kat took out her skinning knife.

Charlie grinned.

"That's it," Matt said, "set him off and send him to me to eat, so he can shoot my damn, fool head off if he doesn't like the food."

Hawk grinned. "You'll just have to make sure it's good."

It was Matthew's turn to growl.

Kat roped the steer's horns, Pete his hind legs. Ned moved in with the branding iron.

Jake pulled another by its back feet before the fire, and he, too, got his brand.

Kid dropped his reins and, with knee pressure, guided his cutting pony through the cows. He indicated the calf he wanted, and his pony deftly pursued it, hardly disturbing the other cows. The calf finding herself outside the herd, turned sharply to get back into the herd, his pony wheeling with her and cutting her off. The calf wheeled, the pony right with her, until she gave up and ran out into the cut.

Kid dropped the noose, nimbly, around her feet, dragging her before the fire.

A gunshot told them company had finally arrived. The hands immediately went into action. Bawling calves, cows and steers stampeded. Hawk swore under his breath. Despite the best laid plans, they went in every direction.

He pulled his Winchester and returned fire. He counted about a dozen men. They rode straight in through the camp. He muttered an expletive. They must have got the guard. He dropped two from their horses, diving from his horse for cover.

They roped the crude, corral and pulled it over. Two of them pulled parts of it through the fire.

Ned dropped one before getting hit in the arm.

Jake rode straight through the cattle. Using knee pressure, he guided his cow pony, while taking careful aim. His nerve undermined McCandle's men, and they scattered. He calmly picked off three of them before they could turn around in the melee.

Kat cut them off and managed to drop two more before the rest slipped by her.

Mandy wrapped a bandanna around Ned's arm and tied it off while Hawk rode out to take a look at the guard. He only shook his head when he returned.

"Okay men," he bit out, "we've got our work cut out for us. So let's get to it."

"What about Jed?" Mandy said, her voice rising with each word as realization dawned on her. This couldn't be happening. *They couldn't have killed Jed.*

Hawk looked, long and hard, at her. "Jake, I want you, and Ned, to take her home."

She struggled to swallow her tears. "Heartless bastard."

"Pete, you and Tommy take Jed's body to town." Hawk turned away. "Jake, don't let her out of your sight," he flung back over his shoulder.

Angrily, Mandy marched over and grabbed her mare's reins. Turning, she stepped up into the saddle, tears streaming down her face. Without another word, she rode out.

"Mandy!" Hawk growled after her.

Jake looked at Hawk, shrugged, then rode out after her. Ned right behind him.

Jake let her ride ahead of them to allow her privacy. When they camped, he cooked and handed her some food, but she never looked at them, and she never spoke. When they reached the ranch, midmorning the next day, she went into the ranch house and flew up the stairs. There, she finally poured her heart out into a pillow.

How could this happen, Grandmothers? I'm completely blocked from all danger! I sensed nothing!

But she could not hear them, and she knew they must tread carefully. The *Grandmothers* had been right, the danger was very real. Their power was just too great.

To Tame a Wild Hawk

It was the next morning before she'd let Lydia come in to talk to her.

"Poor child." She stroked Mandy's hair. "I'm so sorry to hear about Jed. He'll be sorely missed."

Mandy looked at the older woman's red-rimmed eyes. "First papa. Now, Jed. Where will it all end?"

"I don't know, child."

"That bastard...."

"Mandy, don't speak like that. It isn't proper for a lady to talk in such a manner." She tucked Mandy's hair behind her ear. "Now, Ned told me how angry you were with Hawk. But he also told me, Hawk was having a time of it himself."

"Hawk? Upset?" Mandy shook her head. "He started giving orders as though it never happened."

"My dear, men show their hurting different from women. Hawk probably felt as though he'd let Jed down."

"But that's ridiculous. We were all right there. It just happened."

"But Hawk probably feels as though it's his fault—his being the boss and all. When you plan something and things go wrong, it leaves you feeling as though you failed, somehow. And when someone's killed—then, it can be really hard to live with."

Mandy swallowed a sob. "*Oh, no. And I made him think I blamed him.*" She got up. "I have to go back."

"You can't do that."

"I must. Don't you see? I can't leave it like this. What if Ashley's men come again? What if something happened to Hawk? I'd never forgive myself."

She dressed and went out the door in a flash—and ran right into Jake.

He took one look at her split riding-skirt and shook his head. "I'm supposed to make sure you stay right here."

"Then, you'll have to bound and gag me to do it," she snapped, "because, I'm going back, like it or not."

She marched to the barn and grabbed a brush. Giving her horse a quick once over, she saddled and bridled her. Mounting up, she rode out.

Jake right behind her. "Damn women," he muttered, "nothing but a pest."

Early the next afternoon, Mandy and Jake rode back into camp. Mandy didn't feel so brave, now the moment to face Hawk lay before her. In fact, she felt all queasy, just thinking about it.

When Hawk spotted her, he walked dead up to her horse, grabbing her reins. "What the hell is she doing here?" Hawk spoke to Jake, but his eyes pierced her to the spot.

Jake shrugged. "You try to stop her when she's made up her mind."

Disgusted, Hawk walked away.

"Just like that," Mandy muttered under her breath "He walks away." She slid off her mare and ran after him. Grabbing his arm, she pulled him to a stop. "I have to talk to you."

Hawk turned, his eyes narrowing. "You came all the way back here to talk to me?"

"I had to," her eyes pleaded, "I had to apologize. I didn't mean what I said when I left," she hesitated, her voice soft, "please forgive me."

But Hawk's eyes were already soft. "He was killed under my command."

"Hawk. When a warrior is killed in battle, are the others to blame?"

Hawk's jaw pumped furiously. He'd been hurt when he'd thought she blamed him. He relaxed under her hand, and she smiled. He gathered her into his arms and kissed her long and hard—until Jake's growl drove them apart.

"Get back to work," he told the two of them.

Hawk grinned and gave the men, and Kat, their positions. "Mandy, ride with me."

"Hawk," Mandy said when everyone was out of earshot, "I missed you."

He looked over at her, his eyes full of sensual warmth. "I missed you too."

She sobered when she remembered what else she'd come to tell him. "And Hawk. . . ." She shivered, thinking about it.

He frowned at her. "What?"

To Tame a Wild Hawk

"McCandle's man . . . he's successfully blocked the *Grandmothers*—completely."

Hawk turned his back at this news. Every line in his body, rigid. He knew . . . what Mandy knew. . . . Blocking the *Grandmothers* could only mean one thing. They'd had an idea, but this was beyond anything they'd imagined.

Power like that could only come . . . *from—across the veil.*

Charlie, riding in hard, brought them all up short. "It's Pete!" he yelled. "McCandles men threw a rope around him and drug him."

"How bad is he?" Hawk asked, leaping into the saddle.

He's bad." Charlie shook his head.

They rode out, hell bent for leather. When they arrived, Mandy took one look at Pete and turned away, hiding her tears before dismounting to help him.

"We're going to get him for you Pete, I swear it," she whispered to him.

"Rig a travois," Hawk ordered. Jake and kid whirled their horses around, riding out after the poles.

Mandy and Kat made him as comfortable as possible. By the time the poles arrived, they had him set. They grabbed some blankets, deftly rigging the travois within minutes, and the boys carefully picked him up and laid him on it.

"Kid," Hawk growled. "You and Chuck, take him to Docs." His jaw ticked as he watched them ride away. Turning abruptly on his heel, he mounted up.

"I'll be back," was all he said by way of explanation.

He rode away.

Mandy turned to Jake. "What's he going to do?" When he didn't answer, she grabbed his arm, trying her best to shake him. "What's he going to do?!"

His steel, gray eyes narrowed on her, and she let go of his arm. "Don't worry ma'am. He's just taking some time for himself. I believe you call it, blowing off steam."

Mandy worried her lower lip. "You're sure." Her brow furrowed. "He wouldn't take McCandles on himself, would he?"

"No, Ma'am, I'm not sure of anything, right now." He tipped his hat and mounted up. "Let's ride."

Mandy rode with Charlie and Jake the rest of the day. By the time Hawk finally rode in that night, she'd worried herself into a frenzy. If Hawk went after Ashley alone, he might be dead right now What if he was hurt and needed help?

When he walked into the fire-light, late that night, her heart leaped up into her throat at the sight of him. It felt amazing, just to let her eyes travel over him.

He looked down at her, the firelight reflecting the red in her hair—which only came through the color with the light. His gaze moved over her and came back to her eyes. His own lit in sensual warmth. He held his arms open and without hesitation, she stood and went into them.

The hands hooted, and she laughed.

"I'm going to take her home, Jake," Hawk said without turning.

Mandy leaned back in his arms. "What? Hawk, no."

"I'm taking you home. I'll not have you killed."

She frowned at him. It felt good to have him pamper her. But it wasn't necessary. "I'm a good hand, Hawk. Let me work."

"Someone needs to be watching the ranch, Mandy. And that's going to be us."

Mandy relaxed and nodded.

"Kat."

"Yeah." She strode forward.

"You come too."

She scowled.

Hawk turned, and his eyes narrowed on her. "You're coming with us. I need good hands at the ranch. Not everyone can be out here." He adjusted his Stetson. "He's hit here. He'll be after the ranch next."

Kat nodded. "I reckon that'll be all right, then."

To Tame a Wild Hawk

"We'll go at first light."

Hawk was waiting when McCandle tried to hit the ranch.

Despite Mandy's protest, he went out alone. And when she heard a hideous scream, she knew that he'd gone to fight as a warrior.

It was then, she realized Kat was missing.

She couldn't stand it. Grabbing her Colts, she slipped out the back.

She saw Kat grapple with a man near the barn, and something Kat didn't see—the rifle trained on Kat's back.

The man never knew what hit him.

Kat was locked in a battle for her life. She flung her knife, hitting the man square in the chest. He fell, looking at the knife in surprise. She looked over and saw the man lying on the ground behind her—and grinned at Mandy.

"One up on ya," Mandy smiled.

Together, they went looking for Hawk. When he came walking around the bunk-house, Mandy jumped.

He strode towards them, dressed in nothing but a loin cloth. War paint streaked his face and body. His eyes glittered with menace. Without a word, he went to the well. Rolling up a bucket of water, he dumped its contents over his face and head. Throwing his head back, he sent rivulets of water streaming down his muscular back.

She walked forward and touched his arm. He tensed for a moment, then slowly relaxed.

When he finally turned to her, the killing fury in his eyes was gone.

He drank her in, her softness and her beauty. And suddenly, he knew what he was fighting for. Everything, past, present and, now, future, came down to this. This was the moment that defined his existence.

He wasn't fighting for himself anymore. He wasn't fighting for the past. He was fighting for them and any future they could have, together. Their future, and the future of their children, was the only thing that mattered.

"You could have been killed," he growled.

"You could have too," Mandy countered.

"She saved my life," Kat threw in.

Hawk glowered at her. Finally, he relented. "Then, I guess it's a good thing."

"Hell, yes, it's a good thing. I happen to like liv'n."

Hawk grinned, his even, white teeth flashing in the darkening night.

Kat playfully punched him in the arm.

Hawk rubbed his shoulder, laughing and held up his hand before she could do him further damage. He sobered, then. "We've put a good dent in McCandle's men. I think he'll ease up some now."

Mandy sighed, kicking at a clod of dirt. "I hope so. He's been relentless."

"I need some coffee," Hawk growled. He put an arm around Mandy. Together, the three of them walked back to the house.

"We'll keep a few men on the calves," he told them when he had a cup of the hot, steaming brew in hand. "But I'm not keeping every man out there from here on out."

Mandy nodded. "What do you think he'll do now?"

"He's furious." Hawk took a deep swallow of the hot brew. "I think he'll hire a gun."

That night, Hawk took a watch, intending to be out there for most of the night. Mandy quickly realized, she wasn't going to get too many more opportunities, like this one, to find the combination to Ashley's safe—what with Hawk always watching over her, so carefully, and all. She also needed to see her childhood friend. So it was now—or never. She might only get one, or two, more chances—and she had a feeling—everything hung on her success—at getting in McCandle's safe.

She slipped out of the house and down the backstairs. She entered Ashley's house forty-five minutes later and searched for nearly an hour for the combination.

Finding nothing, she left the house, disappointed, again, and rode to meet her cohort.

She whistled, softly, when she reached his cabin, and he joined her, minutes later.

"Anything new?" she questioned.

To Tame a Wild Hawk

He grunted. "Just the usual. We've been taking the cattle down to the Platte now."

She hugged him. "Be careful."

She thought about telling him about Hawk but knew he would be angry about the latest events. And Mandy knew, Hawk could handle things just fine, without involving a half-blooded, Cheyenne warrior, who thought and acted as his mother's people. Her friend would wage a bloody war for what Ashley had done. And get himself hung in the process.

Hawk was waiting for her, leaning against a decorative table, with his arms folded, when she returned. Mandy jumped when she saw him, just waiting, there in the dark. "Hawk?!" She placed her hand over her chest. "You scared me."

"I'm going to do a hell of a lot more than that if you don't give me a good explanation for where you've been tonight."

Mandy slid sideways towards her room, feeling the furniture beneath her fingers, as she moved.

He cut her off.

"I was walking?" she tried.

"You'd better do better than that."

Mandy looked into his glittering eyes and sighed. "I missed my father," she told him, hating herself for lying. "So I walked to his favorite spot on the hill.

Hawk scowled, and Mandy slipped by him and up the stairs. He growled under his breath and let out a sigh of exasperation, watching her go. She was up to something, but he'd be damned if he knew what it was. He went out to the barn and placed his hand on her mare's neck and swore viciously under his breath. She was too warm for, supposedly, having spent half the night in her stall. He picked up her saddle blanket and let out another expletive. It was damp—and warm. Mandy had been out riding. But where had she gone?

And whom had she gone out to see?

The next time she rode out, he intended to be right behind her. Then, he'd have some answers.

Mandy paced her room. He was onto her. What was she to do now? How did she warn White Wolf? She kicked at the blankets, draped over her bed, yelped, and jumped up and down, holding her foot. Sitting down, she examined her hurt foot.

"Mandy, I'm coming in," was all the warning she got before the door swung open.

"Do you knock?" Her voice was sarcastic.

"No." was his only answer. He crossed the room and sat down beside her. Reaching for her foot, he set it in his lap, massaging her bruised toes. "What did you do?"

She scowled. "I kicked the bed post."

Hawk grinned at her. "Giving into that temper of yours again?"

Mandy's eyes snapped, and she tried to yank her foot back. But Hawk easily stopped her, his fingers traveling up her ankle. Her eyes flew wide, and she watched with a helpless little "O" on her beautiful mouth as his hand moved up her calf. Her eyes slid up, colliding with his golden, smoldering ones, and she thought she'd go up in smoke. She gave a breathless little pant, and it was Hawk's turn to lose it.

With a growl, he climbed slowly up her body until his lips were a breath from her own. "Lady, you set my blood on fire."

His kissed her deeply.

"What makes you think we're going to do *that* anymore?" Mandy teased, between soul-shattering kisses. "We can't get it annulled now...."

Hawk cut her off with a deep plundering of her sweet mouth, his hand brushing the underside of her breast, before coming up to cup it.

"Mandy?!" Aunt Lydia yelled from the doorway.

"You," she shook her finger at Hawk, "have a problem at the barn. And, for heaven's sake, you should close the door."

"Yes, ma'am." Hawk stood up, holding his hands up in mock innocence, and with a definite swagger, made his way to the door. He turned, just before he went out and gave Mandy a look of clear intent. Then, he was gone.

Mandy giggled, breathlessly. "You enjoyed that, didn't you?" she accused.

Aunt Lydia smiled, then gave a girlish giggle of her own. "I will admit. It was kind of fun." She harrumphed. "Serves him right."

To Tame a Wild Hawk

"Aunt Lydia!" Mandy laughed, blushing.

"Well." The older woman gave a look of innocence. "It does. Besides, I wasn't sure you didn't need help, since I overheard your conversation down in the foyer, and knew he'd caught you in one of your nightly outings." She raised a brow at Mandy, as dawning broke in the younger woman's eyes. "Did you think I didn't notice that you were missing from your bed, every week?"

Mandy's mouth dropped open. "How long have you known?"

"Several weeks." Her Aunt Lydia shook a finger at her. "How much did he figure out?"

Mandy's shoulders dropped. "I don't know. And if you've noticed, he's sure to figure me out."

"Then you better stop, child."

Mandy frowned and shook her head. "I can't Aunt Lydia. Not—quite yet."

In the parlor, Hawk poured himself a drink. "Damnation!" he muttered.

"Women trouble?"

Hawk rounded, pistol in hand.

Jake's grin was full of glee, from his comfortable seat on the chair in the corner. "One up on you, old man."

"Damnation," Hawk growled, again, "she's making me soft."

"She's not making you soft," Jake scowled. "You're doing that all on your own because you can't get her off your mind. Do us all a favor, will ya? Put yourself out of your misery. Hurry up and admit the truth to her before you get us all killed."

Hawk's cold, green eyes raked his friend. "This, from a man who gets his nose bent out of joint every time he sees me kiss the lady. When she learns the truth, I'm done for. She'll hate me." He ground his glass down on the counter. What the hell are you doing here, anyway?" He raked Jake with a cold stare.

Jake shrugged, placed his drink on the small table beside him, and stood up. "Just figured you were right about McCandle hitting here next. Looks as though I missed the show." Picking up his Stetson, he placed it on his head. "She's good for you, old man."

"Yeah, well," Hawk tossed back his drink, his teeth pulled back when he swallowed, "you just wait."

Jake grunted, and they left the house.

Chapter Twenty-One

Mandy slipped out of the house three nights later. She saddled her horse with practiced efficiency and walked her down the lane. When it was safe, she put a dark hood over her hair and tied a dark bandana around her neck for when she got to McCandle's place. She was about to mount up—when she heard a lone horse behind her. Her heart took off, thundering in her ribcage. She'd been caught! What to do now? She almost sagged with relief when she recognized Kat. "You scared ten years off my life," she said in low tones.

Kat's, cat-like, eyes shown, even in the moonlight. "I don't know what you're up to," she tossed her curly, golden mane behind her shoulders, "but I want in on it."

"Hawk doesn't know," Mandy warned her. "And if he ever finds out, there'll be hell to pay."

Kat grinned at her. "Then, I guess he'd better never find out." She looked behind her. "By-the-way, I already made sure he didn't follow you tonight." She looked back at Mandy with meaning.

Mandy choked on a laugh. "How?"

Kat gave her a conspiratorial smile. "I just made sure he would be busy for a while—with some calf troubles. Us women gotta stick together."

"*Have* to stick together," Mandy automatically corrected. Kat had asked her to help her to speak better, since she had her cap set on Kid.

Lenore Wolfe

Kat's smile shown like pearls in the moonlight. *"Have* to stick together," she repeated. "I am going to speak like a real lady in no time. She reined her horse around. "But I sure don't know about *acting* like one." She grinned.

Mandy's own smile flashed in the moonlight—but an eerie shiver crawled up her spine when she thought about Hawk. She sure hoped Kat was right, and whatever she'd done to keep him busy, kept him there till well after they got back.

She tossed Kat a dark hood, out of her saddlebags.

"Here. Put this on." She mounted her horse and reined her around. "Come on, I'll explain on the way."

Mandy stood behind the curtain, Kat behind some furniture in the corner, when Ashley finally did the thing Mandy had been waiting for, for over three months, and approached his safe.

With baited breath, she watched as he twirled the dial to unlock the door. Slowly, inch by painful inch, she moved up behind him. As the door swung open, she raised her colt, butt first, and swung at his head.

Surprise caused her to drop the gun when he suddenly whirled to face her. The sound of her gun, clattering to the floor, dismayed her. He moved easily behind her, his arm going around her throat, cutting off her air in a painful grip.

"Finally," he snarled in her ear, "we're going to find out who our little nightly visitor is. I have been waiting, patiently, for you to make you're move all week."

Despite her desperate hunger for air, Mandy couldn't help feeling elated. She hadn't been a complete ninny. A ninny, yes, but she had fooled him for a little while. It seemed, *everybody* had figured her out."

He reached up to yank the hood off her head. Mandy cringed, knowing the time was at hand. It was over. She had lost.

She heard a sickening thud, felt his arm go slack, and she was free. She turned and grinned at Kat. Guess it's a good thing you spotted me tonight."

Kat looked, stupefied. "Well, if I hadn't been here, looks as though she has," she nodded at the woman behind Mandy.

Mandy swung around, quickly realizing just who had knocked Ashley out. She knew how Kat felt. She'd had much the same reaction the first night she had met her. Star Flower was, by far, the most exotic woman she'd ever seen.

To Tame a Wild Hawk

"Hurry," Star Flower told them, moving to bind Ashley's hands and feet with a length of cord in her hand. "Get what you came here for."

Kat looked from Mandy to the young woman who'd just saved Mandy from Ashley's, sure, murderous rage. "Who are you?"

"Oh, sorry," Mandy whispered. "Kat, meet Star Flower, Ashley's sister. Star Flower, this is Kat." She looked at the bewilderment on Kat's face. "Star Flower found me, my third night here. She's been covering my tracks ever since—even doing some searching of her own. Ashley would have noticed something was going on here, a long time ago, if it were not for her help. She's saved my hide more than once."

Kat smiled at this. "You're Indian? But your eyes. . . ."

"Are my pa's spring-green."

Mandy frowned at that but didn't have time to examine it any closer at the moment. She moved quickly. "He'll kill you for what you've just done?" she told Star Flower. "And he's going to be in a rage from what we're *about to do.*" Taking her bags, Mandy handed one to Kat, and they started loading it with the contents of the safe.

"He'd never believe we would cross him. He's cruel, and we're all terrified of him."

"Obviously, not all," Kat retorted.

"But he must never know that—or all is lost." Star Flower stuffed a rag in his mouth, then bound it with a handkerchief around his head

"Hurry," she urged. "I must leave, in case he wakes."

She started for the door but came back to the safe to whisper, "Be sure and take the papers," she pointed them out. "They are all the deeds he holds to those poor people's lands, and the notes he waves over their heads.

Elated, they grabbed them all. "I must talk to you," Mandy told their ally. "Where can we meet you? Can you sneak away?"

"I will let you know the time and place," Star Flower replied. Helping Mandy to fix her disguise, she told her, again, "I must go. He must not awake and find me here."

Mandy nodded and hugged her. "Be careful. You live with a demented man. You should come with me. You would be safer with us."

Star Flower shook her head. "I'll be of more help, here."

"But he's dangerous!" Kat exclaimed in a heated whisper. "He'll kill you if he finds out you've betrayed him."

"I cannot give up now," Star Flower replied firmly. "I've come too far, to let go now. It is good, you finally got what you were seeking."

Hugging her again, Mandy watched their friend leave. Kat nudged Ashley, hard, with the toe of her boot. His moan told them, he was still, pretty much, out. Then, as quietly as they'd come, they picked up their hard won treasure and made they're escape.

Two hours later, they sat on her bed, staring in surprise at the papers they'd recovered. Mandy giggled, softly, and threw the papers in the air in barely suppressed glee.

Oh sweet, sweet revenge. She had finally got a lethal swing in on Ashley McCandle. "This is going to hurt him where it counts," she told Kat. "This will put a dent in Ashley's pocketbook that will have him reeling." For she held in her hands all the deeds for the lands he had captured along the railroad. And more importantly, to her anyway, she held every note he had against her friends and neighbors." She sobered when she realized the killing fury this would send Ashley into, when he woke. She sent up a silent prayer to up above—for Star Flower. "Maybe we should warn Hawk." She frowned at the thought. How would she ever explain this to him—and all she had done in the past?

"But, I see, you won't."

Mandy shook her head. "He'd be impossible to deal with . . . seeing this . . . realizing. . . ." It was with a heavy heart, Mandy hid her hard won treasure in the safe in the library. Her heart beat a heavy tempo of dread. In all her planning, she had never contemplated Ashley's reaction, if and when she'd succeeded.

Now—well, this would probably force Ashley's hand—and his resulting fury.

And if he killed Star Flower . . . or Hawk. . . . She had to warn White Wolf. He was in the gravest danger of all. She had to get him to stop—at least for a while.

She put her hand on Kat's shoulder. "I have to go back out," she told her friend. "And this time, you cannot go with me."

Kat's eyes narrowed on her. "It's too dangerous for you to go alone."

"I've been doing it for some time now, Kat. I'll be fine. You must trust me on this."

To Tame a Wild Hawk

Kat shrugged. "If you must, but if you don't return soon, I'll be coming after you. So you might as well tell me how long—and which direction. It'll save me a lot of time."

Mandy smiled at her friend and told her what she wanted to know. For the second time that night, she stole out of the house, and off the ranch.

The night was still and eerie. Mandy's heart beat like a drum, every muscle in her body telling her, bad times lay ahead. And lately, she could swear she was being watched, maybe even followed.

She knew where Ashley was on those nights.

That only left a certain . . . White Indian.

The moonlight shone on the path in front of her, her horse's hooves ringing out on the road, beneath its feet. She winced. She could really do with an unshod pony right now. Her Henry lay over her lap, her Colts in their holster on her hips.

She was taking no chances.

There was a time, she had visited her friend, and cohort, without hesitation. But now, thanks to Ashley, she had to ride as though armed for war.

When she reached the cabin in the woods, she whistled softly, so she wouldn't get her head blown off.

He let her in and closed the door behind her. "Why do you only come out here in the middle of the night, now?"

"It's no longer safe to meet you during the day," she answered. She looked at her childhood friend. "I have hired *the Hawk.*"

He went still, then nodded. "This is good."

"You know him?" she asked.

He nodded, again. "I know him."

"What about you," she asked, "now that we're not stealing McCandles cattle?"

"I will join my people."

She took his hands into hers. "It is very dangerous times for the Tsistsistas, right now."

"A time when I belong with my people, now, more than ever."

She lowered her head. "I will miss you my friend."

"You love *the Hawk.*"

Her eyes flew wide, meeting his. "What told you that? Is it written all over my face?"

"It is written in your eyes." He took hold of her shoulders. "May your love be long, and full. I will miss you, too."

She told him everything that had happened with Hawk and McCandle recently. Then, with tears in her eyes, she left.

She was half way home when she became aware she was being followed, again.

Like a dark thunder cloud, he rode out of the night. Before she could kick her horse into a full run, he was beside her, sweeping her off her horse. She fought as though she were a wild cat, until she heard his low growl. "Be still Mandy, or I swear I'll paddle you, right here, right now."

She went completely still. "Hawk?"

"You put yourself in danger," his tone was far to calm.

She lifted her chin. "I can take care of myself." Hawk growled, and Mandy jumped. "However," she got out, "I never have to sneak out again."

"Out here, with no one to protect you!" His arm tightened with threatening intent.

"Look how well armed I was."

"Why were you out here?"

"I was saying goodbye to my friend," she told him.

"In the middle of the night," he eyed her in disbelief, *"without anyone with you?"*

"Think what you will. I was saying goodbye to my friend," she reiterated.

They had reached the barn, by then, and Hawk ordered the horses put up. He walked her to her bedroom door. "Remember what I said would happen if you placed yourself in danger? If you risked your life? Do you remember that I said I would not be held responsible for what I did to your pretty little back-side then?"

Mandy winced—and nodded.

Hawk turned and walked away.

To Tame a Wild Hawk

She sagged against the door. He was really angry. Imagine how angry he'd have been if he had caught her the first time she'd rode out, breaking into McCandles house.

Hawk stood in the night, every muscle of his body tense, in reflex of how angry he really was.

If he hadn't walked away from her when he did—he really would have paddled her backside, all right, and as angry as he was, he might have hurt her in the process.

He'd had to walk away.

It took him until dawn to feel calm.

Chapter Twenty-Two

Mandy bolted upright on the bed. Throwing off the covers, she hurried into her robe. Hawk was already in the hall, buttoning his pants. Another bellow, and the sound of glass breaking, had them racing for the stairs.

"Stop it, wild-cat!" Kid growled from behind the kitchen door. Opening it a crack, he jumped behind it as a plate sailed though and crashed against the wall to the far side, shattering into a thousand tiny pieces from the force."

"You fish eyed, yellow bellied, son of a whore," Kat screeched.

Spotting Tommy, Kid waved him over. "Pretend you're me and keep her busy. I'm gonna sneak in the back way."

Grinning, Tommy opened the door, fully staying behind it. He watched as a plate sailed through it and thudded at Jake's feet. Tommy slammed the door shut and heard another dish slam against it. Holding his breath, he tried to gauge Jake's mood but could read nothing in those cold, steel-gray eyes.

They both looked back at the door when Kat's screeching became two-fold.

"Put me down, damn you." This, followed by a loud crash, took both man and boy through the kitchen door. Hawk came through the doorway on the other side, followed by Mandy, who was pulling the belt tight on her robe.

Hawk met Jake's eyes over the couple sprawled on the floor—and grinned.

"You little, spitting, fire-cat." Kid huffed. He grabbed both of her arms and pinned them to either side of her head.

"Yes, she is," Hawk answered.

Kid grinned. "Here that, wild-cat, he agrees."

"And she needs some taming," Hawk added—and grunted when Mandy punched him firmly in his side.

"That, you do," Kid agreed. "You definitely need taming."

Hawk grabbed Mandy and hauled her to his side, a firm band of steel holding her in place. "And you're just the man for the job," he went on.

Kid adjusted his hands when Kat tried to scratch his hands to free herself, then to buck him off.

"Definitely, I'm gonna tame you, wild-cat."

"In a pig's eye," Mandy hollered, trying to dislodge the arm holding her.

"That's why you're going to marry her," Hawk finished, and Mandy went still.

"Yeah, that's why I'm gonna—what?!" Kid's head jerked up, his gaze meeting Hawk's. His mouth rounded in shock at the very idea.

"Marry her," Hawk grinned, unrepentantly, and Mandy wrapped her arms around his waist, settling to his side, seeing his intent.

Kid stared at him, then at Kat. She'd gone completely still and was watching him.

"Yeah," Kid said softly, "That's why, I'm gonna marry you. Will you have me?"

Kat bit her lip, tears running down her face. She nodded her head, and Kid gathered her into his arms.

"That's it!" Jake roared. "Hawk, you'd better find a way to finish this war, 'cause whatever disease is going on around here, it's catching, and I'll be damned if I'm going to get it."

"Hee hee hee," Charlie chuckled, coming up behind Jake, seeing another way to rib him. "Could just see you gett'n hitched, Jake."

Jake glared at him with a fury, which would have stopped most men in their tracks. But Charlie only grinned at him. "Gonna fall in love, Jake? Come to think of it, I know a pretty little thing with red hair and the most livid green eyes you've ever seen," he added, then shot out the door as fast as his old bones would take him, chuckling the whole way.

"I need a drink." Jake stomped his way to the liquor cupboard.

Chapter Twenty-three

Kid and Kat took turns taking a shot, with a bow and arrow, at the target they had set up on some bales of hay. Kid's landed in the bull's eye, Kat's right beside it. Mandy watched them shoot from where she stood, hanging the week's laundry out in the sweet sunshine. When they invited her to try, she was unable to resist the temptation to show off a little. What could it hurt? Hawk was out on the range anyway.

Smiling at Kid, she took the bow from him. It was larger, and stronger, than what she was used to, but with some concentration, she managed to put the arrow right between Kid and Kat's."

Hearing a familiar growl, she swung around, like a mouse caught under a cat's paw. He was coming across the yard, heading straight for her, and his eyes were flint-steel lethal.

She was tempted to use Kid as a shield, but unable to be that cowardly, she stayed right where she was. He came straight for her, Mandy backing up a step, with each one he took towards her, until she bumped up against the wall, her escape cut off.

He grabbed her wrist and turned to haul her into the house when with a whistle and a thud, he found his arm pinned to the wall. He looked down, stunned to find Kat's blade holding his shirt sleeve firmly in place.

"I would never hurt her, Kat," he said softly. "You must know that.

Blushing, Kat removed the blade. "Yeah, I guess I do. Sorry about that." She placed the knife in its sheath.

Kid was grinning. "Where did you learn to throw a blade like that, Kitten?"

Hawk and taken Mandy's arm and started for the house, again—when Kat's answer brought them both up short.

"What did you say?" Mandy was the first to choke out.

"I said, I learned it, growing up with my grandma's people. They were Blackfoot," she added. "I lived with them most of my life." She looked at their faces. "Why?"

Stunned, Kid looked at Hawk. Hawk looked at Kat, and Mandy just concentrated on breathing evenly.

Mandy took a deep breath and let it out. "He really is insane."

"Kid, Kat—and me," Hawk's golden eyes fastened on Mandy with an intensity that stripped her soul bare. "If that's the connection. Then, that's why—you, too, Mandy." He looked dumbstruck. "I thought it was because of the plantation . . ." He looked at Mandy. "Is there anything you know—that would explain this. . . .?"

Mandy lowered her lashes before he saw all. "I only spent those few years with the Lakota, and you know all about that. Other than that, he needs my land. He wants control of the river—and the railroad."

He laid a finger under her chin and slowly lifted it until she looked up at him. "Where did you learn to shoot a bow like that? Not from the Lakota, I can assure you of that. So where?"

With an effort, she drew in a ragged breath into her lungs. She licked her dry lips and caved. She just couldn't lie to Hawk. "From a Cheyenne friend." She glanced up. "We couldn't let people know of our friendship. He and his mother lived with his white father. We learned, early on, how it would go if it were to become known that a white girl and an Indian boy were friends."

Hawk's gut clenched. Her friend was a man. "Apparently Ashley found out!"

Mandy opened her mouth to deny it and realized her mistake. "Yes, that must be it."

Hawk gave her a smoldering look of intent. "Mandy!"

She nearly jumped. "How is Kid involved?" She tried to change the subject.

His look was measuring . . . searching. "He is my brother."

To Tame a Wild Hawk

Kid grinned when her eyes met his in shock. "Welcome to the family."

"He was ten when our family died of cholera. Another family adopted him when I left. He was twelve when his small village was attacked by whites. I found him years later. They were working him like a dog at Fort Laramie." Hawk's lips quirked. "I took him to Doc, but after I left, someone started harassing them. So Doc finally sent him back-east to school. When Kid returned, he took to cattle drives."

And Ashley wants you because you used to live with the Cheyenne?" She tilted her head to see his eyes in the sun.

Hawk opened his mouth to deny it. Then, his lips turned up in a smile. "Yeah, that must be it."

Mandy glared at him. "But what does any of this have to do with Ashley? Why you? And why Kid? Why not someone else?"

Kat shook her head in thought. "And I can see no connection to me—other than my grandmother's people. Why would he do this?"

Hawk mopped his brow with a red bandana. The heat was relentless. "Something else is bothering me, too." He looked straight at Kid. "Someone beat me to inviting you here, when I was laid up." He turned, then, and went in the house.

Kid frowned at that. "You Mandy?"

"I didn't even know of you until you arrived."

"So you're all saying, Ashley has murdered my parents because of our connection to our people." Kat's eyes glowed with rage. "Has he done anything, I mean, specific, to you?" she directed the question at Kid.

Kid frowned. "He was the white man at the head of the slaughter of my village that day," he quietly answered.

Mandy winced.

Kat stared intently at Kid. Her large, yellow eyes, unblinking. "Then, you know how I feel. Why I have to get him."

"Yeah. I know." Kid cocked his head. "We'll both get him, okay."

"But why? Why is Ashley doing all this?" Mandy asked, unseeing.

"Because, his father—our father, kept leaving his mother to come to my mother," came a young woman's voice from behind them.

Mandy spun around. "Star Flower!"

"Star Flower?" Kid frowned.

Ignoring him, Mandy rushed to her side. "Star Flower. If he finds out you were here, he'll kill you."

"I had to come." She hugged Mandy. "I had to warn you."

"Warn her? About what?" Hawk's masculine voice broke in from the porch. He sipped a glass of lemon-aid, his golden eyes appraising the beautiful Cheyenne maiden. "I thought you said your friend was a man?"

Star Flower stared, speechless, at Hawk.

"Well!"

As though shook out of a trance, she turned and clutched Mandy. "He knows!"

"Oh, no," Mandy whisper, clutching her middle.

"Who knows?" Hawk frowned, then, noting Mandy's chalky appearance, "Knows what?"

Star Flower turned to plead with Hawk. "She's in grave danger." She grabbed Mandy's arm. "He's unhinged. You've ruined him, you know."

Hawk's consternation was like a dark thundercloud. He pinned Star Flower, then Mandy, with a look of pure fury. *"What does he know?"* he asked in a voice, all the more deadly for the quiet way with which he spoke.

Without another a word, Mandy took her friends arm and led them all into the house. When they reached the den, she moved the painting and opened the safe. She removed a canvas bag and dumped the contents on the desk. Not once, did she look at Hawk, too afraid of what she would see there.

He had told her not to lie to him. He'd even given her plenty of opportunities to tell him. But here she was, caught before she could finally tell all. He'd never believe her, now. Worse, he'd hate her

She knew, without watching, he was sifting through the different papers—heard him lay one down and pick up another. She never even noticed, Kid was doing the same. Her every nerve vibrated on every move Hawk made.

She noted, beneath lowered lashes, when he picked out, what she knew to be, several promissory notes, which held in ruin so many people, and finally, she noticed Kid doing the same. Kat caught onto which ones they wanted and was handing hers to Kid while he explained what they were. Only Star Flower stood by, quietly watching.

To Tame a Wild Hawk

Turning, Hawk placed his in the fire, and it wasn't long before Kid did the same. "I wonder," he mused, "how many of them were, in some way, connected to our people?"

Mandy's body vibrated with tension—and fear. When would he break this calm?

She didn't have to wait long. . . .

With a murderous look, he swung on her. "Where did you get these?"

"I stole them?" she tried.

He clamped his jaw down so hard it flexed several times before he could ask, "How?"

Mandy glanced frantically at Star Flower, and stepping forward, the young maiden laid her hand on Hawk's arm.

He looked down at her hand, his gaze raking her. *"Who are you?"*

Mandy saw her take a deep breath before answering "I am Ashley's sister."

Hawk went stone cold still. He blinked, as though to clear his head, then blinked again. "Jason's daughter?" he croaked.

"That's right," she replied, softly.

He turned and walked out.

Star Flower went after him, and Mandy stared after them, confused. Something didn't fit here. Her heart slammed in pain, deep within her chest. Her shoulders dropped in grief. She didn't understand why Star Flower would care what Hawk thought and . . . and Mandy had lied to him. He was never going to forgive her.

She had lost him

Star Flower found him in the kitchen. She touched his shoulder, and he turned and folded her in his arms, hugging her so tight, she protested her bones would pop.

"How?" his voice was thick with unshed tears.

"Our father searched for you for years." She winced at the hate she saw in his eyes. Pulling away, she went to the window. "During one particular search, he—met my mother."

"That son-of-a. . . ."

She held up her hand. "Yeah, well, we both know he's a cruel man. But at least I'm here." She smiled. "I have waited so long. . . ."

He put his hands on her shoulders. "I have a sister. . . . A beautiful, charming sister." His eyes turned dark. "And I'm going to kill Ashley."

Star Flower smiled. "He hasn't been too bad to me, Hawk." She closed her eyes. "How I dreamed of you, when I was little. . . ."

"I heard all the stories about you, you know. And what I couldn't get out of father, I searched every paper to find out." She laughed at his surprise. "Yes, I taught myself to read, just so I could find out, all about, my big brother."

She easily read the pain, and regret, in Hawk's golden eyes. "No, Hawk, I did not tell you this so you would feel guilt. I am happy they did not touch you with their evil."

He touched her face as if to examine it for injury. "Did he hurt you?"

"Father wouldn't let him."

"So the old man was good for something after all."

"He helped." She headed for the door and glanced back. "I have to get back. Ashley cannot find me gone. He will know where I went."

"Absolutely, not! You're not going back there!"

She was half-way out the door, but she turned and smiled. "I always knew you'd be this way. That you'd be kind. That you'd ride in on a dark horse, and save me from our cruel brother. Like I said, I dreamed of you." She looked into his eyes. "But I have to get back."

He folded his arms. "I will not allow it."

"You must." She stepped back towards him, close now, placing her small, slender hand on his arm. "If we're to catch him, and bring him down, I must stay—where I can help you—all of you."

"It's too dangerous!"

"I've been there since I was five years old," she said in a quiet voice.

Hawk shook with the magnitude of his emotions. First, there had been nothing inside him but a burning need for vengeance. Then, a slip of a woman had brought him to his knees with the depth of his love for her. Now, he'd found he still had family, he would claim that is, and his beautiful sister, whom he'd only just found, was telling him he had to let her walk back into dangerous territory, and making him feel damn ridiculous because he wanted to protect her from the very family with whom she'd spent her entire life.

"Mandy knew you were there." It wasn't a question. "She left you in danger, without telling me."

"I insisted on staying. And," she quietly reminded him, "she doesn't know I'm your sister, does she, Hawk? Because, she doesn't know Jason's—your father. . . .?"

"How old are you?" Hawk asked, amazed.

"I thought so." She smiled.

"At first, I was too full of hate to share it." He swallowed. "Then, I was too afraid she wouldn't understand. Afraid, she'd never let me near her if she knew who she was trying to hire for a gun. That she was hiring the son of the very man she'd been trying to keep *away* from her ranch."

He laughed harshly. "Can you beat the irony? She was being forced to marry Ashley. So to save her ranch, she unwittingly marries, no other, than his brother." He turned to the window and slapped his hands on either side of it. "She'll never forgive me when she learns what I've done."

"You have to tell her Hawk. She has to hear it from you before it's taken out of your hands by circumstance, such as by Ashley." She touched his back, and he turned and hugged her.

"Tell her," she whispered, "before it's too late."

"Mandy, how did you get these?" Kid asked to sidetrack her, when she looked toward the door for the fifth time in the past ten minutes. He held up his hand. "And I know you stole them, so no sarcasm please," he teased.

Mandy looked at what was left of the papers. "What do you think Ashley will do?"

He raised his brows in perfect imitation of Hawk, telling her he was having none of it. "Thing's will just tighten up around here. Maybe it'll be the thing that blows this whole business wide open."

Kat smiled. "Purrrrfect," she said, in great imitation of her name's sake.

Mandy couldn't help but grin.

"Women." Kid threw up his hands. "Do you realize, the two of you, and now Star Flower," he added pointedly, "have managed to stir up more trouble than all the cattle rustling combined." Kat jabbed him in the ribs with her elbow. "Dangit, Kat," he bellowed. "You're gonna crack every rib I've got."

Mandy grinned again. There was never a dull moment with these two. As a matter of fact, there was never a dull moment with this war—but she could really use an end to the war.

Kid sobered and pinned Mandy with a look, by far too unnerving for a man his age. "How did you get these, Mandy?"

Mandy sighed. She really was going to have to a find better way of keeping these men off balance. "I broke into Ashley's place. I've been breaking in, methodically looking for his safe combination, for the past several weeks. Star Flower has been searching too—and covering my tracks."

"She found me the third time I broke in, and she wanted to help," Mandy smiled, despite her fears. "She'd noticed the door kept getting unlocked, and things seemed different to her, I guess." She sighed. "Looks as if, she wasn't the only one to notice."

"Looks like," Kid frowned.

"Either that, or he recognized my face before Star Flower knocked him out," she mused to herself, not even aware that she'd spoken out-loud.

"Mandy!"

She jumped when three voices yelled her name.

The only one she focused on—was Hawk's. Damn the man. How did he always manage to do it? Once again, she found him coming straight for her, with lethal grace. And, once again, she found herself backing away. His growl sounded like a cougar as he strode to reach her. She jumped and placed a chair between them. With lithe ease, he threw the chair out of the way. She raced behind the desk. "Kat," she yelled. But when she glanced up, Kat was leaving the room, upside-down, over Kid's shoulder.

She took a cue from Kat's battles and hurled her first missile at Hawk's head. He ducked. And she actually breathed a sigh of relief when it crashed harmlessly against the door. In the next instant, he was upon her. "Oh, you arrogant pigheaded," Mandy screeched when Hawk grabbed her. She found another missile and flung it at him.

He blocked her arm, and it crashed to the floor. He threw her over his shoulder and strolled to their room. When he reached the upper landing, he strolled into the room and tossed her on the bed.

To Tame a Wild Hawk

Mandy scrambled to the other side, watching him warily when he took his bandanna from around his neck. He, then, grabbed her wrists and bound them above her head. "Damn you, Hawk,"

He rolled her to her side and delivered a stinging slap to her backside.

She growled her temper in a long infuriating snarl.

He reached up her dress. And she sucked in her breath. He pulled one of her stockings down her leg and off her foot. And then, he tied her feet to the foot of the bed.

"What in the hell do you think you're doing?"

He rolled her to the side and delivered a second stinging slap to her bottom.

"What," she gritted through her teeth, "are you doing?"

"I'm saving your beautiful backside."

"You can't keep me tied up here forever," she yelled in fury.

"No. But I can sure keep you tied up here until we're done dealing with McCandle," he stated this with infuriating calm.

"All right!"

A dark brow shot up.

She glared at him, a mutinous look on her face.

He turned for the door.

"I'll behave," she yelled in alarm.

He stopped. "Not good enough."

"I'll . . ." she breathed through her anger. "I'll—do what I'm told."

He raised both of those damn brows of his.

"What else do you want?" she screamed.

"I want the truth," his voice dropped low in anger. "No more lies. No sneaking out of here. No more secrets. Agreed?"

Her chin lifted in rebellion.

He turned to leave.

"All right!"

He turned, slowly, around. His gold eyes searched hers for the truth.

"I promise," she breathed. Her heart picking up, now, with a familiar flutter.

He waited.

She sighed. "No more sneaking."

Still, he waited.

"No more lies," she promised.

He didn't blink.

She sighed. "No more secrets."

And still, he waited.

"Well!" She pulled at her bonds. "Let me up."

He grinned at her. Then, he turned and left, shutting the door firmly behind him.

"Damn you, Hawk!" She screamed every word she could lay hand to. She yelled until her voice gave out, and still, he did not come. Finally, in total exhaustion, she fell asleep.

When she woke, sometime later, it was dark. Although, she couldn't see him, she could feel him watching her.

"Don't ever risk your life like that again," his voice was subdued and slightly slurred.

Her eyes fought to see him in the dark. "I won't," she said, just above a whisper.

He pulled his hand across his face. It still scared the hell out of him. She had been breaking into McCandle's. And while, he'd known she was up to something, he'd never dreamed she would do something so dangerous.

"I'm sorry, Hawk," Mandy whispered, tears slipping down her face.

He heard the tears in her voice, and with a groan, he stumbled from his chair and freed her bonds. Then, he hauled her into his arms. "How long?" was all he could get out.

She stroked his face, searching his features with her fingers, reveling in the feel of his embrace—the fulfillment his arms brought to her.

To Tame a Wild Hawk

Before I met you," she finally answered, "I stole his cattle." Hawk growled, and she gave a nervous grin. "Then, one day, I realized I'd never ruin him that way. I had to do more, so I started breaking in and looking for the combination to his safe."

The thought of her in such danger made his physically sick. He held her so tight, she protested, and he had to let up. Again, he made her swear to him.

"I swear," she said, softly. Then, she frowned.

"Why isn't Lydia up here raising cane?"

"Because, after your latest escape, she's decided you're safer in my hands. She said, she never dreamed you were doing something so dangerous."

She should take exception to that—really, she should—but it was too hard to do so when he was holding her like this.

And he held her long into the night.

Chapter Twenty-four

The day Hawk finally relented and let Jake, and Charlie, escort the women to town, was cause for celebration. Mandy and Kat chatted excitedly and made plans throughout the ride there. Mandy hadn't seen Meg for days, and she had so much to tell her.

They left their mounts at the livery, and she led Kat towards her friend's house. Meg smiled in happiness, seeing Mandy standing at the door, and she gave her an enthusiastic hug, pulling both her, and Kat, into the house. "So how's married life? As if I didn't know." She rolled her eyes, laughing.

Mandy grinned. "Kid and Kat are now getting married. You will attend their wedding, won't you?"

"I wouldn't miss it. Come in, we'll have tea and you can tell me everything." She ushered them to the parlor. "Don't you dare leave anything out."

They spent the next hour filling Meg in. Some of it had her laughing, till the tears rolled down her face—the sad parts had her crying with Mandy.

"Ashley's really angry," Meg warned her. "Your marriage to Hawk has put him over the edge. And now whatever you did may have ruin him. The whole town's talking about it. He'll do anything to get to you."

"Just don't give him any excuses to come after you to get to me," Mandy ruefully shook her head. "It's because he knows my ranch is lost to him. That everything is now lost to him. He won't stop until he kills each and every one of us—or we kill him."

"I'm thinking you're right Mandy," Kat agreed. "That man's crazy, and noth'n will stop him 'till he's dead."

While waiting for the women, Jake had Charlie had laid in supplies. Finding they still had time on their hands, they went into the saloon and ordered drinks. At first, Charlie took his and went to a table, but seeing Jake was staying at the bar, Charlie grabbed his bottle, and glass, and started making his way back across the barroom floor.

As he crossed through the sunlight from the saloon door, suddenly Jake grabbed iron and shot past Charlie's shoulder. Behind him, Charlie heard the soft thud of a bullet, hitting flesh, and a man's yelp before he hit the floor.

"Only had two drinks," he muttered.

"Sorry about that, old timer," Jake replied.

"Dag-nabbit." Charlie turned on him. "You are gonna go and punch holes in every one of the yarns I spin, ain't ya?"

Surprised, Jake stood, unmoving.

"I was just gonna give ya a hard way to go about being a greenhorn and hold'n your drink with your gun-hand." He set down the bottle and glass. "Then, you go and draw like that with your left."

Jake relaxed. "Is that what this is all about? That's just a little trick I use to catch men, gunning for me, unawares."

Charlie gave him a look of pure disgust, then turned and shuffled his way to the dead man lying in the doorway, just as Mandy and Kat came running up the boarded walk.

"Where's Jake?" Mandy said, out of breath, relieved to see Charlie was all right.

"Inside," Charlie muttered. "Only had two drinks. Boy was drink'n with his gun-hand, then all a sudden he goes and draws like greased lightening with his left."

Mandy smothered a smile with her hand at Charlie's grouching. Looking up as Jake approached, she searched for signs of injury. Finding none, she smiled openly.

To Tame a Wild Hawk

"I'm *supposed to tell people* you can draw *like that*. You ain't actually supposed to *be able* to draw that leghorn that fast."

"Well," Jake growled. "I can do better with my right if that's what's bugging you."

Charlie squinted up at him, unblinking. "Was that supposed to make me feel better?"

"What's your problem, old timer?" Jake growled.

Kat laughed. "Seems to me, you can draw faster than some of the gunfighters Charlie likes to spin yarns about."

Jake grinned. "And here I thought you had a problem with my gun-play. Well, hell, Charlie," he couldn't resist. "I guess you never saw the Hawk . . . "

Charlie rounded on him. "Don't even know if this is someone Ashley hired, or someone gun'n for you, just to prove who's faster. Now, you're gonna go and tell me the man protecting my little girl, is faster!"

"He saved my life because he's that fast, Charlie," Mandy chided, softly.

All the wind seemed to go out of the old timer. "Been alive all these years. Ain't never seen noth'n like that." A small trace of pride tinged his voice. "You should'a seen it." He drew faster than a rattler can strike." He shook his head and started shuffling down the boarded walk. "Tommy won't even believe me when I tell him."

Stepping down off the boarded walk, out into the sunlight, Jake slowly looked around. Standing next to him, Kat felt him tense. "What is it?"

"Hawk was right, Ashley's hired himself some killers."

"Man's got a sixth sense." Mandy's eyes narrowed on the gunfighters before looking away. "Guess it's all out in the open now."

Jake nodded. "How long before you're ready to leave?"

"Can we have a half-an-hour?"

"Yeah. I'll meet you at the store. We're going to need some extra supplies for the ride home." He indicated the men down the street with a nod of his head. "First I'll see the sheriff."

Mandy hadn't drawn attention to the Colts strapped to her narrow waist when she rode with Jake. She'd waited until they were away from the house to dig them out.

Kid would have turned around and hauled her straight home, but Jake hadn't said a word. Now, she wished she had them on. The folks in town already tended towards gossiping about her—without her wearing her Colts to town. But the risk was too great not to be well armed at all times, now.

She wasn't used to having such hardheaded males around. She wondered if Jake had guessed at how well she could use them—and doubted he'd have let her keep them if he hadn't. Jake unnerved her. His steel gray eyes didn't seem to miss anything, always seeming to assess all their secrets, like there wasn't anything they could hide.

Mandy hoped he couldn't see all of hers.

The women quickly picked out all the items they were going to need for the upcoming wedding. The gunmen outside lay like a wet blanket on the previous laughter.

"How do you know Hawk?" Mandy finally got up the nerve to ask about halfway into their ride home.

"We were kids together."

Mandy frowned. "But he left when he was six. How could you two still be such good friends after all these years? Besides, you know how to fight together."

Jake glanced at her, brows raised.

Mandy shrugged. "I can tell by the plans you two lay. And the way you fought on the roundup."

Jake went back to scouting their surroundings. "He came back to the South. We fought for the North together."

"And when his sister and nephew died—were you there?"

Jake's eyes snapped back to her with a killer's lethal flame, and Mandy froze. The dangerous, but calm, man, she'd come to know, had suddenly become a blazing inferno.

"Oh, Jake!" she whispered. "Not your wife?"

The fire went out of his eyes. His face, once more, became impassive. "I told Hawk, you're too sharp. You're good for him, you know. Not some fancy lady, who can't get dirty."

Mandy thought about taking exception to that. "Thank you . . . I think," she muttered the last. His next words stopped her.

"But a lady, who sure looks fine in a dress."

To Tame a Wild Hawk

She blushed and looked away "I'm sorry, Jake," she said after a moment.

He shrugged.

"Why didn't you tell us? Why didn't Hawk? Charlie wouldn't have been ribbing you like that, would you have Charlie?"

"Women," Jake hissed between his teeth.

"I think he's been so cold so long, he'd forgotten that side," Charlie mumbled.

"Charlie!"

"No, Mandy," Jake broke in, "he's right. I haven't known anything but an unrelenting hatred since I came home that day."

Mandy blinked, so many words from Jake at one time, and with feeling too. An improvement. Maybe he had been cold, and full of hatred, but she suspected, time was healing those wounds. And when his shell of hatred came off, the true pain, and healing, would begin.

That's if the ice wall around his heart melted before it became a permanent fixture of stone.

"Get down!"

Mandy was snapped out of her thoughts by Jake's barked order. Instinct took over, and she obeyed without hesitation. The four of them were on the ground, and scrambling for shelter, when the first shot kicked up the dirt by Kat.

Kat, of course, immediately returned fire, along with a few choice words. Within seconds, they were surrounded by gunfire and returning some of their own.

"I swear, I'm going to shoot that no account, Ashley McCandle, right in the butt the very next time I see him," Mandy bit out, reloading her gun

Kat laughed. "Then one toe, then another . . ."

"And another, til he can't walk."

"Then, we can start in with his fingers . . . "

By that time Jake was looking at the two women as if they'd grown horns. "Next, the two of you will be burying him up to his head in an ant hill."

"Not a bad idea," Kat quipped.

"You'd think you'd both been raised by Indians."

Eyebrows raised, the two women looked at each other.

"As a matter of fact . . . " Kat started.

Jake raised his hand. "I don't want to hear it."

Kat looked at Mandy, smiling, and shrugged. "Suit yourself."

"See anything from your position, Charlie?" Jake called out, softly.

"Nope. But them snakes, out there, are just wait'n for us to raise our heads, so's they can blow 'em off."

Jake grunted and reloaded his Winchester. "What about you, Mandy?"

"I think, if the one I've got lined in my sight pops up just one more time. . . ." She pulled the trigger and heard a yelp. "Stop whining, it was only a shoulder wound," she called out. "If I had wanted you dead, you'd be dead. Now, go home and tell McCandle to leave my ranch alone, or the next time I shoot you, believe me, you won't be crying about it."

A bullet splattered the rock next to her face, the fragments hitting her cheek.

"Well, it was worth a try."

"Next time you shoot," Jake growled. "Shoot to kill. Or you'll be the dead one. That's the unforgiving code of the west."

Duly reprimanded, Mandy watched for the next shooter.

Two hours later, they hadn't heard a shot for some time. "Do you think they're gone?" Kat called softly.

"Nope," Jake hissed. "They're just waiting us out."

"Damn this heat," Charlie complained.

"Yep, that's what they're counting on." Jake checked his surroundings, yet again.

Mandy shifted to a more comfortable position. "Do you think Hawk will be coming?" she directed at Jake.

"Not for a while," Jake answered. "He won't notice, till we don't come in for several more hours. Then, he'll head right out."

"How do you know?" Kat questioned.

To Tame a Wild Hawk

"Because, that's how we operate. That's how we know something's gone wrong, without wasting precious time deciding."

"Should a known," Charlie grumbled.

"I said to keep your head down." Jake frowned in Charlie's direction, then went back to watching their surroundings.

"Come on out," one man yelled. "And we'll take ya in to talk to the boss."

"Yeah, over a saddle," Mandy snapped.

"Sell your land, and we'll leave ya alone."

"Over my dead body," Mandy yelled.

"That can be arranged."

"Where have I heard that before," Mandy bit out.

"We can sit here," Ashley's man called back, "until you change your mind, or you're all dead, your choice, ladies and gentlemen."

"You've only got one problem," Jake called back.

"What's that?" someone answered.

"Nobody's mistook me for a gentleman—in a long—long time."

"So?"

"I don't live by no one's rules."

Mandy's brows shot up.

"I make them."

"Big talk. Big man. Let's see how you're talk'n in a few more hours."

Jake turned and got comfortable against the rock.

"And now?" Kat asked.

"We wait."

"Do you think we could get near the water canteens?" Mandy asked almost an hour later. "My tongue feels like old shriveled up wool."

Jake squinted at the sun.

"Probably wouldn't be a bad idea. By the time Hawk realizes we're late, then rides here, we'll still have about a two or three-hour wait."

Without further urging, Kat jumped up. Dodging from rock to rock, she went around the other side of the closest horse, led them to a safer spot and grabbed two canteens. Heading back, dirt kicked up around her feet as she slid safely around a rock. She tossed one to Mandy, who took a grateful drink and tossed it to Jake.

Back-handing the moisture off her face, Kat threw hers to Charlie. "Let me sneak around 'em," she directed this to Jake.

"No," he grated out. "Nobody's going to play hero when a little patience will bring us all what we need."

Kat made a face and kept her sights on a hat that kept popping up. "If you say so."

"I say so."

By the time, Jake had figured Hawk would show, Charlie was shooting at anything that moved. "Set on us, will ya!" He shot again. "Well, come on out and get us."

"Easy, old timer," Jake soothed. "You're wasting ammunition."

"Hee hee hee. Shooting at McCandles men," he racked his Winchester, "ain't never a waste." He shot again and was rewarded when someone swore viciously.

The sound of several horses, riding up, held them all in suspense for a moment, until the new arrivals started shooting at McCandles men, this causing Mandy and Kat to hoot, and rendering more vicious swearing from Ashley's men. They dodged bullets and mounted up, one catching a bullet in the leg. Another pitched off his horse on their flight out.

Hawk rode right up to Mandy and dismounted. Before she could say a word, he pulled her up into his muscular embrace. "I was afraid I wouldn't get to you all in time," he whispered into her hair.

"You came," she whispered back. "And pretty much, right when Jake thought you would."

Hawk chuckled. "Military tactics." He led her over and set her on his horse. She just shook her head. She was getting used to his highhanded methods. A girl could get really used to having a man like Hawk around. And she didn't want to let that thought go too far.

Or she'd also have to think about the day he'd be gone.

Chapter Twenty-Five

Jason McCandle rode in slow, careful not to make any sudden moves. He kept his hands in plain view and prayed Hawk's men were not the trigger happy sort. His weathered brow was furrowed in deep concentration.

What was Hawk doing here, anyway? Why was he fighting for the Kanes?

When Jason had come home this morning, he'd been visibly shaken to learn Hawk was nearby. So much so, he'd sent Ashley into a rage.

He raised his eyebrows at the number of guards he'd seen posted the past five miles. There had been one every mile. What the hell was going on?

He rode straight up to the porch.

Hawk was coming across the yard when he spotted him. Seeing the visitor, Mandy had come out on the porch

But Jason's eyes were riveted on Hawk.

Something on Hawk's face made the hairs stand up on the back of Mandy's neck. Her gut clenched. She didn't know why, but she felt sick.

"Hello, son," Jason said in a rough whisper.

Hawk didn't answer, he merely stood there—casually, some would say. But Mandy sensed the underlying rage, beneath the complacent facade.

Lenore Wolfe

And she'd swear, she sensed pain, too. But that couldn't be right. Hawk didn't even know Jason. Or did he? Was this part of Hawk's personal reasons for entering this war? Mandy didn't know why, but she felt tingly and—afraid.

She couldn't shake the feeling that something—was about to shatter her world.

Jason's eyes hadn't left Hawks. He seemed bone weary, as though the whole world pressed down on his shoulders. "You did it son. You gained the ranch. I couldn't be prouder. I was wrong, you know—wrong to reject you when you found me," he sighed, "when you finally left them savages. But you gotta understand, son. You looked so much like 'em. I just couldn't stand how they'd changed you—your long hair—your buckskins. Hell, you *couldn't even speak English anymore . . .*" his voice trailed off, his eyes seeing the past.

Mandy was no longer looking at Jason.

She was staring at Hawk.

And when Hawk finally looked at her, the pain in her eyes nearly doubled him over. For a moment she just stood there, still and pristine, like priceless china, shattered—and then, she turned and ran.

Hawk's eyes glittered like cold steel. "I didn't get this ranch for you, old man. *I came here to keep it out of your hands!*" his voice was sharp and deadly, like a razor. *"Get off my land. Or—the next time I see you—I'll kill you."* He turned and, without another word, went after Mandy.

Jason stared after his oldest son. Hawk wouldn't dare challenge him.

But Hawk was gone before he could reply. He got down of his horse and went into the house. He crossed to the cabinet and poured himself a drink—and sat down to wait.

The hands just looked at one another, unsure of what to do. Jason had simply walked into the house, uninvited. Hawk hadn't stuck around long enough to stop him, and not a man among them knew, for sure, what they were supposed to do. Nobody knew what to make of such blatant arrogance, and no one wanted to cross Jason McCandle without Hawk.

Seeing this, Tommy ran to get Kid—or better yet, he thought, he'd get, Jake. Yeah. Jake would take care of Jason McCandle.

"Get out Hawk!" Mandy screamed when she saw him at the door. "You get out—and get off my land."

"I'm not leaving, Mandy," Hawk's reply was quiet.

To Tame a Wild Hawk

Mandy bit her lip to keep it from trembling. "Then, I will."

Hawk was jarred out of his calm. "You're not going anywhere." He strode toward her, and she jumped and took a step back, than another.

"You can't stop me, you arrogant, over-grown, insufferable...."

"You're wrong, Mandy," he softly told her. "You are my wife. I can do anything I want." He roughly grabbed her by her shoulder, "—*and you're not leaving.*"

Mandy wanted to slap him. "What are you going to do, Hawk," she sneered his name, "lock me in?"

"Stop it, Mandy!" he roared, his hands slipping down her arms to manacle her wrists.

Mandy laughed, a laugh fraught with pain—and betrayal. It knifed through Hawk, leaving him wounded and bleeding, like Mandy.

"I didn't marry you to get this land for my father," Hawk growled.

"Didn't you?" Mandy's voice was thick with scorn. "All these years, he's been after my father's land. He even killed papa to get it." She took a deep shaky breath. "And now, he got it, by a single stupid move on my part. *I handed it over on a silver platter—along with myself.*"

Hawk grabbed her chin in one hand. "Hear me well, woman," he bit out. *"I did not get this land for my father.* I'll admit, at first, I thought it was a perfect way to get revenge...."

Mandy wrenched away and turned her back. *"Get out, Hawk,"* her voice was cold. *"I never want to see you again. I will spend the rest of my days wiping you from my memory...."* and from my heart, she silently cried.

Hawk heard the hate in her words. He stared at her back, knowing he'd lost her, feeling the pain slice through him. Then, he left the room with a deep hole in his chest, where his heart had been.

It remained back in the room—in Mandy's slender hands.

He never saw the tears that ran, unchecked, down her face.

When Hawk came back down stairs and found Jason, sitting in his comfortable chair, drinking his whiskey like he owned the place, he nearly gave into the desire to kill his father.

Lenore Wolfe

For the first time, in all the years since he'd learned his warriors training, he almost went mad and let his emotions run him. His eyes glittered with such unsuppressed fury, it had Jason clutching the arm of the chair.

He took one menacing step towards Jason, his hands clutching the air "I could break your neck with my bare hands."

"So," Jason smiled. "I see both of my sons are in love with the wench."

With a growl, Hawk lunged forward and yanked him from the chair. He didn't stop until he had pulled him through the front door and thrown him, face first, off the porch.

"You're going to regret that," Jason told him in unruffled calm.

Hawk was impressed. He was more like his father then he cared to admit. And it made him want to vomit. The thought made him want to do bodily harm. He looked up to see Kid—and Jake, coming from the barn. It was probably a good damn thing they both showed up when they did.

Having just come in off the range, and been appraised of the situation by a frantic young Tommy, they were only too happy to deal with Jason.

In fact, they were looking forward to it.

At the look on Hawk's face, Jake drew his Colt and stuck the barrel in Jason's face. "Get on your horse, McCandle. I assume you must be the eldest McCandle, since you got Hawk, here, in such a killing fury," he stated in a voice, so calm, the hair stood up on the back of Jason's neck.

"I am," he replied, getting slowly to his feet. "Too bad my son hasn't listened to reason. It would have saved you all a lot of trouble. But Jordan is bent on trouble. Aren't you son?" he asked Hawk. He picked up his hat. "I see Jordan told you all about me." He grinned.

Kid's eyebrows shot up in a perfect imitation of Hawk. "The cold-blooded killer of friends, women and children. Yes, he's told us. You ought to be hung for the vile bastard you are. And . . . " He smiled back. "Isn't that, *McClain?* He looked around at the hands. "Boys, meet your real neighbor. This is Jason McClain."

That caused Jason's calm to slip. In fact, the cold that came to Jason's eyes was almost demented in appearance.

Again, Kid's brows shot up. "Ah. . . . a glimpse of the monster—behind the mask." He grinned. "It's always nice to know who one's enemy really is, now, isn't it?"

"Does he always court danger with such aplomb?" Jason asked Hawk.

To Tame a Wild Hawk

"Always," was the only reply he got

Jason clucked his tongue. "Too bad, I rather like you boy. Don't reckon I'm going to enjoy killing you. Are you certain you're on the right side?"

Kid inclined his head in a mock bow. "Quite certain." He grinned. "I do believe I'm going to enjoy bringing you down." He looked at Hawk. "I owe you one, brother."

"Think nothing of it," Hawk replied dryly

Jason flinched at the word brother, and his eyes narrowed, dangerously, on Kid. But before he could say a word, Jake indicated Jason's horse with a slight move from his Colt.

"Get on."

He complied, but gave one parting shot before he turned his horse to go. "I'm glad *one of my sons* has tamed the little minx." He grinned. "Either way, I've already won, you know. The Northern Rose. . . ." he made a face, "I hate that name. Anyway, *it's in the family.*"

Hawk groaned. So this was how Mandy saw it. He couldn't blame her for her hate. He'd delivered the land, she'd fought for, for so long—the land, her father had given his life for—right into the same, thieving, hands she'd hated most. Why hadn't he realized she would always see this as the worst betrayal? In his love for her, he had betrayed her.

Hawk drew himself up tight. "The only family I claim—the only father I knew, they're all dead." He stood, proud and strong, placing a hand on his chest, he said. "I am Hawk, son of Standing Bear. Brother of the Lakota." His eyes flickered on Jason with deadly menace. "They, Star Flower and Mandy, are *my only family.*"

Jason glared at him, hearing this. Then, turned and left.

Chapter Twenty-six

Hawk wasn't surprised when Mandy didn't come downstairs that evening. But when she didn't come down the next morning, he'd had enough.

No one answered when he knocked, and without a second thought, he kicked in the door. His heart was pounding with fear.

The fear mounted when he found a note lying on her bed. Sometime during the night, she must have found a way to break out. Since Hawk had heard her pacing late last night, she couldn't have been gone too long. But just how long? And where did she go?

Hawk,

I know you're furious right now, but I'll be fine. Really, I will. At any time, in all these weeks, you could have told me the truth, but you didn't. So I can only assume the worst. I could never live with that kind of deceit. You have what you were after. You're the owner of The Northern Rose. As I said before, I shall spend my life—wiping you from my life—and memory.

Mandy

Lenore Wolfe

Hawk crumbled the note and threw it. In a flash he was down the stairs, barking orders at Ned, Kid and Jake.

Kid, himself, brought him his horse, while Hawk threw some things together. He was on her trail within the hour, Kid with him. By mid-day, he seriously questioned his tracking abilities. Unless he missed his guess, she was headed straight for the Lakota. He sent Kid back with a message. They were to run the ranch like their own.

And it might be weeks before he returned.

Hawk knew this tribe, although only briefly. It would not be a short trip. They would be heading for wintering grounds.

Angrily, Hawk signaled his horse to pick up speed. Did she think this was the one place she could hide, where he would never think to look? She would have succeeded, too, but for Hawk's tracking abilities. He'd nearly missed the, almost too well covered, trail when it had deviated from the main road to town. Hawk's gut clenched. In fact, he had been heading straight for town, believing her to be going out on the next stage out. It was going to be, too, easy, bringing her back.

Again, he nearly missed her trail, but once again, it had stood out, too well, from the rest of the land, to a man who'd spent years hunting, and tracking, his sister's killers. A man taught from a young child to track.

When he thought of how easy it would have been to miss, to a man with less experience, how easily she could have disappeared out of his life—forever, he went into a cold rage. His heart pounded, then, at the thought of the years of he would have searched—at the thought of the loss of his only true love.

She would have, quite simply, seemed to drop off the face of the earth.

But the *Grandmothers*, who watched over her, now led him to her.

Hawk peered hard at the trail. She'd done well, had taken no chances. Several times he'd lost it, had spent quite some time picking it up again, crossing back and forth until he found it.

She must have been about eleven when she'd been bought back from the people, since he knew it was about the time her father moved to this area. That was during the same time Hawk was living with Doc, relearning the white man's ways.

Ashley had used her Lakota background to force her to submit to his threats. Ashley had known her witchy ways ruined her chances for a decent marriage proposal, and he'd been using it to get her to break. Hawk knew

To Tame a Wild Hawk

thinking about these things wasn't boding well for him keeping a clear head. He should have come for her years ago, when the *Grandmothers* had first sent him the dreams, not off seeking an old revenge.

It was near noon, the next day, when Hawk entered the village. Children ran up to him, excited to greet him. When he reached the center of the village, he stopped in front of Chief Ten Bears. The old chief stood there for a moment, his face lit up in recognition, and welcome.

He let his old eyes travel over Hawk before he finally spoke. "It is good to see the son of Standing Bear. It has been too many moons since my old eyes have looked upon your face."

Hawk dismounted and embraced the old chief. "It is good to look upon the face of my father's best friend, once again. It brings my heart much joy to see you enjoying good health. We will see each other for many more moons while we walk on this earth."

The old chief grinned. "You are probably right. I am still strong, and I walk upright. My mind is still clear, and I still chase after my wife."

Hawk nodded, smiling. "And you will continue to do so for some time."

Chief Ten Bears sobered then. "But I see many hard times ahead for our people. I see much sadness. Much death and hunger. The bellies of our children will rumble, and the women will weep and gnash their teeth in their grief." He looked up at Hawk with a sad smile and shook his head in bewilderment. "I can see no end to it."

Pain lanced Hawk's heart, for he, too, could see there was no stopping what was fast approaching.

When Mandy entered the tipi, she ran into a brick wall and went completely still.

He had found her. Well, of course he had found her .Double damn. He'd been sent the dreams too, no doubt about it.

When she finally got the courage to look up, his green eyes glowered down at her.

"I suppose you want an explanation."

"Something like that." He grabbed her shoulders before she could get away. "It seems I wasn't the only one with secrets."

That observation had her spitting like a wild cat.

He grabbed her hands and pinned them behind her back.

"Your woman?" The old chief broke in.

"My woman," Hawk agreed. "My wife."

The old chief grunted. "She said she had married a great warrior. I thought she said this to keep the other men at bay. But she has indeed married a great warrior. He indicated to his wife to get the two young people their own tipi. "Have Two Stars come stay here. I think these two have much to talk about."

Mandy shook her head, and Hawk gripped her arm so tight it hurt. "We would be happy to accept such kind hospitality. I so, indeed, have much to say to my woman."

After the evening's supper, they were finally free to go their tipi. Hawk grabbed Mandy and pushed her through the flap, closing it behind them.

"There is nowhere you can hide from me." He stepped up close to her while she looked wildly around for a means of escape. "You married me for better or for worse. You may be, even now, carrying my child."

Mandy's mouth dropped open in shock. Her eyes wide as she circled the fire, out of his reach "I want you out." She indicated the door.

"Not on your life, darl'n." His eyes were slits. "Till death do us part. Remember?"

At this, she laughed. The sound of it was brittle. "Hah! Not here." She grabbed his saddle bag and roll, and opening the flap, she tossed them out before he could stop her.

"Damnation!" he thundered, "Do you realize what you've done." His eyes narrowed on her. "Yes, I think you do." He stepped out and picked up the bags, ignoring the snickers when he stepped back inside.

Mandy swallowed "You can't do that."

"I just did."

She dove toward the door, but his arm snaked around her waist, bringing her to an abrupt halt. Deftly he drew her down to the mat. He kissed her, while she punched him. He kissed her, until she brazenly kissed him back. He kissed her, until she begged for more. And then, he made love to her.

That night he never let her go.

Chapter Twenty-Seven

When Mandy woke, Hawk was gone, and Two Stars was setting breakfast in front of the fire.

"*Hihani washday*—good morning. You're man went hunting with the others."

Mandy nodded and thanked her, then went out and bathed in the creek. When she returned, she ate with Two Stars.

"We will gather berries today," the young woman told her.

Mandy nodded, absentmindedly. She could sometimes here the *Grandmothers* here. The *Grandmothers* had not been happy that she had come here, neither had her teachers. They had not been happy she had tried to spurn the Hawk. They had warned her, she must return in all possible haste. But first, they said she must marry in the true circle.

But Mandy couldn't imagine that they still thought her future, her path, lay with him.

They gathered berries in the morning and sat beading all afternoon. It felt good to sit with her friends again. "I have missed you, my friend."

"You will visit more often?"

Laughing, Mandy nodded. "I will visit more often."

Late that afternoon, Hawk sat behind the tent and played a flute. Her Lakota friend giggled, shyly. But the tempo sent Mandy's heart thundering out of control. It was sweet and lulled her. She repeatedly had to tell her heart it was over, finished, he'd lied to her.

Two Stars laughed. "You're man weaves a love spell around you."

Mandy made a face at her. "It doesn't move my heart at all," she denied.

The young woman leaned forward to put more buffalo chips on the fire. "I think you lie to yourself."

Mandy scowled. Seeing it, Two Stars giggled.

A young Indian brave also played a love song. He told Hawk, she had thrown his belongings out of the tent. That she was free to marry someone else. Embarrassed, Mandy looked at Hawk for help, chewing on her lip.

"She was angry," Hawk growled. "It comes from the whites to let emotions rule your head. She has not divorced me." He looked at Mandy. "Have you?"

Mandy's eyes flashed with anger. She was stuck. He knew it—and she knew it. If she didn't go along with him, she would have this brave laying claim to her.

Only Hawk's reputation, with the people, saved her now. He was highly respected. If she caused any more waves, she would pay the price. Reluctantly, she relented. "It is as he has said, I lost my temper last night. It is why the people call me, *Eyes that Flash with Fire.*" She saw Hawk grin at this piece of news and made a face at him. "But I am deeply honored you would look at me favorably," she told the brave.

Hawk scowled, and that made Mandy want to grin.

Mandy could see the young brave was disappointed. She lowered her eyes with the guilt she felt over starting this. She should have known it would lead to this. If she had been a captive, the first warrior who claimed her would have owned her, and Hawk would have had to fight to the death to have her. With her Lakota family, who was there to protect her, Mandy was free to choose her husband. As far as they were concerned, she had chosen the Hawk. Still, she would have every brave who chose to court her, coming over here, if she disclaimed Hawk.

She didn't want that.

She should do it, just to irritate him, but it would cause her much grief with the young braves. She couldn't toy with them in such a manner. After all, she still was Hawk's wife, no matter how she sliced the pie. In the white man's eyes, she couldn't just throw out his possessions and say, *be gone.*

To Tame a Wild Hawk

She looked up now to find Hawk's green eyes burning into hers. Involuntarily, she flinched. "Don't look at me like that. I'm not the one who lied."

"Didn't you?" His eyes bore into hers a moment more, and he was gone.

"Did I?" She muttered. She thought of the many times she had lied. The many times she made promises to him and broken them.

That didn't give him the right to trick her.

She thought about what he'd said in the very beginning, not to ask what his part in this fight was, or he'd be gone. Technically, he had never lied.

"Don't go feeling sorry for him," she muttered. He'd left out the fact that he was McCandle's son. She realized what he'd meant, just now, when he'd asked her if she had lied. She had married him, for better or for worse. The worse being, he was her most hated enemy's son. She knew better than to think he loved his father—or his brother.

His brother.

She just couldn't get over the simple fact Ashley was Hawk's

Brother—even if it was only half-brother. How could two brothers be so different?

She stood, suddenly, in surprise. "Star Flower!" She raced through the village until she spotted Hawk, and then, as calmly as she could, she stood quietly and waited for him to notice her.

He came to her within seconds, which pleased her immensely.

"Star Flower?" She questioned, "Is she. . . . ?"

Hawk closed his eyes and nodded.

"Oh my—that's why she followed you out of the room."

He waited.

"She's in extreme danger, Hawk. Don't you know that?"

"I know." His jaw flexed. "But she wouldn't listen—anymore than you will."

That stung. Mandy turned and went back to her beading.

She fixed his dinner that evening, and they sat in silence eating. They didn't observe Lakota tradition with the meal—of her serving and him eating. She had started to, but he indicated for her to sit, so she sat and ate.

Lenore Wolfe

Mandy lay down on the buffalo furs, towards the sides of the tipi. Her stomach was tied up in knots.

Would he make love to her again tonight? How long could she hold out in her anger? It wasn't even anger anymore. And it wasn't hurt. She was simply disillusioned. Her heart was reaching for him, and her reasons for holding out were fast crumbling.

He stood and held his hand out to her.

Trembling she placed her smaller hand in his, and he gently pulled her to her feet. He placed his palm on her face. "I'm going to give you time to think."

She nearly shook her head, no.

"I won't let you go," he growled. "But I want you to be happy. You need time to think everything through."

She looked up into his green eyes and swallowed. Watching him leave, she almost cried out in pain. She lay down and curled up in a ball.

Hawk entered the sweat lodge the next morning, he felt he needed this. He had to figure out what to do about Mandy, and he had to have a clear mind to do it. The sweat lodge was just the place to do that.

The sweat lodge cleansed both the body and mind. He breathed in deep, knowing every detail of the sweat lodge reflected something. The dome stood for the universe. It was usually made of bent willow, which stood for birth and renewal—and it was covered with buffalo hides. A hole was dug in the center, where they placed hot stones. Dirt was strewn across as a sacred path, leading to the fire, symbolizing the sun, where stones were heated.

Within the dark interior, the sweat lodge stood for the womb, from which all were born.

Hawk sat naked, on pads of sweet smelling sage, with the other warriors. The hot stones were brought in, and they offered prayers, and chanted. Water was sprinkled on the hot stones, filling the lodge with steam. A pipe was lit, and passed. Someone cried out *mitak oays' in*—all my relations—a kinship to all creatures. And they did it all, again—and again.

Early the next morning, the Crow raced down the hill. Their faces, bodies and horses were painted for war. They screamed their vengeance, and Mandy realized this was an aspect of the life of the Lakota she had never missed.

To Tame a Wild Hawk

The Lakota warriors were caught unawares, many still sleeping. Shaking the sleep from their eyes, they grabbed their weapons and went out to meet their hated enemies. Women and children raced in every direction, screaming—wailing when they saw their loved ones struck down. Mandy picked up a rifle and shot, first one crow warrior, then another. She didn't back down, didn't flinch, until a bullet spun her around.

Hawk saw it, raced to pick her up and hauled her into the trees to where some of the women and children were hiding.

He had to get back out there. They were holding their own, but he had to help make sure it remained that way. He asked the women to take care of her and went back to fight, knowing he would die if anything happened to her.

When it was over, they stared at the destruction left behind by their enemy. The women wailed their grief for their lost loved ones. Once more, an enemy had wrecked destruction on their lives, and with the ever-present danger of the encroaching white man, they were finding little peace. They would mourn their dead, then leave this place.

They sent scouts out to find the buffalo. It was, again, time for a great hunt.

Hawk had other plans at the moment. He walked over and drew back his fist. The Crow, they'd captured, took the brunt of his temper in a brutal punch. Hawk felt the man's nose break and only received little relief for the terror he'd felt. He realized then, he'd let his emotions rule him—one of the few times in his life—and drew back sharply. He swore, viciously, and swung around, heading for Mandy.

When he located her, he was relieved to learn the bullet had only grazed her arm. The women had her bandaged up, and they were all working diligently to pull up camp.

They pulled down the tipis and loaded the horses. They would look for the buffalo.

Once there were thousands of them, roaming as far as the eye could see. But now, the buffalo hunters dropped hundreds of them at a time, and their numbers were dwindling. The people were going hungry.

Hawk rode up with some of the other warriors and scouted for signs of the buffalo. What they found turned his stomach. He was sickened by the sight of buffalo, dropped dead in a wide swath by buffalo hunters—sickened by the sight of the buffalo calves left behind. The buffalo hunters had killed the buffalo only for their hides and their tongues, the rest left to rot. Enough meat was left to rot that it would have fed several tribes through the entire winter. There was anger and hatred in the warrior's eyes, and Hawk knew, they looked forward to a bloody war. One they could not win.

It made him sick.

There were tears in the eyes of the women, and Mandy was no exception. The beasts were beautiful, huge animals. How could anyone abide by such waste?

They rode, silently, along for several days, and when the buffalo were spotted they set up the tipis and the celebration began. The drumbeats filled the air, the tempo of Mandy's heart matching the rhythm. The bodies of the men glistened in the firelight. Their chanting and singing joined the throb of the drums.

They painted a silhouette of a speared buffalo on the grass and danced around it—because of its importance, and strength, its spirit praised before every hunt.

The warriors readied for the hunt, taking special care of their horses. The horse he chose for this hunt was treated with high regard. Even a mortally wounded bull could run a good distance before dropping.

Hawk wore only his breech-cloth and moccasins with only a knife in his belt. He also carried a short bow and quiver of arrows. His horse had a leather thong around his neck in case he fell from his horse and needed it to remount.

Once the deadly ride started, Hawk moved in behind a huge bull, using his knees to guide his horse. The sheer size of the animal was an impressive sight. A bull could weigh up to two thousand pounds. And he wasn't to be messed with when angry. The bull thundered along with the others. Hawk aimed for a spot behind the bull's last ribs, hoping to puncture the diaphragm and collapse the lungs.

His second aim was true, and the huge bull dropped.

Hawk moved off towards another.

Thirty minutes later, the hunt was over. They finished off the wounded buffalo and claimed their unbroken arrows.

The women moved in with their cutting tools. Each woman claimed the meat she wanted, and the hides, from the animals brought down by her man. But then, they shared the rest of the meat with the poor—especially the women with no men to hunt for them.

There would be a great celebration for the success of the hunt.

To Tame a Wild Hawk

They were relaxed, and well fed. Mandy could have stayed this way forever. But the wonderful feeling, the full bellies, the laughter and the celebrations—could never last.

"I am going with some of the warriors for a few days," Hawk told her, almost though he knew her thoughts.

Mandy looked up sharply. "You're going after the Crow." It wasn't a question and panic thrummed through her. They'd just had a successful hunt, and she knew the proud Lakota would not let their hated enemy get away with what they had done.

"Jake was right. You're very quick. Yes, we go after the Crow."

She hugged him to her, afraid to let go. "How long do you think you'll be gone?"

"A week, maybe more, maybe less. I know we should return, Mandy, but I have to do this." His gold-green eyes pleaded with her for understanding. Jake will run our ranch like his own. I know he'd understand."

"I know, Hawk." She hugged him. "Hurry back."

There were tears in her eyes when he left her early the next morning. When he was gone, she went back into the tipi and lying down, she cried herself back to sleep.

Mandy and Two Stars sat and sliced the buffalo meat thin and set it on racks to dry. When it was done, they made, *Wasna*, pemmican, which would keep forever. A wintering band could survive weeks on *Wasna* and dried buffalo or Jerky. But it wasn't as good as fresh meat, and hunters often went looking for fresh meat.

They laughed and told stories as they worked, teasing one other whenever a young brave came by to smile or court one of the girls.

The next few days were spent on the buffalo hides. Mandy and her friends were about to spend as much as ten days preparing a hide. The hides were scraped clean. They immersed them into a solution made from ashes and water to loosen the hair so it could easily be pulled.

Two Stars prepared a tanning mixture of buffalo brains and other things. She wanted one of the hides to be white, so the bones were pulverized and the oil extracted and added, which they worked into the skin for hours.

Lenore Wolfe

They folded the hides and left them overnight so the mixture would penetrate. The next morning they stretched them back out and worked it over with elk horn, then smoked them to make them pliant.

Mandy set aside hair to stuff for a pillow for each of them. One of the things Mandy liked about the people was they didn't take anything for granted.

They made use of all they could and didn't waste, like the white eyes.

The horns were carved into cups, or boiled and shaped into spoons or ladles or used for glue, their bones made into sled runners and hoes, their hair braided into lariats, the sinew used for thread. Dried dung was used for the fire or baby powder. It took a dozen or so hides to make a tipi, but once done it belonged to the woman. If she divorced, she took her tipi with her. White women always lost everything to her husband and never stood a chance of keeping her home.

Mandy walked through the village. A bed of grass carpeted the ground, the scent of pine and cooking fires filled the air. Warm sunshine, and the laughter of children, surrounded her. She sighed peacefully. She could stay here forever.

Here, away from ever present danger of Ashley McCandle.

But peace was only an illusion among the people. The long-knives made peace impossible. From what had she heard, broken treaties were like broken glass—impossible to mend, and razor sharp. Her sigh was tinged with sharp regret now. It would be a sad day, indeed, to watch these proud people forced to knuckle under white man's laws.

And for what?

Why did they have to live the white eyes way? Why did the treaties have to be broken? These people would have lived in peace if promises had been kept.

She had reached the edge of the camp and reached to pluck a wild flower. Twirling it between her thumb and forefinger, she held it under her nose to smell.

Hawk came up behind her and pulled her into his embrace. She knew it was him, instantly, with awareness—a powerful woman's intuition. She fought not to lean into him, and lost. He was home, and he was unharmed. It was just too easy to feel safe in his arms. They were a safe haven from all that was wrong in the world.

"Are you okay?" His voice was husky.

To Tame a Wild Hawk

She nodded and for some unexplainable reason, broke into tears.

Hawk held her close. *"Ceye Sni yo*—don't cry."

When she had sobbed her heart out, he dug out a bandanna and dried her tears. She tried for a lighthearted joke. "A hundred uses for a bandanna."

"Do you carry my son?"

She went still as death. All the color left her skin.

"I see the possibility hadn't occurred to you."

She shook her head, too shocked to speak.

"When was the last time you bled?" he persisted.

She swallowed hard, trying to think. But it was nearly impossible to think through the haze that had dropped over her head.

"Two weeks before we married," she finally got out

That makes you about two weeks late." He looked down at her, an unnamed emotion shinning in his eyes. We have to return home. This Indian summer won't last, then it will be impossible to return through the deep snows."

She nodded mutely.

He rested his forehead against hers, relieved as hell she wasn't fighting him. She was letting him take her home. That was a great start in his book. He could deal with anything as long as he knew he stood a chance of righting things. He'd spend the rest of his life making it up to her, as long as she gave him the chance. He rained kisses all over her face and down her neck.

Later, when Hawk was called away to play some games with the warriors, Mandy sat and watched the children play, remembering when she and her friends had played these same games when she was young.

The little girls put up tipis, and the young boys brought them small game, pretending to be great warriors. Mandy smiled at their antics and laughed out loud when she spotted two boys snatch some meat off the drying racks and run.

She sat trying to picture having Hawk's son. What would he be like? Would he have Hawk's golden-green eyes? Would they sparkle with mischief like these boys? She placed her hand over her lower abdomen. Was it possible, that even now, she carried his son under her heart? In the heat of the sun, she lay back and went to sleep on the grass.

In her dreams, she ran like the wind. She had done it now. He would paddle her for sure. She'd been teasing him all morning, making him want her, then eluding him. She had no more guards to put against him. It didn't matter whose blood ran in his veins. She loved him with all her being.

And when she woke, she knew—she would run from her husband—no more.

She was laughing, running though the creek, near where they bathed, when he caught her. She went down and came up sputtering. "Damn you, Hawk." She looked down at her beaded dress. "You've ruined it."

He picked her up and hauled her to shore. Setting her down, he pulled the dress off over her head.

She shivered, not from the cold but from the heat in his eyes and the answering tempo in her body.

"I can see it in your eyes," his husky voice settled over her like his fingers on her skin. "Now, say it."

"I don't know what you're talking about."

"I've waited for you to decide," he growled. "Only your stubborn pride is stopping you from saying the words."

She lifted her chin, and he pushed his hand though his hair in frustration. When he looked at her again, his eyes were warm. He cupped her face. "I need you, now. I know you want to be with me, Mandy. You set me on fire. You're making me crazy."

She looked up with tears in her eyes. She lowered them, but he hooked his finger under her chin and brought her eyes back to meet his. "Say it, Mandy. Say, you don't want to leave me. Say, you want to be with me."

Her breath shuddered within her when she looked into his eyes. The emotion she saw there completely undid her, and she did him one better. "I love you."

Hawk went completely still. Every beat in his heart had waited for this moment. Every dream a man could dream but was too afraid to hope, lay suspended on a silvery thread in that very moment. "Say that again. I need to be sure I heard you right."

Mandy smiled at him, her heart in her eyes. "I love you, Hawk. I love you with my whole heart, and my whole being. I love you with everything there is, and everything there ever will be inside me."

To Tame a Wild Hawk

He crushed her to him. "And I love you," he whispered in her hair. He laid her in the grass. He kissed her, ravaging her mouth with a fierce love, born from the fear he'd felt when he'd thought her lost to him. She matched him, kiss for kiss, raking her fingers over his naked, muscular back. "*Skuye*—sweet." He possessively laid claim to her breast. "*Wiwasteka*—beautiful Woman." He teased her until she whimpered and begged for more. Only then, did he move between her legs and enter her in one hard thrust.

With each rock of his body, he brought her with him, took her to a place only lovers go. And when she climaxed violently, he was with her. Then, he lowered his head to hers, and with warm tears in his golden eyes, he said those words again. "I love you, my woman. *Mitawin . . . wastelakapi*—forever beloved."

She turned on her side, watching him. Taking a piece of grass, she tickled his nose until he playfully swatted at her. "What were you thinking about?" she asked, softly, when he had successfully pinned her down.

Hawk smiled, wryly, and flopped back over onto his back. "A lot of things," he answered with a sigh.

"This is the first time, in seven years, I've slowed down long enough to do much thinking. Truth be told, I think I ran away from having to do any thinking."

She gave him a soft smile. "That's understandable. Many people run from pain."

They lay there, in the grass, enjoying the warm autumn day, listening to the babble of the brook and smelling the warmth of the sunshine on the grass, with the lingered scent of autumn flowers.

"Tell me how you were captured?" she asked after a moment.

His expression turned stony, and she instantly regretted the question. "I'm sorry, I shouldn't have asked. I didn't mean to bring back bad memories."

Hawk watched her for several long moments. "My mom died when I was six. One day she was there—and the next. . . . She died giving birth to my sister."

"My father wouldn't even look at her—I guess he blamed her. Then, one day, several months later, he took me and headed west." He stared at her, but didn't see her. He was deep in the past. He absently rubbed a lock of her hair between his thumb and fingers. "He was never the same," he nearly whispered. He cleared his throat. "One day, weeks into the long wagon ride west, he told me to go to the river, and no matter what, not to come back until he came for me."

"When I heard the gunshots, I disobeyed him and came back. I hid in the nearby bushes, frozen with fear." Hawk paused, lost deep in thought, seeing it all again as though it were yesterday. "They were white men." His voice went hoarse. "They killed every man, woman—and child. And then, I got the biggest shock of all—my father was one of them." His tone held so much hate, Mandy wanted to cry. "He helped them kill our friends."

Mandy gasped, her hand flying to her throat. He must have thought her mad when she'd accused him of getting the ranch for such a man.

"Anyway, when it was over, the burning wagons drew a hunting party, and a Cheyenne warrior, from the party, adopted me as his son. They raised me as one of their own. I knew much love and happiness there." He laughed, remembering.

Mandy was speechless, imagining it all. "Why did he do it?" she whispered. "Why would he do such a thing?

He looked at her, his eyes flinty. "For the money." Mandy shook her head, unable to imagine such butchery—and for so little gain. Fighting for survival was one thing. It was what the Lakota fought for, and while she didn't always agree with their methods, she did understand them. But this. . . .

"I told you the Crow killed my Cheyenne father," his voice pulled her back. "White man's disease killed my Lakota family, and almost half my tribe, as the doc told you if I recall right."

Yes," she said softly. "I remember." That's when you met Doc, after you were beaten for being an Indian."

Hawk nodded. "And you know the rest."

"Your father said he was sorry he rejected you. What did he mean by that?"

Hawk scowled. "I found him after my Lakota family died, right before the doc found me." He flipped over on his stomach. "He wasn't too pleased with the changes in his son."

Tears welled in Mandy's eyes. She reached out and touched his shoulder, and he rolled over onto his side and kissed her. "You're all that's right in the world," he whispered in her hair. And he made slow passionate love to her again.

Mandy was flabbergasted when Hawk, and several of his friends, came over that evening, leading nearly a hundred horses loaded down with

To Tame a Wild Hawk

blankets, guns, bows, arrows, and other such items. They staked these horses outside the tipi.

So many horses were unheard of. What was he doing? She was already his wife.

Ten Bears didn't even look up for several long moments. Finally, when Mandy knew her heart would leave her chest, Hawk's emissary entered the tent and when invited to, sat down, and they smoked and made small talk.

Two Stars took Mandy's hand and led her away.

"What are they doing? I'm already Hawk's wife?" Mandy exclaimed.

Two Stars shrugged. "Your man wants to do this thing the Lakota way. It is good he wants this." She giggled. "Father is enjoying this."

"Too, much," Mandy growled in perfect imitation of Hawk.

She watched Hawk's emissary leave, then her eyes widened to see all the male members of her adopted family enter the tent. "They're taking this way too seriously," she muttered under her breath.

Two Stars took Mandy's hands in hers. "Father will not refuse him. Your man is a great warrior. He will welcome him into the family.

But Mandy didn't relax until they had distributed the horses amongst the relatives—a signal they had accepted the match.

Two Stars painted Mandy and braided her hair. Then, she brought out a beautiful white buckskin dress.

"It's beautiful," Mandy breathed.

Two Stars giggled and lowered her eyes. "We worked on it all night—to surprise you."

Mandy's eyes were shining. *"Pilamaya*—thank you.

When they had her all dressed, Two Stars stood back. "You are *wiwasteka*—a beautiful woman."

They heard the laughter, then, and the many people approaching the tent, long before they arrived. The closer they got, the harder Mandy's heart drummed in her chest. She had married Hawk in the way of the white eyes. Now, she would marry him in the way of the Lakota. Somehow, this time took on much more meaning. Maybe, it was because, this time, she knew Hawk wanted this—as much as she wanted him.

When he came for her, she closed her eyes and concentrated on breathing normal. When she knew that he was outside the tipi, she thought she would strangle from her thundering heart.

He rapped on the tipi door, and she called, *"Tima hiuwo*—come in." He threw back the door and entered the tipi and just stood there for a moment. All the love he felt for her, shinning in his golden eyes.

Finally, he strolled forward and took her hand. "I love you, my woman. My wife."

She breathed deep—and trembled. "I love you, my husband."

He led her outside to a beautiful mare. Mandy's eyes flew wide, when he set her on the mares back.

"For me?" Mandy whispered.

Hawk nodded. "You may name her whatever you wish.

An old woman, named Twin Flowers, led the mare to the tipi of the family who had taken in Hawk

One of Ten Bears wives followed, leading several of the gift horses.

Several of Mandy's Lakota male relatives carried her in and set her on the blankets. There, several of the females redressed her in the new buckskin dress they'd specially made for her. Then, they re-braided her hair and reapplied her paint. When they were finished, she stood beside Hawk as Ten Bears said a few words.

Hawk turned to her when he was finished. "I promise to love you, provide for and protect you, all the days that I live."

With tears in her eyes, Mandy squeezed the hand holding hers. "I promise to love you. I will cook for you and keep your home. I will bear you children and keep you warm at night."

Hawk chuckled and hugged her. "You better," he whispered in her ear.

"But I won't promise to obey," she whispered back.

"You already did—in the way of the White eyes." She scowled at him.

All the women sent up a cry into the wind. The warriors all whooped as Hawk led her to the tipi. And long into the night, the Lakota celebrated their union.

Hawk and Mandy had a celebration of their own.

Chapter Twenty-eight

Mandy breathed deep the smells of autumn. It was just her and Hawk out here. It was so nice to have some time alone together. She just couldn't figure out why Hawk was so quiet. He'd hardly said a word all day.

Hawk pulled up. "We'll camp here tonight."

"Why are we stopping so soon? We still have plenty of daylight left."

"You have been looking pale all day, and I don't want to push it too hard. We don't want anything to happen to you, or the baby."

"Is that why you have been so quiet all day?"

"I suppose it is." He helped her down from the mount, and pulled her bag off the saddle. "I've been thinking about you—and the baby."

"Here I thought I had done something." She started to unsaddle her horse.

Hawk stopped her. "Let me do that." He pulled her hands gently from the straps. "There's a hot spring just through those bushes." He nodded in the direction he wanted her to go. "You could go have a nice long soak. I'm sure it has been a long day for you."

Mandy squealed in delight. "Oh that sounds so wonderful, but are you sure?"

"Of course," he grinned. "But only if I can join you in a few minutes."

"Mmmm, that sounds marvelous," her voice was husky. She went to get her soap and a clean night shirt out of her saddle bags.

"I'll be along shortly then."

Mandy walked away smiling. Things were okay after all. She could barely keep herself from skipping along. Coming to the small pond, it looked like she had found heaven. Everything was green. It had grass banks on one side, and a cliff going straight up, on the other, with a waterfall coming over it. Lush green trees and bushes made it completely secluded.

She took her off clothes, slowly, indulging in how it felt to stand gloriously naked, there, in the warm fall breeze—it felt more than a little erotic. Letting her hair down, one pin at a time, until it fell loosely down her back, she shook it free and reveled in the feel of it against her skin.

Hawk stopped as he came around the corner, all the breath sucked out of his lungs. She was beautiful standing there. He felt as though someone had granted him a special spot in the circle of things, to be a part of her life. They would be together—for always.

Coming up behind her, Hawk reached up and ran his fingers through her hair, a hiss escaping through his teeth.

Kissing the side of her neck and nipping at her ear lobe, Hawk whispered, "I love you." Mandy giggled at him and went to pull away, but instead, found herself pinned—in his embrace.

He picked her up and set her gently on the grassy bank, loving her with slow, silky caresses.

Laying contented in Hawks arms, later that evening, she watched him sleep. Mandy wondered if there was any way possible they could be together, forever.

The next morning, Hawk woke Mandy by tickling her nose with a feather.

She kept rubbing her nose, trying to brush away the tickle, finally opening her eyes to find him grinning down at her. "Oh you—what a beast."

"What am I supposed to do? Let you sleep all day?"

"I'm sorry. I didn't realize it was so late." She stretched and started to get up. "We'd better get going."

"That's not exactly what I had in mind. I was thinking more along the lines of this." Hawk leaned over and kissed her. Then, kissed her again, and again, until his kisses were no longer soft—but passionate, and her responses matched his own. They made love all morning, then went for a long walk.

To Tame a Wild Hawk

Late that afternoon, Hawk went hunting. While he was gone, Mandy straightened up the camp. Then, she sat down to finish beading a pair of knee high moccasins she was making for Hawk, barely getting them hid before he came back to camp, carrying a small deer over his shoulder.

"Is that dinner I see slumped over your shoulder, or do you always go around offering rides to the game." It was lame, and she blushed, but she had accomplished what she set out to do—in sidetracking him.

"Actually, it is dinner, and you could be a good wife and cook it for me. But if I were to be offering rides to anyone. . . . " He gave her a lecherous, suggestive gaze.

Mandy blushed, promptly changing the subject.

After skinning the deer, they relaxed while they were waiting for it to cook. Hawk went to move the lump under his back, pulling out the moccasins she was beading for him.

He looked at her, uncertainty, showing in his eyes.

"What are these for? Why did you hide them?"

Mandy couldn't look up, suddenly shy. "They were a present for you. I just finished them while you were gone." She finally managed to look at him. "I've been working on them since we went to the buffalo hunt. I had a hard time keeping them a secret from you."

Realizing she was rambling, she bit out. "Why don't you try them on and see if they fit?"

Before she even got finished, Hawk was taking off his old moccasins and putting on the new ones Mandy had made for him.

"Do they fit?" She bit her lip. "Do you like them?"

"I love them. They're perfect. Especially since, they came from you. I'm sorry I reacted that way. It's just nice, you making me moccasins."

Looking into Hawk's eyes they seemed so soft, like melted butter. He pulled her into his arms, kissing her so softly she wanted to weep with it. "I have never had someone do something so special for me before. I don't know what to say."

"You don't have to say anything at all."

Lenore Wolfe

The forest smelled with the fresh scent of pine, as the sun warmed the trees, causing the sap to run. A warm breeze lifted Mandy's hair as they rode along the trail.

She breathed a contented sigh as her horse slowly picked its way through the rocks. The warm sun shone on her face, and she felt as though she could smile forever.

If only there wasn't the, ever-present, shadow of Ashley, McCandle looming over her shoulder.

She watched Hawk riding his horse ahead of her, the muscles in his back rippling. She could watch him forever.

"If you keep looking at me like that, we're going to take another break."

Mandy giggled. "And how exactly am I looking at you?"

Hawk growled, swinging down from his mount.

Mandy laughed and swung her horse around, to run, but Hawk drug her off into his arms.

He made love to her, slow, with hunger, right there in the grass.

Tears stung her eyes, her emotions overwhelming. He pushed her hair back from her eyes and kissed her face. "I love you," she told him and buried her face in his shoulder

"I love you." He kissed her gently. "And we are never going to make it home."

"Maybe. But we're having so much fun trying."

They camped, early, near a creek. Hawk left to scout the area, his gut telling someone was nearby. He circled around, determined to get the drop on whoever it was.

Unaware of what Hawk was doing, Mandy dug out a change of clothing. Humming as she headed for the creek.

The warm, autumn evening was just warm enough for her to strip naked. The creek wasn't warm, and she nearly yelped out-loud. She washed quickly, goose bumps covering her skin. When she washed her hair, the cold water on her scalp was downright painful.

To Tame a Wild Hawk

Clenching her jaw and dipping her head, she came up sputtering. When she wiped the water from her eyes, there were three dangerous looking men sitting on their horses, watching her.

Mandy's first instinct was to dip low in the freezing water and try to cover her breast with one arm. She moved towards her clothes, and one of the men laughed.

"Where do ya think you're going, girlie?"

"To get my clothes," Mandy grit out.

He drew his pistol and waved her away. "I don't think that's a good idea."

Mandy's legs were going numb. She knew if she was going to move, she had to move, now, before her frozen body prevented her.

She dipped near some boulders. The desperadoes didn't think anything of it—until it was too late. She raised, and cocked, the pistol with a speed that would have made Hawk proud if he'd hadn't been about to tear someone apart with his bare hands.

Her first shot hit one desperado full in the chest before she rolled out of reach behind the boulders, her knees and elbows taking a bad beating in the process.

She, simultaneously, came up shooting, hitting a second desperado before Hawk had moved in position to kill the third.

The forest was dead silent. Not even the buzz of an insect could be heard. Mandy stood dripping wet and gloriously naked, goose bumps covering her golden skin.

Hawk didn't know whether to beat her—or kiss her.

"You knew they were there," she hissed.

He strode right into the creek and took the pistol from her hand. "I knew." He picked her up and hauled her to the embankment.

"Where did you have that gun hidden?" he growled.

"Between two rocks," She raised her chin. "Nobody would ever let a woman near her clothes, it's the first place she'd hide a gun."

Hawk grinned, setting her on her feet, then sobered. "I should have given you more credit."

Mandy sniffed. "You shouldn't have treated me as if I were a simple-minded female."

"Believe me honey, I won't make that mistake again."

"You should have trusted me." Mandy lowered her eyes to hide her hurt.

He lifted her chin with his fingers. "I didn't want to worry you. I was wrong."

"Oh my . . . " she breathed.

"Don't push it," he growled.

Mandy fought hard not to grin, and lost.

With a growl, Hawk kissed her senseless. And it was much later before she could savor her triumph.

Mandy's horse was picking its way down a particularly steep path, early the next morning. The sun was warm, just as the day before. She was deep in thought, worrying about what they would find when they reached the ranch. Perhaps that was why she was caught so unawares when a cougar screamed. Her mount stepped sideways, then bolted.

Only Mandy's excellent horsemanship kept her in her seat.

Her horse went wild, striding forth—each step taking her faster—at a deadly speed. Mandy fought for control. She took the lead rope and yanked her with all her strength, trying to pull her head around. Under different circumstances it would have worked. But the mare was crazed with terror.

She was hurling herself forward with the strength of two horses. At that moment, Mandy knew, she probably wasn't going to survive.

In the next instant, two strong hands gripped her, and she was yanked from her horse onto Hawk's steed and surrounded by the steel bands of his muscular arms. He drew his stallion to a halt and crushed her to him, pressing kisses into her hair, whispering in her ear. He carried her on his mount until he found a good place to camp. Mandy was white as a sheet, and Hawk was determined she was going to rest for the remainder of the day.

When she realized what he was doing, she fought him. "I'm fine, Hawk. I don't need to be pampered."

"You're resting, Mandy, and that's the end of it."

To Tame a Wild Hawk

Much later, they sat in front of the fire, eating a delicious stew Mandy had prepared. Mandy licked her finger tips and saw the answering fire leap in Hawk's eyes.

"Do you ever think of settling down?" she whispered, her eyes shining.

Hawk's golden gaze probed hers. "Are you asking me to stay?"

Swallowing, Mandy nodded.

He set his plate down and crawled to her. Kissing her softly, he whispered, "I thought you'd never ask."

Her eyes widened and filled with tears. "I was afraid to. Afraid you'd say, no."

He kissed her again. "Well, the answer is, yes, lady."

She touched his face. "You mean it?"

"I'll love you forever, Mandy." He cupped her face in his palm. "I'll never let you go."

They reached the ranch early the next morning. Mandy stared in horror at the spot, where one of their barns had once stood. Nothing but burned rubble lay there, now.

She scrambled from her horse and raced into the house. "Aunt Lydia!" she screamed.

Aunt Lydia came around the corner and took a long look at Mandy. Tears welling in her eyes, she came forward and folded her into her arms. "You're all right. Oh child, you had me so worried."

"The barn..." Mandy choked out. "Is everyone all right?"

Lydia took her face in both hands. "They got a hold of Ned and drug him, like they did Pete."

Mandy's hands flew to her mouth. "Oh, no! I shouldn't have left. I took Hawk away, and now look what's happened."

Aunt Lydia gave her a gentle shake. "Now, you listen to me, child. We have good hands out there. Ned was just in the wrong place at the wrong time. It's nobody's fault but that monster, McCandle."

Mandy wiped the tears from her eyes. Pulling herself together, she straightened her shoulders.

"What else did they do?"

"They burned two line shacks," Lydia said gently. "And cattle have been disappearing faster than we can keep up with them."

Mandy felt sick to her stomach. "He's going to ruin me," she whispered.

"Like hell!" Hawk growled, and she jumped. He strolled towards her. "You're a fighter, Mandy." Reaching her, he grabbed her by the shoulders. "Now, stand up and fight."

"We've been fighting." Her voice was hollow. "And look what happened."

"We've only just begun to fight."

She bit her lip and looked at him. She looked so tired, and it made Hawk angry.

"What are you going to do?" she finally asked.

"First thing I'm going to do is go out and have a talk with Jake. We'll figure out where we go from there." He placed his Stetson back on his head and adjusted it. "I won't be back 'till tomorrow."

Chapter Twenty-nine

Meg showed up early the next morning. "Lord Mandy, don't ever do that again," she breathed. "You scared ten years off my life."

Mandy dimpled and hugged her friend. "It's good to see you too. I'm so glad you came, I've got much to tell you." She pulled Meg into the kitchen.

Ned had been taken to Doc Mallory. And Meg updated her on his condition as they sipped on tea. "He's going to be okay, Mandy. It was mainly surface bruising and scratches, though patches of his hide were peeled off."

Mandy breathed a sigh of relief on hearing this.

"What about you?" Meg asked. She dimpled. "How are you—and Hawk—coming along?"

Mandy blushed, giving everything away. "Things are wonderful. Heck, they're better than wonderful!" She grinned.

"Does that mean . . . ?"

"He loves me," Mandy answered, tears in her eyes.

Meagan rolled her eyes, dramatically. "Well, I could have told you that, you dolt. I tried to tell you when you were beaten up by that no good McCandle. He mooned over your bed as if he were a lovesick cowboy."

Mandy blushed. "I know you did, but I couldn't see it."

"So how are things with the Lakota?"

"They're doing as well as can be expected, but I don't think it will last long." Her eyes were sad. "However, all my friends were all grown up, and I had a wonderful time."

Mandy poured her friend some tea and refreshed her own cup.

Meg took a sip. "I heard Hawk's related to McCandles. The news about floored me."

Mandy scowled in answer.

Seeing it, Meg made a face at her. "You already said it, remember, he hates Ashley more than you do."

"I know."

Meg's eyes narrowed on her. "Oh, I see." She set her cup down on the saucer and folder her hands. "You can't handle whose blood runs through his veins."

"I'm getting used to it," Mandy countered, her tone warning Meg she was in dangerous territory.

"Really," Meg said, sardonically. "And how do you think he feels?"

Mandy's heart dropped to her stomach. "I've been selfish, haven't I?"

Meagan readily agreed, and within minutes the two women were laughing together, like they had as children.

Mandy sat in her favorite comfortable chair, in front of the fireplace. It felt wonderful to be home, she thought, sipping on a cup of tea. She snuggled deeper into the chair, sighing with pleasure. When she looked up, Hawk was leaning against the door jam, watching her.

"Come upstairs," his husky voice settled over her, strumming something vital and alive inside her.

"Mum . . ."

He took her hand, pulling her gently out of the chair. Picking her up, he carried her up the stairs. Inside the bedroom, Mandy looked around at the tub of steaming scented water, with drying towels lying close by. Candles sat burning on the highboy—and around the room.

To Tame a Wild Hawk

"Oh Hawk," she whispered, her eyes shimmering with tears. How did you manage to sneak in here and do all this?" she indicated the room.

Hawk smiled and slowly undressed her. He picked her up and set her in the scented water. Mandy sighed as the water closed around her. Her body relaxing as Hawk soaped up a rag and ran it over her skin. Inch by inch, with slow sensual movements, he washed her. All the while, Mandy sighed—even wept a little. When he finally lifted her from the tub and dried her, she was frantic with need of him. That night, he made tender love to her. Talking to her—loving her, again—and again.

Very early the next morning, Mandy rolled over with a sated sigh. When her hand touched empty sheets, she sat up with a frown. She slipped out of bed and dressed, apprehension filling her for some unexplained reason.

She found Hawk and Kid downstairs, already eating breakfast. "You two are up bright and early." She frowned.

Hawk came across the kitchen, kissed her, then poured her a cup of coffee. "I thought you might want to sleep in."

"We're going to check out the trail leading to the cliffs," Kid told her around a mouthful of biscuit.

Hawk scowled at him.

"What?" Kid asked innocently.

Mandy's brows shot up. "Where you got shot at?"

Hawk gaze pinned her. "Who told you about that?"

Mandy placed her hands on her hips. "It doesn't matter who told me," she railed at him. "That's where you're going, isn't it?"

Hawk set his cup down and strode purposely towards her.

"Oh, no." Mandy evaded him, going around the table. "Not this time."

"Mandy!"

Kid chuckled.

They both glared at him.

He held his hands up. "Pretend I'm gone."

Hawk took a threatening step towards him, and Kid shot out of his chair, laughing. "Touchy." He left the kitchen.

"I'm going with you."

"Mandy . . ."

"I'm going with you!"

"Who's your Cheyenne friend?"

Mandy sighed with exasperation.

"All right," Hawk caved in. "You can come."

"Thank you." Mandy laughed and ran to get ready.

"I've really got it bad," Hawk growled.

The sun was beating down, the air heavy, when they finally hit the trail, near the canyon. It was turning out to be a very warm autumn. Mandy hoped it would cool off soon, since they still had a lot of calves to brand. And branding was a hot, dirty job as it was, without the sun adding to it.

Damn Ashley McCandle's hide anyway. He'd managed to put them weeks behind. Cattle continued to disappear on a regular basis, and they couldn't seem to pick up a clue about where they were going.

That's why Hawk had been checking out this canyon, before he'd had to follow her to the Lakota village. He'd seen tracks leading towards here, periodically, for no good reason. Especially since, the canyon appeared to be a dead end. At least that's what everybody in the area thought it to be.

Now, they were beginning to wonder. It had been a two hour ride there, and Mandy was anxious to see what they were going to find.

She needed answers. Time was running out on her. The cattle needed to be brought in and sent on down to the market. They needed to get ready for winter.

It was all getting close—too close.

They had reached a fork in the trail, took the one more beathen down, from use, and started a steep climb up through the rocks. Occasionally the trail took them right next to the edge. If this was it, there had to be another way in, because, there was no way McCandle was bringing a bunch of cattle up through here.

She looked down over the edge as they once more came perilously close. It was a long way down. One slip and . . .

To Tame a Wild Hawk

Hawk drew to a halt and peered at the trail. "Well traveled, I'd say," he muttered.

"Is this where you were shot at? Mandy looked around.

"Yeah," Hawk squinted up the trail. "I've got a gut feeling this leads to all our answers." He looked down over the cliff again. "Or our deaths," he muttered.

"Well come on," Mandy shivered, "we won't know anything standing here."

Kid looked around. "I've got a gut-feeling, too," he said in low tones.

Mandy jumped at the sound of a gunshot, turned and saw Hawk fall over the cliff.

Screaming, she scrambled off her horse. Kid's arm closed around her waist a split second before she would have gone over the cliff after him.

She fought like a wild cat. "No, no, no . . . Let me go. He's hurt. We have to help him. He's hurt. Let me go!"

She never saw the rifles that surrounded them. Kid never stood a chance in stopping them. He was having all he could do to keep her alive.

She went to her knees, screaming. She never knew when a rifle butt knocked Kid unconscious, was unaware of the hand that hit her so hard, she was nearly rendered senseless. She knew only of her need to get to Hawk.

She wouldn't remember, until much later, how she fought when they set her on her horse and lashed her hands to the saddle horn. She never saw the toughened men, who shook their heads, half afraid to touch her, muttering how her grief had left her touched.

She knew, only, she had to get to her love.

She rode, staring straight ahead, unblinking, while they led her deep into a hidden canyon, which led to a valley.

Some hours later, someone yanked her off her horse, not bothering to catch her when she hit the ground, hard. They yanked her up and pushed her forward towards a huge ranch house. When she looked into the face of Ashley McCandle, she jerked out of her catatonic stupor.

She lunged at him as if she were a mad woman. "Damn you!" she screamed, her bound hands slamming into his chest with force of two women.

Lenore Wolfe

"You murdering bastard, as the Goddess is my witness, I swear, I will kill you." She hit him again. *"I will kill you!"*

She was pulled, brutally so, off of him. Someone backhanded her, and this time, she was rendered senseless.

Ashley hit the man responsible, with a bone-cracking force. "I told you, she was not to be harmed."

The cowhand propped himself up on one elbow, and wiped the blood form hip lip with his free hand. He knew better than to say one word in his own behalf, when McCandle was like this. It would only enrage his boss further. He got up, dusted of his hat and limped away.

Leaving Mandy lying there, in the dirt.

A man on a dark horse rode in along the canyon wall. He'd been hunting—but now, hearing the distant gunfire—he turned his horse in the direction of the sound.

He wore a breech-cloth and beaded leggings. His hair flowed down past his waist. His jaw was hard. His eyes dark, and, women would say, beautiful.

He was Tsisastas, Cheyenne, from the beautiful people. And he had returned with a warning from the teachers, who sent their warning—from the *Grandmothers*.

Chapter Thirty

When Mandy woke, her head was throbbing. She gingerly reached up and touched her jaw, her fingers running lightly over the bruised swelling. With full dawning, the past few hours flashed before her eyes like a bad dream. Wave, after wave, of pain rolled over her, until she screamed.

Grief tore through her, and she sobbed, gut retching sobs, which shook her to her depths, leaving her empty when they were gone. She couldn't believe Hawk was gone, couldn't accept it. She needed him to hold her, comfort her.

He would never do so again.

Ashley was unfortunate enough to walk through the door, when she'd reached anger. With a hideous scream she attacked him for the second time that day, beating him, kicking him, clawing his face.

He backhanded her, sending her flying against the far wall. Her head cracked against it, and she slid to the floor. He walked over and yanked her up, and with a single rip, tore her blouse from top to bottom. For the first time, Mandy was afraid.

He was going to finish what he'd started that day in the barn, weeks ago.

And this time, Hawk wasn't here to rescue her.

When he came at her again, she viciously slapped him. Welts immediately rose, outlining her fingerprints. With a violent yank, he tore her skirt from her. Piece, by piece, he tore every inch of clothing from her body, while she fought him, until she stood, trembling with rage—and totally naked.

"Ashley!" Star Flower yelled from the door.

He rounded on her. "Stay out of this!"

Star Flower raced across the room and grabbed him. "Ashley, stop this!" she yelled.

He viciously slapped her. Picking her up by one arm, he dragged her through the doorway. Turning, he closed, and locked, the door behind him.

"No! Don't lock me in here. You bastard, don't lock me in." Mandy screamed. "There are no windows! Ashley . . . " She beat on the door, crying and hitting it.

She paced back and forth . . . back and forth, like a caged lion. Every once in a while, thinking of another swear word, or a name she could call him from all the ranch hands she could remember in her past, she'd start screaming at him again.

Twice she managed to rile him enough he came to the door, and she wondered what had gotten into her, provoking him like this. But, she just didn't care. She was beyond caring. They were right, when the said, the world lost all color when grief cut you deep enough.

By the last time Ashley came to the door, she realized he didn't have a shred of sanity left.

And she shut up.

He had ranted as he paced the room outside hers. He was screaming, now, like a man gone mad, telling her she would come around when she got tired of being locked up in the room naked. And when she did—she *would* marry him. He took pleasure in letting her know how he didn't acknowledge her marriage to Hawk. He said, he was waiting her out, waiting for her to marry him, and then, he was going to enjoy taking her. But he'd have *the marriage first*.

He'd have it all, everything Hawk had taken from him.

He had lost all touch with reality, and this is what scared her most.

She wondered where Star Flower was. The danger to her friend was greater than her own. The fact he'd brought Star Flower here scared the hell out of Mandy. He wouldn't have shown her his secret, hidden valley, unless he had nothing to fear from her knowing.

To Tame a Wild Hawk

That meant, he never intended for her to leave—alive or dead.

Later that evening, a Spanish woman brought Mandy her meal. Mandy peeked around her, knowing she could easily overpower this woman.

She saw her opening, made her move, but the instant she made it through the door, she was seized in a brutal grasp and thrown, headfirst, back into the room by one of Ashley's men. She hit her head on the bedpost and slid to the floor, fighting not to pass out for the second time that day.

When she finally managed to stand up, she went to her little table next to one wall, sat down and tried to eat, knowing she needed to keep up her strength. She needed to stay alive—long enough to kill Ashley.

She pushed food around on her plate, for what could have been minutes, or hours. Mandy no longer knew, or even cared. Hawk was dead. The light had gone out of her life. When the pain, that lanced her heart, was overpowering, she wept, rocking back and forth moaning and wailing her grief. She violently wished for a knife, so she could hack her hair or slice herself. She'd seen tribes who did this and had never understood it—until now.

Later, when she felt a little better, she managed to eat a little more food.

The room closed in on her at times, causing her to claw at the door. She longed for a window, begged for one, desperately craving fresh air. She felt as though someone was sitting on her chest, and she couldn't breathe.

Hawk wasn't here this time, she thought again, and again. Hawk would never rescue her, again.

The next morning, the same woman brought her breakfast. She shook her head in sympathy at the distraught Mandy. It was obvious the young woman couldn't handle confined places. If Ashley kept her here much longer, it would probably drive her mad.

Mandy picked at her food for the better part of two hours. She backhanded the juice from her lips. She didn't bother to move her hair out of her face. In truth, she didn't even notice it was there.

Her heart ached like nothing she'd ever felt before. She knew without being told, the pain would not ease for a long, long time, and she didn't have a clue how she'd ever manage to survive it.

When Ashley finally showed his face again, her appearance riled him. "What the hell is wrong with you?" he raged. *"You couldn't have loved that no good drifter."*

Mandy didn't even look at him. She just continued to stare at the wall. What did it matter anyway? Hawk was dead. Nothing could equal what she'd felt with him.

"Fine, you can stay in here until you rot." He slammed, and locked, the door.

Mandy only stared after him, a single tear sliding down her face.

Ashley threw a vase against the wall, sending two of the girls, he kept around, running in terror.

"What's the matter brother?" Star Flower hissed.

He twisted his face in a snarl. "Get out of my sight!"

"She will never love you, you know, no matter what you do. She will never forget him," she softly taunted.

He rounded on her, backhanding her, sending her flying against the wall.

She sat, holding her cheek, glaring at him with murder in her eyes. "You can kill me. But you will never change the facts—she hates you."

His eyes glittered, when he turned. "You better hope she doesn't." He walked over and grabbed her by her hair, hauling her to her feet. "You better damn well hope she doesn't," he brought her face with an inch of his, "because, your very life depends on it."

"You cannot change what's in the heart," she spat, Despite of the pain. "She hates you."

He flung her away. "Then, you better change her mind, hadn't you."

And as he left, she hissed, "She hates you brother, *almost as much as I.*"

Chapter Thirty-one

Hawk tried to move and groaned out-loud with the effort. He was alive. Every bone in his body felt as if it had taken a brutal beating, but he was alive, none-the-less. He moved each limb, checking for broken bones. Finding none, he slowly stood up.

He was a long way from the ranch, without a horse, and his hands were bleeding from every purchase he had gained on his way through—the trees.

He'd never been so happy to see trees. They weren't very big, but they sure were welcome.

He stared up the cliff. He shouldn't be alive. It was one hell of a long way up.

When he'd gone over the cliff, he was sure he was about to meet his maker, but Hawk had been a fighter too long, to just go over the edge without a struggle, and he managed to catch hold of some bushes and tree roots near the edge of the cliff—could have, in fact, climbed back up, if he had not been dead certain he would be shot for his efforts. Part way down was a small ledge. And that was fine—if he had stayed there and waited for help. But he didn't have time for that. McCandle had Mandy—and that didn't sit well with Hawk.

He was in a rage, consumed with thoughts of what McCandle would do when he got his hands on her—demonized by mental images of Ashley's assault on her in the barn.

There was no way he was staying on that ledge and waiting for help.

It was finding his way down—that proved to be a problem.

He had lowered himself, part way down, on limbs and jagged outcroppings of rock. He was agile, and strong, had even had to climb up or down one or two cliffs before in his life, had made it, in fact, part way down this one, without incidence, but lost his footing about thirty feet up and hit the trees below.

They had broken his fall, but he'd taken off much of the hide on the palms of his hands for his efforts.

Well, there was no other way around it. He was going to have to walk out of here. He made himself a makeshift cane and wrapped it with his leather vest. Shaking, he struggled to his feet.

The sun's rays beat down on him with excruciating intensity. He gripped the cane so hard, his bleeding hands cracked back open, causing fresh blood to ooze from each open sore. Everything smelled hot, and it wasn't long before his throat was burning, his lips cracked and bleeding too.

It angered Hawk every time he was forced to stop and rest. It frustrated him to no end. He needed to reach Mandy, now. Time was the enemy at the moment. Every moment, another moment she was at Ashley's mercy.

Every time he had to rest, he had to pull his beaten, and bruised, body back up and, somehow, continue on. He had to make it.

He had to find her.

She was in the hands of that monster. His beautiful, fiery Mandy had been captured by one of the most brutal bastards Hawk had ever known. If he harmed her, Hawk knew, he'd never forgive himself. And he'd never stop until he'd hunted Ashley down—and exacted a warrior's revenge.

He couldn't believe how firmly she had anchored herself in his heart, in such a short time. A few months ago, he would have never have imagined caring so much. Now, he didn't know how he'd ever live without her. She was his life. The air he breathed.

The beating of his heart.

He chuckled through his cracked lips, almost missing his step. Hell, she was his heart. How did one live without his heart?

The sun was beating down hard, an hour later. Hawk was about to go down to his knees, from the pain in his head. He wiped the side of his head, where it throbbed the worst, his hand coming away covered in blood.

To Tame a Wild Hawk

He'd been shot. How could have he forgotten the gunshot that had knocked him over the cliff. The thought gave him renewed determination to get to Mandy. Like a chant, it kept him putting one foot in front of the other.

McCandle'd had his own brother shot, much like their father had killed their friends so many years before. Nothing would stop him from harming Mandy—or his sister.

Nausea and frustration made him sit down. He ripped off a piece of his shirt tail and tied it around his head. With shear grit, he drug himself to his feet, again, to continue on. He was staggering by the time he stopped again, nearly two hours later, judging by the sun. He'd been going on anger now; it was the reason for taking one more step forward. Anger was what forced hot air into his lungs, ignoring the burning of his throat, which was, by now, on fire? He knew, he had a fever, and the fever was working against him, but he'd never quit. Then, anger gave way to hallucinations. He spent most of his time, now, with his mind roaming free, touching Mandy's hair, running his hands over her creamy skin, making love to her. He was no longer aware of anything around him, although some sounds managed to rouse him. But he still managed to pull his gun at the sound of a lone horse, although it was years of training, and instinct, which did it for him.

Squinting through the red haze in his eyes, and the sweat on his brow, he was slow to recognize the Cheyenne warrior on the horse. When he did, he stepped out from behind the rock he had taken for cover and dropped to his knees in relief and pain.

Jake's eyes scanned the horizon in the direction that Hawk, Mandy and Kid had taken, earlier that morning.

Beside him, Kat frowned, watching him. "Something's gone wrong." It was a statement. Hawk hadn't met the dead line he'd set when he went out.

"Yeah," Jake settled his hat back on his head.

Kat headed for the house.

"Where are you going?" Jake growled.

"I'm going look'n," Kat shot back, slamming the door.

"Women," Jake growled under his breath.

She came back out within minutes, dressed to ride, and armed for battle. Heading toward the barn, Kat was surprised when Jake came out, leading their horses.

Jake handed her the reins to the bald faced stallion she had picked up earlier that week. "They said they were heading towards the canyon."

She mounted up, and they headed out at a brisk pace. When they reached the canyon, a couple of hours later, they easily followed the tracks, and reading the sign, they picked up the signs of a scuffle.

Jake looked down over the edge of the cliff, where it was obvious something heavy had fallen, his jaw flexed heavily. "Someone went over the cliff."

"I'm going on—to scout the trail," Kat told him.

Jake looked over the ledge, then back at her. "It's better if I go alone," she told him.

He nodded, "I'm going to find out what happen here" indicating the cliff.

"Don't reckon I can give you much of a time frame. It's whatever it takes, go'n in there."

"You got till morning," he said dryly

Kat scowled, then reined her horse up the path, barely seeing one of the rare grins of approval Jake gave her.

He went back down to the bottom of the mountain and began the tedious job of making his way along the base of the cliff.

His horse took him across boulders and hundreds of small rocks the size of a man's skull, crossed trees and forged creeks. When they reached the spot, where he could see someone had landed, he scoured the ground for a clue to who it was.

He picked up Hawk's medicine bag and scowled menacingly. He touched the blood in the sand—it was dry. He, then, began to carefully track Hawk back out of the canyon base. Nearly an hour into it, he picked up the tracks of a horse. Moccasin feet had stopped beside Hawk, and the heavy indentation indicated he'd been picked up. But by whom?

Friend or enemy?

It was dark when he tracked him to a small cabin. Guns drawn, he stormed his way in, and was relieved to come face-to-face with Hawk, who had yanked his Colt from where he was being bandaged an the table.

The Cheyenne warrior, standing there, was ready to fling a deadly looking knife.

To Tame a Wild Hawk

Hawk grinned and winced. Seeing this, the Cheyenne warrior relaxed. "Jake, this is White Wolf. White Wolf, Jake," Hawk said by way of introduction.

Jake let his Winchester relax at his side and nodded. But it took a long moment for the menace to leave his eyes.

White Wolf grunted. "Shut the door."

Jake did, and his eyes narrowed on Hawk. "You got the lives of a cat."

Hawk looked at his hands, and Jake's eyes dropped to them. "Yeah, well, I scaled most of it, probably grabbed everything that stuck out, most of the way down. It was the last thirty feet that was the kicker.

"You alone?"

"Kat's gone on up the trail."

Hawk stood and grimaced, touching his wrapped ribs.

"Relax," Jake growled. "We can't go anywhere til daylight anyway. You sleep. I'll get you a mount."

"Give the hands their orders." Hawk slumped down to the bed White Wolf indicated. "Make sure they cover the ranch."

White Wolf gave Hawk something to drink and the next thing he knew, he was being shaken back awake.

"We're burning daylight, old man."

Chapter Thirty-two

Kid woke to a terrible pain in his arms. It took him several moments to realize he was hanging from them, and they had beaten him—even while he was unconscious, if the injuries he'd sustained were anything to judge by.

He groaned.

He saw something yellow dart from one stall to another—and groaned again. Now, he was hallucinating. 'Cause if that was his kitten, he'd just seen streak by, he was going to blister her backside.

He licked his cracked lips.

She appeared at his side, and with a quick slice from her deadly blade, he landed, hard, on the barn floor.

She was by him in a flash.

"I-I'll be—talk'n to you—later," he gritted out, when he could catch his breath.

"Shush." She disappeared and was back, seconds later, with two horses. She helped him to his feet and after several attempts, managed to get him on his horse—face down. He'd have never stayed any other way. When he wouldn't shut-up, she tied him there—and gagged him.

She was never going to hear the end of it.

They were nearly off the deadly mountain when they came across Hawk. Jake had headed into what had always appeared to be a box canyon, to find the hidden passageway. It had to be there. It was the only explanation. If it was there, Jake would find it.

Hawk's eyes narrowed, dangerously, when they lit on Kid.

"He'd alive," she grinned. "He was about to get us both killed."

Hawk chuckled, then winced from the pain that shot through his head.

"And Mandy?" he said this in a deadly tone.

"She's locked in a room in the back of the house, screaming the door down."

Hawk's eyes narrowed in question.

She held up her hand. "She was just screaming at him to let her out. Calling him every vicious name she could think of," Kat laughed, "and every single way she was going to kill him. Could hear her all the way to the barn."

Hawk chuckled. "That's my girl."

"Hawk," Kat's beautiful cat, yellow eyes were serious now. "There's probably five, six hundred head of cattle in that valley."

Hawk nodded. "When you get down to the base, tell the men to wait. Tell them to be ready to go through the hidden passage through the gorge," he told her." We'll be ready to show them where."

Kat cocked her head. "Hidden passage?"

Hawk nodded. "Jake's looking for it now, should be right behind me soon."

"Will do." Kat tilted her hat at him and headed on down the trail to the ranch.

Hawk was heading up the trail. Jake had said he'd catch up as soon as he checked things out. Hawk peered over the edge. If anyone could find that passageway, it was Jake. That had to be the way they were bringing in the cattle. Half way up the trail, Hawk heard a lone horse behind him. He muttered an expletive under his breath. That better be Jake, cause he was wide open with nowhere to go, and whoever it was, was coming up fast.

He leveled his Winchester at the bend. Seeing Jake come around the corner, he sheathed the rifle.

It was Jake's turn to swear, having been caught with his pants down.

To Tame a Wild Hawk

Hawk chuckled. "Got the drop on ya."

Jake more snarled than smiled.

"Did you find it?"

Jake actually grinned, then. "Did you think I wouldn't?"

It was Hawk's turn to smile. "Come on, let's make tracks." The two lost no more time finding the ranch house.

Late in the afternoon, they had located the cabin and circled the entire area, getting a good layout of the land. Jake went down to meet Kat, and the hands. She had left Kid in Lydia's care and returned. Kid was grumpy that he was about to miss all the action. One of the hands had gone for the doc. He was to let the doc know, he might want to stick around . . . cause it was time for a showdown.

"Got a plan for all those cattle you put the hands on?" Hawk asked when everyone was in place, and they were within sight of the cabin again . . . as if he hadn't guessed. Jake had taken several of the hands and been gathering cattle for the past hour. It hadn't been too difficult. Kat had been right. There were several hundred head of cattle gathered in the valley, hidden beyond the passageway. Mandy's cattle, their cattle—and cattle from every ranch from miles around.

Mandy couldn't have stolen near as many cattle from McCandle.

"Yeah," Jake drew up his rifle. "A stampede."

Moments later, Hawk let out a chilling, war cry, and within minutes, they had several hundred head of cattle thundering towards the ranch. The thunder of hooves shook the ground like an earthquake.

Gunshots rent the air.

Hearing it, Ashley took out his field scope and got a good look at who was coming. Surprise, had him swearing a blue streak, when he got a good look at who was in the lead. "Man's got nine lives," he sneered. He ran for his office.

Seconds later he hit Mandy's door in his rage, sending it splintering against the wall. Mandy jumped when he entered her room, an insane gleam in his eyes.

She stared, wide-eyed, at the shackles in his hands.

"What are you going to do?"

"He's come," Ashley laughed like a lunatic. "But he'll never get you, my sweet." He laughed. "You're going down with me."

Mandy tried to bolt past him, but he easily caught her around the waist. With the power of the insane, he shackled her to the wall. She never stood a chance in fighting him, though she bit, and kicked, and scratched his face.

He picked up the lantern and walked out the door.

"Goodbye love, may we be together again in paradise."

"Goddess," Mandy whispered, "he's going to burn the house down." She tore at the shackles, tears rolling down her face, oblivious to the fact she was tearing her fingernails from their beds. "Oh Hawk," she cried. But Hawk wasn't here. He'd never help her again. Perhaps it was just as well if she died. For her, life would be an empty shell without him.

Something wooden, and far too calm, stole over her. She was surprised to realize her panic was gone. She slid to the floor, her back against the cabin wall—to wait.

Tears rolled from her eyes, and she centered on her *Grandmothers*.

Have faith, child. Your time has not come yet.

Oh sweet Goddess, she could hear them again.

How, Grandmothers. The house is on fire.

Have faith, you will soon see.

Even Mandy couldn't see how she would escape this one, so she couldn't believe what she saw appear at the door, through the shimmering, haze of her tears.

"Hawk?!"

He'd never looked so good, striding straight for her.

Her tears came, now, in ragged sobs. "You're alive. Oh, Hawk." She wanted to put her arms around him, but the shackles brought her up short.

Hawk's eyes narrowed on the shackles. "I'll kill him." He grabbed them and tried to yank them from the wall. Again, and again, he yanked at them, to no avail.

"I love you, Hawk."

"I'm not leaving you here, so just get that out of your beautiful head," he growled.

To Tame a Wild Hawk

Jake came through the door, and seeing Hawk give a thunderous pull on the chains, quickly joined him. With a violence born from deep hate, for the man who'd killed his wife and was now trying to kill his sister-in-law, Jake yanked on the chains.

"You've got to get Hawk out of here," Mandy pleaded with him.

"We're not leaving without you," Jake answered. His tone brooked no argument.

Mandy wasn't listening. She only knew, they'd die if they didn't get out of there now. "You have to get him out of here."

"No! Get that out of your head." Hawk growled. "We are not going anywhere until we get you free."

"That's right." Ashley said from the doorway. "Nobody's going—anywhere."

Mandy knew they were in real trouble. She could see it in Hawk's eyes. She looked up at Jake, saw him register the same realization. The two of them still had their guns strapped to their sides, but in such a small room—they'd all die.

Hawk rounded on him. *"What is your problem, brother?"* he sneered.

Ashley's eyes were filled with menace. *"You are my problem.* You! He just had to go looking for you. Year, after year—*hunting for you!"*

"So daddy wasn't there for his baby boy," Hawk growled. "That doesn't explain why...."

"It explains everything!" Ashley eyes held an ugly gleam. "The bastard took me with him. And...." he paused, "they took me!"

Mandy frowned. "Who took you?"

"I never knew what tribe they were from," Ashley sneered. His eyes took on a feral gleam, staring off into space, seeing what no one else could see. When he spoke again, he was speaking to someone visible only to him. "But we took care of those heathens. They got what was coming to them *in the end."* He stopped when he realized what he'd revealed.

Mandy swallowed. "Who, Ashley?" Who took care of them? What did you do?"

Ashley cocked his head to the side, staring at her as if to contemplate how much to tell her. "I suppose it wouldn't hurt anything, telling you." He waved the gun at Hawk, and then Jake, as if to remind them, he still watched them.

"We'll all be dead soon anyway." He smiled that nasty smile, he'd perfected so well.

Mandy caught herself *wondering* if he'd stood in the mirror, for hours, practicing it.

"We sent them the blankets." He watched her face. She knew he wanted his final great act, his great finale. She schooled her face as her brain fought *not* to understand what he'd just said. She *didn't want* to understand what he had done, what he'd been a part of, but her brain was putting the pieces together in rapid succession, and she saw the feral gleam in his eyes as dawning struck in hers.

She saw Hawk and Jake both step forward at the same time, and Ashley waved the gun, like a lunatic bent on destruction. "Go ahead. Give me a reason to shoot you right now. I've been waiting for this moment, for all of my life."

He looked back at Mandy, smiling at the shock in her eyes. "Yeah, *you know what blankets I'm talking about.*" His lip curled around his words like he was sucking on sick—sweet syrup.

Mandy hit the end of her chains in her rage to get to him. *"How could you, Ashley!* How you could you do such a thing! There is *nothing* more evil than that. Do you have any idea how many people died of that small pox? *How many woman and children died?"*

"They can't be allowed to live," was his only answer.

Mandy was taken back by the nasty gleam in his eyes. "Why? For protecting their home? For protecting *their way of life?"*

McCandle just smiled for a moment, waving the gun around at the three of them. "No. I can respect a man, protecting his home. *But they would have known. They would have seen,"* he nearly whined.

"They would have seen, what?" Mandy nearly yelled, then, for the second time, dawning came, and with it, realization. "They would have seen *who* was responsible. What *few* can see."

Ashley saluted her with his pistol tip."

And that was all the time Hawk needed. His gun cleared leather in the blink of an eye, but Ashley was just as fast, and his was trained on Mandy.

Hawk glared at his brother with deadly intent.

"Yes, brother, I can see just how bad you want to kill me," Ashley grinned.

To Tame a Wild Hawk

Actually, grinned.

He looked at Mandy. "So you see. We can't have a people giving us away."

"Us?" Mandy asked. Her delicate brow shot up.

"Oh, yeah. You mean the man who wears the dark suit in the middle of summer in a hot, dusty cattle town. That, us."

Her sarcasm wasn't lost on McCandle, who glared at her for her effort.

"They needed him to be sure their work was being done, correctly," he sneered. "Damn waste of money, if you asked me. They had *me!* Nobody hates those damn renegades more than me. I was bound to do a better job than any one of them!" He backed towards the door.

"Where is he now, McCandle," Hawk asked, drawing Ashley's attention off Mandy.

Ashley smiled. "Wouldn't you like to know." He waved the pistol around as he spoke. "I'm sure he's around town somewhere."

"What else could he possibly want to do?" Jake asked.

Ashley cocked his head at him. "Well, see, people are blind. They just want to be led. They're like lambs to the slaughter. They select their leader, or whatever, and they believe their job to be done, that they're now taken care of. And they'll do what they're told." He stepped forward a step, aiming the gun right at Jake's chest. "But you watch, and mark my words. One hundred years from now—two hundred years from now—they will be the one's ruling the world. And no one will even question who's really in power."

"That will never happen," Mandy said, drawing the attention back to her.

"It already is," Ashley sneered. "Why do you think the United States capital flies their own flag? Why do you think the Vatican flies their own flag? Why do you think there's a place in England—who also fly their own flag?"

Mandy swallowed. "And they are a power who is more spirit, than man," she whispered. "Which is why they fear a people who might betray their secrets."

She leaned out towards him as far as her chins would allow her. "But no one would believe them. They'd see them as heathens. They'd never believe their words about an unseen force."

"Not now, they wouldn't," Ashley said. "But someday. . . ."

"And they couldn't risk that."

"And now, you know." Ashley saluted her, this time with his free hand, smiling at Hawk. He looked back at Mandy. "I tried to keep you where you couldn't do any harm. I tried to keep you alive. But you had to go and chose—him." He waved the pistol towards Hawk. "They knew you were to help save the people. I tried to keep you where you wouldn't. But you just wouldn't listen. . . .so, now, you have to die." He leveled his pistol on Mandy. He looked a bit regretful. "You should have listened."

Mandy tensed—waiting for the shot.

This was it.

This was the moment you know you have to face, all of your life. But what about the life her and Hawk were supposed to have? What about their children? She'd seen, it in them, in her dreams.

When it came, she jerked—but felt no pain.

She opened her eyes to see Ashley sliding to the floor.

Chapter Thirty-Three

The gun slipped from Star Flowers fingers. Jake caught her just before she hit the floor.

"*He beat her!*" Jake grated out.

The muscle in Hawk's jaw pumped furiously.

Star Flower's eyes opened. "I had the right," she whispered. "I know you—wanted him, Hawk. . . . " she looked up at her brother, "but he killed my mother—and our father."

"Jason?" Hawk stared at her, speechless.

"The key," she breathed.

"Where?" Hawk asked her, gently.

"My skirt pocket. I followed him. I saw where he. . . . " She passed out.

Hawk found the key and unlocked Mandy's shackles. Wrapping her in the blanket off the bed, he picked her up.

The smoke in the hall was thick, now. He couldn't see a thing. It wouldn't be long before the fire reached them. They felt their way along and found themselves in the kitchen. He set Mandy down and poured water from the basin over cloth, pressing it over Mandy's mouth and nose, handing another to Jake for Star Flower before getting two more for them.

Finding their way into the next room, Jake pointed to a large window. He lay Star Flower down and picked up a chair, heaving it through it. He grabbed a large braided rug, and threw it over the frame, then lifted Star Flower through it. Hawk followed with Mandy.

Outside, they gulped huge breaths of fresh air.

They turned and watched as the fire reached the part of the ranch house, where they'd just been. Within minutes, it was all gone, like flames to dry kindling.

Mandy cupped Hawk's face with her small hands. "You're alive," she breathed, covering his smoke, covered face with kisses, tears coursing down her own face. He hugged her so tight, she thought her bones would pop. "For a few minutes, I thought I wouldn't make it."

He squeezed her again. "My life would be meaningless without you."

Remembering their audience, they both turned to look around, expecting to find Jake scowling. To their amazement, he hadn't been paying any attention to them.

He was too busy, staring at the vision in front of him. "Hawk, is she okay?" Jake had more than a little panic in his voice.

Hawk let Mandy go, upset to realize he'd forgotten his sister.

A moment later, Star Flower groaned, and there was a collective sigh of relief.

"Let's get her to Doc." Jake picked her up and headed for his horse. He didn't wait for the others to follow.

Charlie had come around the barn, leading several horses. When he saw Jake doting over Star Flower, his jaw fell open. He started chuckling. "Done caught what's go'n around?" he teased.

Mounting up behind Star Flower and reining in his horse, Jake glared furiously at him, then turned and headed down the trail.

Hawk picked up Mandy and headed for his own horse.

"I can ride." Mandy protested.

Hawk put her on his horse, mounting behind her.

"Bring her horse," he said to Charlie. "Put the rest of the hands on bringing the cattle home."

"Got it," Charlie grinned.

To Tame a Wild Hawk

Mandy snuggled close to Hawk's chest, and they headed down the trail.

Two hour later, Hawk had laid Mandy on the bed waiting for Doc, hovering over her for a moment. He looked at her for a second, then his sister, then back at her.

Mandy saw the confusion in his eyes and instantly knew what the problem was. Taking his hand in hers, she gently squeezed it. "It's all right Hawk. I'm fine—truly. Except for some lumps and bruises, I'm not hurting anywhere. And except for worrying about Star Flower, I couldn't be happier." She smiled at him, gently. "After all, it's not every day a woman gets a second chance at life with the man she loves."

He squeezed her hand in return and kissed her softly. "Have I ever said what a fortunate man I am?"

Mandy giggled. "No, but I'll be waiting to hear it—later."

"Witch," he growled, and Mandy laughed.

He went to Star Flower's room and took her hand in his. "How is she?"

Doc had examined every inch of one side of her scalp, looking for signs of why she wouldn't wake up.

"She looks to have some cracked ribs," he answered.

He turned her head and examined the other side.

"Her abdomen isn't distended, or hard, so I don't think she's bleeding inside. She has a couple of nasty bruises on her head, probably why she hasn't woke."

Hawk's dark eyes pierced him. "Her head, Doc?"

Doc shook his head. A great weight pressed down on his shoulders. "Only time will tell."

When he was done with everything he could do for Star Flower, he went to Mandy. "Hawk, here, tells me you might be carrying a little one."

Mandy blushed. "I'm fine, Doc."

"Just the same, I want'a take a look at ya." He waved Hawk out of the room, letting Meg—who had shown up by that time and was raising a ruckus—stay.

When he came out a few minutes later, Hawk was pacing the hall, a muscle in his jaw ticking.

"Practicing?" Doc couldn't resist.

Hawk let out a heavy breath, "Is that your roundabout way of telling me they're all right?"

Doc grinned. "They're both fine. Mandy's healthy as a horse, and the babe looks like he's staying put."

Hawk smiled. Jake, who'd stepped out in the hall on hearing the doc telling Hawk the good news about Mandy and the babe, broke into a full grin, slapping Hawk on the back before going back in to watching Star Flower.

"Now," Doc told Hawk, "it's your turn."

Glaring furiously at Doc, he relented and sat down, letting him take a look at his head and ribs. Doc was just finishing bandaging his ribs, when the sheriff walked in.

"I hope you have a good explanation as to why both the McCandles are dead, and nearly half their men with them."

Hawk turned deadly eyes on him. "You take a good look at Mandy. Then, you take good look at my sister, and then, you come and ask me that." He waved his hand towards Mandy's room, cocking one brow at him.

Hat in hand, the sheriff walked past him into Mandy's room. He did take a good look at her and expelled a sigh. "Why is it, everywhere you go, people wind up dead?"

Mandy laughed at him. "Are you sorry to see McCandles gone?"

The sheriff shook his head. "Nope, I ain't gonna say that. But I had better see it a whole bunch quieter around here, from now on."

Mandy nodded. "I'll give it my best sheriff.'

Sheriff Tucker stared dubiously at her. "Somehow that doesn't make me feel any better," he muttered, doffing his hat as he left the room.

He went over to Star Flower's room next and stood for a moment, once more, hat in hand, looking down at her. "What a shame." he said under his breath. He turned as Hawk entered the room. "Let me know when she wakes up." Hawk frowned.

The sheriff shrugged. "I just want to know how she's doing, is all."

Hawk relaxed and nodded.

"Well, I'll see myself out." The sheriff set his hat on his head and adjusted it. "Stay out of trouble, hear?"

To Tame a Wild Hawk

Hawk went back to watching his sister sleep.

They took turns pacing the hall throughout the whole of the night. Mandy begged to have her turn, but Hawk wouldn't hear of letting her out of bed.

Jake tried to get himself royally drunk, but his body wasn't cooperating.

Finally, just before the dawn lit the sky, Doc came out, whipping his hands and beaming. "She's awake," and when everyone started whooping, "she has a splitting headache, which, I'm sure, you all just added to."

Everybody looked properly remorseful for all about five seconds, then went back to grinning and congratulating one other.

It was three days before Hawk would let Mandy out of bed, and another week before Doc released Star Flower. Mandy moved her right into the ranch house, and Aunt Lydia clucked over both of them, like a mother hen.

In fact, it wasn't too long before the two women were planning their next escape.

On Star Flower's third day home, Perry rode up in his black buggy. When Aunt Lydia had him comfortably sitting in the Parlor, and all was quiet, everyone stood around, or sat, looking at him expectantly.

Perry cleared his throat and adjusted his spectacles.

Mandy smiled. Having three gunmen so close was clearly setting him on edge.

Hawk's gaze narrowed on him. "So what did the old man want?"

Perry looked, askance at him.

"I assume that's why you're here?"

Perry nodded. "But . . . "

"Save it," Hawk settled his Stetson on one knee. "There was no love lost between me and McCandle."

Perry settled the papers into order in front of him. "He's left you the ranch and everything that goes with it."

Hawk didn't move. Only a muscle, ticking in his jaw, betrayed what he was feeling. "What the hell am I supposed to do with that? I don't want it."

"Well, it's yours, regardless."

Hawk looked up at Jake. "Can I do what I want with it?"

"Yes"

"Anything?" Hawk reiterated, looking back at Perry.

Perry nodded.

Hawk grinned. "Good."

Jake shifted, uncomfortably, his steel-gray eyes trying to gauge Hawk.

Hawk stood and turned his back, then turned back to Perry. "I give half to Jake and half to Kid."

Perry's face registered surprise. "As you wish."

Kid grinned at Hawk. "I've always wanted to raise this one breed of horses. I'll give you a third of the proceeds, or in horse stock, whatever you wish."

Hawk nodded "And a portion of the cattle to the Lakota and Cheyenne already on the reservation."

Kid's eyes lit up. "An excellent idea."

Jake scowled for a moment. Then, Star Flower walked in the room and his eyes cleared. "I'll accept," he stated simply. "I've always wanted to breed this new stain of beef cattle. I think they'd do well. And—I, too, would be willing to be part of taking cattle to the Lakota and Cheyenne."

Hawk nodded, and Mandy sighed and settled to his side, her arms around his waist. She laid her head on his chest with such an intense feeling of contentment she could have wept with it.

Perry picked up his papers and set them in his case.

"I'll have the papers ready for you in a few days." He moved to leave the parlor.

"Perry?" Mandy asked before he reached the door. He turned and gave her a questioning look. "You haven't seen that man who was hanging around all summer, have you? You know the one in the long, dark suit. He would have stood out in the middle of summer in such a suit?"

She was surprised to see a guarded look reach Perry's eyes. She felt the tension in Hawk and knew he'd seen it too.

Perry pursed his lips as if thinking. "No. I never saw him."

Mandy's brow shot up. "Oh. Okay. Well, you'll let us know if you do?"

To Tame a Wild Hawk

"Sure," Perry turned his back. "I'll let you know." He turned at the door. "But I've never seen anyone dressed like that around town." He left the parlor.

They all looked at each other in stunned surprise.

"Well," Jake was the first to speak. "Doesn't that beat all. Guess we better keep an eye on that one. I'm sure our friend will turn up one day, again. I just hope not so soon."

Mandy hugged Hawk. The *Grandmothers* warnings sounded in her heart and head. Their warnings had returned to her of late. Maybe that had something to do with the man in the long, dark suit, leaving town.

White Wolf had said as much, too, before he returned to his people, that they had not heard the last from this man, that he would return one day, and they would need to be ready.

She missed her child friend. The future of the people was growing more and more uncertain with each given day. And she knew, one day, there would be trouble like non they had ever known.

But for now, there would be peace. Kid and Kat would live nearby, and Jake, and maybe Star Flower, would too.

She had Meagan in town. Mandy hoped, soon, things would work out for Meg. She smiled a secret smile, then scowled. Soon, before Meg's family forced her into a marriage she didn't want.

Later that evening, Mandy wrapped her silky thighs around Hawk as he plunged his way into her soft flesh. She breathed her need, and he answered her—each thrust bringing them closer to paradise.

Then, with a cry, she was swept into a violent storm of passion, her body clutching, her honeyed mouth breathing his name. With an exultant cry, he followed her over.

When their breathing returned to normal, Mandy ran her fingers over his bare flesh. "Do you know how much I love you? How very happy I am?"

Hawk leaned up on his elbow and looked down at her. With a gentleness that brought tears to her eyes, he stroked her face. "Once I was lost. A little boy, with no idea who, or what, was real. Then, a family took me in and taught me about love. But love was often an illusion, always slipping out of my reach.

Lenore Wolfe

And loneliness and longing were my cold reality." He kissed her gently, his dark eyes moist. "Then, you came into my life—and all the things that were out of my grasp were suddenly handed to me. You filled my dark world with your sunshine. I will always love you, my woman—my wife."

Epilogue

Cheyenne, Wyoming July 1873

Mandy sat gingerly down into her chair, her bulk making it difficult to get around these past weeks. She couldn't sleep. Her back ached lately. Her ankles were swollen, and no matter which way she lay down, or which way she sat, she was miserable.

Aunt Lydia puttered around her like a mother hen. Hawk was relentless in his vigil to watch over her, making sure she didn't do anything to harm herself, or their child.

Mandy wanted to scream.

The worst part was the way everyone had been looking at her lately. People who came to visit her would say things to her like, I see your still here. Of course she was still here. Where the hell did they think she was?

She propped her aching feet up on the stool and placed her hands over her swollen abdomen. She had been up cleaning her bedroom and looking over the nursery, one more time, when she'd been caught. Hawk had carried her back downstairs and placed her on the couch.

She went to the kitchen to get some tea, and Aunt Lydia sent her back to the parlor, promising to bring it to her.

Lenore Wolfe

Mandy closed her eyes and saw herself flying through the fields bareback, her arms spread wide, her beautiful mare's mane flowing with the wind—lightening tearing through the sky, and the rain on her face.

Soon, she promised herself.

She didn't resent being with child, just the ceaseless pampering.

She wasn't china.

The clock on the wall chimed in the hall, its loud bongs standing out starkly in the quiet house. Mandy peeked over her shoulder. No one was around. Aunt Lydia had gone back to the kitchen after bringing her tea, and Hawk had gone outside somewhere.

She quickly put on her slippers and quietly left the house.

She walked down the porch steps and around the side of the house. Seeing no one around, she went as fast as her bulk would let her, past the new barn and down the grove.

She walked up the hill, taking frequent breaks when she became short of breath or her back got to aching too much. Once she reached the top, she breathed deep the sun filled air. Looking over the ranch, she knew such an inner contentment, it filled her soul.

Hawk had the ranch prospering beyond anything it had done before. His ideas, and dreams, were taking the ranch forward in ways she'd never imagined. And as promised, they were taking cattle, and horses, to the Lakota. In a few years, Mandy would fulfill the *Grandmothers'* prophecy and help hundreds of Lakota cross safely into Canada—but that was White Wolf's story.

For now, Mandy sat down under the tree her papa had planted when he'd first moved here, a place he'd pretended her mama lay. He'd spend hours up here. It gave him peace.

After a while, she figured she better head back.

Turning on her side, so she could push herself up, Mandy started to rise—and gasped.

A pain split through her abdomen, and Mandy bit down on her lip to keep from calling out. Warm water gushed between her legs. For a stunned second, Mandy realized why everybody had been so careful with her.

Then, she calmly reached in her pocket and pulled out her trusted colt, yes, she hadn't lost the habit, yet, of carrying it, firing two shots in the air.

To Tame a Wild Hawk

Within a couple of minutes Hawk, and several of the hands, converged on her.

Hawk leaped from his horse before it skidded to a halt. "What is it?" He had reached her side and now placed a gentle hand on her abdomen. "Is it the baby?"

Another pain tore through her, and she could only nod, biting her lip hard enough to draw blood.

"Kid," Hawk threw over his shoulder, "go after Doc."

Kid was already tearing down the road before he could finish his sentence. He swung her up into his muscular arms. Her soaked skirts weighed down on her. She groaned with the movement. "I'm going to carry her," he bit out to Jake. "It'll hurt her too much to put her on a horse."

Ned came forward and took control of his horse, and Tommy ran down the hill to warn Aunt Lydia to get things ready.

"I'm sorry," Mandy whispered between contractions.

"No," Hawk murmured looking down at her for a moment, "don't be sorry. I understand what it was you needed."

She reached up and pushed a stray lock of hair from his forehead before another retching, contraction took its grip on her, and she groaned, clutching at her abdomen.

Once he had her back at the house, and settled on the bed, he helped Aunt Lydia get her changed into a fresh gown. By then, the contractions were coming every five minutes and with a pretty heavy intensity.

Every time Mandy had another one, she concentrated on Hawk's face. It was what she saw.

Her only focus.

Hawk watched her moan through another contraction. His gut clenched in agonizing fear. He did this to her. If this was what she had to endure, he'd never touch her again.

Seeing his face, Aunt Lydia laughed. "You men," she clucked her tongue, "if it were up to you, the human race would die right out."

Hawk ran his hand through his hair and started pacing the floor. But when Mandy called out, he all but ran to the bed.

She clutched his hand with a death grip, pulling him towards her, during her pain, with a strength he'd never thought her capable. Aunt Lydia tried, a couple more times, to send him out, but Mandy wouldn't hear of it, and Hawk wouldn't cooperate any more than Mandy had. She finally gave up.

To Hawk's mind, Mandy had to endure, she couldn't escape it—so neither would he.

When her contractions were two minutes apart, they knew Doc wasn't going to make it. Nearly twenty minutes later, she began to push. "Help me up," she breathed.

Hawk leveraged her up like the Lakota women. A couple of spine chilling screams later, Mandy bit out, "Put something in my mouth." She was drenched with sweat and panting to keep control. Hawk grabbed a piece of leather and rolled it up. Mandy bit down hard with her next contraction—and pushed.

Twenty minutes later, their son emerged and made his life known with a lusty cry. Hawk kissed her brow, his eyes warm and wet with unshed tears. She looked up and gave him a tremulous smile. Reverently, he lifted his son's tiny hand, watching as his tiny fingers curl around one of his own.

A moment later, Doc walked in. Seeing the baby in his mother's arms, he beamed. "I see you made it through without me." He came over and picked up the boy. Laying him on the bed, he thoroughly examined him. Then, handed him to Hawk with a happy chuckle.

Next, he examined Mandy. "Mother and son are doing fine." He looked up to find Hawk's golden gaze watching him intently. "I'll leave you two alone with your son."

Mandy stared down at her son. "He's so beautiful." She touched his downy dark hair. "Absolutely perfect, just like his father," she murmured softly.

Hawk chuckled. "Men are not supposed to be beautiful, remember. But I agree. My son is beautiful, just like his mother." He sat in silence for several moments, watching mother and son. "I don't think I can do that again."

Mandy laughed.

"I mean it," Hawk growled.

"I recall being the one to handle it." She wrinkled her nose at him. "Not you."

Hawk pushed a hand through his dark hair. Mandy watched him, trying not to laugh. The big, dangerous gunfighter, brought down by his woman and his son.

To Tame a Wild Hawk

"Well," he said finally, "maybe we could wait a little while."

Mandy raised a brow at him. "I think that would be a good idea. We do have to wait a few weeks, but then that will give us some time to play together first."

There was hunger in Hawk's golden gaze when he looked down at her. "Woman, you are going to get yourself into heap of trouble, real quick, talking like that," he growled. "It's going to be a difficult several weeks as it is."

Mandy settled their son down for his meal and looked up innocently at her husband. "Well, then, don't be talking to me about making babies if you don't want to know where it leads."

Hawk strolled towards her, and Mandy smiled at him. When he reached her, he stopped, looking down at her. He, again, pushed a frustrated hand through his hair, and Mandy's smile widened. She was going to be the death of him.

"Oh, yes, I think it's going to be a lot of fun behaving," she said impetuously.

And Hawk leaned forward and gave her a kiss, full of promise for all tomorrows.

When they took the steers to the Lakota, Mandy was with them. Their son anchored, securely to her back in a Lakota papoose. They crested the rise and looked down on the Lakota village. Mandy looked up, with love in her eyes, and caught Hawk's golden gaze on her and their son.

That promise would be coming true, very soon now.

That evening, they gave their son his Lakota name. Hawk held their son up and declared his name, Young Hawk.

His Christian name was Colt McClain.

LOOK FOR MY NEW RELEASES:

DOORWAY OF THE TRIQUETRA

FROM THE CHILDREN OF ATLANTIS SERIES

BY LENORE WOLFE

Free Sample Chapter

Mira Levine flattened the back of her five-foot-nine, athletic frame agianst the apartment, seeing it as the closest protection. Well, it wasn't like you something like that walking down the street every day .

Working up the nerve for another look, she pressed her face next to her trembling hands on the cool bricks, digging her perfect manicure into the stone until pain shot through her fingertips, forcing her to ease up. Her mind warned her not to, but Mira never was one for caution. At this moment, she needed things to make sense, more than she needed caution.

Chewing on her lower lip, she peeked around the corner at the street—and fought to take another breath. Sure enough—there it stood! Mira shook her head, pressing her face back against the bricks, squeezing her grey-green eyes shut in the kind of denial the mind takes when something doesn't fit. Her brain scrambled to make sense of what she was seeing. She stood there, her body uncooperative and fought to breathe—fought to stay standing, her knees threatening to buckle. She opened her eyes, arguing with herself not to take another look.

She peeked again.

Lenore Wolfe

There, at the end of the street, stood a full grown, black as midnight, live, man-eating, jungle cat. A jaguar—judging by her heavier frame, a female—judging from her smaller stature.

She shook her head. She wasn't having this conversation with herself, in the middle of the street, in the middle of the night, in the middle of St. Louis where there was no way this cat could possibly be.

The cat chose to defy her careful logic by letting out a loud cry, sending shivers skittering down Mira's spine. Fine hairs stood up on her arms. She froze for what seemed like an eternity, told herself not to move—if she didn't move, she wouldn't be detected. If she wasn't detected, she wouldn't be eaten. She was doing it again. She lost the argument and peeked, again, if only to convince herself that this was happening—and to be sure that thing was not headed her way. Which, in fact, was exactly what it was doing.

The cat was heading straight for her!

For a second, Mira just stood there, trembling lips compressed against a scream. Then, she was propelled into action by the force of her ramming heart. Glancing down the barren alley, she fought a fresh wave of panic. There were no doorways or stairways leading out. There was only a gate at the end of the alley with an overly large paddle-lock and the ripe dumpster overflowing with garbage and cardboard boxes. There was no place to go—no place to hide, no place to climb. No place to keep her from becoming that beast's dinner, anyway.

She peeked around the corner, again, in a kind of morbid torture the mind takes when it doesn't want to look—and can't seem to stop, her hand over her hammering heart. Blood pounded in her ears, drowning out all other sound. She let out a small cry. Scrambling for the cell phone in her pocket, Mira flipped it open, punching 9-1-1 with fumbling fingers. Peeking around the corner, yet again, she dropped the phone. There, not two feet away, stood an old woman.

"Wha-at?" she said, trying to see around her.

The cat was not there. She turned swinging this way, like a crazed thing, bobbing, then that, trying to locate the cat. The old woman watched her, skin crinkling around wizen old eyes in what appeared to be patient amusement. Without looking, Mira picked up the phone and went to press the call button when the old woman's words stopped her.

Doorway of the Triquetra

"Dear, I wouldn't do that," she said, not unkindly. "I mean, what are you going to say? Officer there is a very large jungle cat outside my place."

Mira turned for another glance down the street, when something about the hag snared her attention. She stopped, now, staring at the old woman's eyes. She knew she stared, rudely so, but couldn't help herself. Nothing about tonight made sense. She looked down at her phone, not seeing, her ears buzzing. Somewhere, out in the city, a horn blared.

The crone actually smiled. Mira didn't have to look to know she was smiling, she could hear it in her words.

"Actually, it would be quite amusing," she said, drawing Mira's attention back to her, wrinkled hands folded in front of her long, black dress. The dress, itself, falling in folds of black and silver, interlaced with, what looked like—black fur. "Ma'am, did you say, jungle cat?" she mimed. "Yes, are you deaf?" She smiled, again, at her own joke. "Ma'am have you had something to drink." She laughed. No, Mira was quite sure it was more of a cackle.

Mira glared at her, shut the phone with a snap, feeling coming back into her limbs as anger coursed its way through her limbs. She took one more look down the street before she met the crone's gaze.

The woman's eyes were as yellow and metallic as the cat. She'd swear for just a moment, they'd been the same shape. Black hair, with two large silver streaks, fell down the crone's back. Black fur, like that interlaced into the dress, the same midnight color of the jaguar, lay twined into her hair. "Who are you?" Mira demanded, the last dregs of fear giving way to anger, relishing the feeling. It gave her back her control. "You frightened me half to death. Or rather…" she gestured with an erratic jerk in the direction behind the hag, where the cat had stood. No words could explain what she needed to say. Not giving the hag a chance to speak, even if she'd intended to—which she looked in no hurry to do so, Mira finally blurted out, "Where is that cat, Old Woman?"

She realized she yelled the question, but even that couldn't be helped. Mira was quite certain she was about to do a lot more than yell.

The old crone smiled. Mira frowned. Something about this woman was strange. One moment she appeared old, the next years younger. Mira wrestled, for several long seconds, with a crazy thought. No, she was not going to pile on that thought to the already bizarre things she'd witnessed this night. She tried to block it out—and failed.

"Who are you?" she demanded again.

"So many questions, child." The old woman smiled at her. "I see…."

Mira cut her off. The crone's amusement was too much, coupled with the other strange occurrences. "You see! What do you see? That you have frightened me half to death? Or that I am quite, incomprehensibly, about to accuse you of being a cat! So now, not only am I seeing things, I'm going crazy. And to top it all off, I'm doing something I find reprehensible—I'm yelling like a banshee at an old woman."

Mira knew, with every word, she was back to panicking, and a panicked state was never a good state to be. But somewhere between being angry at the hag, and voicing the impossibility she'd even seen a large jungle cat, more-or-less accused the old woman of being that jungle cat, she'd stopped caring that she was not making sense.

The old woman stepped forward and put a hand on Mira's arm. "Calm yourself, child."

Mira found the gesture strangely comforting, fear and panic melting away, giving way to an odd feeling of familiarity.

The crone's gaze narrowed on her. "I needed to know how well you see. You have advanced quite nicely. You saw the cat because of this."

Mira frowned. "You still have not told me who you are?"

"My name is, Amar. I am of the Jaguar People. I have brought you a message." She slipped her hand into her pocket and brought out a disk, an ancient looking medallion. "And this…"

Mira reached out and accepted the disk. It felt cool beneath her fingers. She stood, tracing the ancient symbol. She had known this symbol before.

The old woman nodded, as if she somehow approved of Mira's reaction to the medallion.

Mira looked up at her. "I don't understand."

The old woman turned to go. She turned back as if she had a thought. Looking at Mira, she pointed to the west. "You must go to a place that is a

Doorway of the Triquetra

mile high, and so wide, you cannot see the end from the tallest building there."

Mira frowned at her. "Are you talking about Denver? Speak plainly, Old Woman. I mean—Amar."

"Four await you there. They will help you find the answers you seek."

"I don't remember telling you I was seeking any answers."

The old woman only smiled, as though she held some hidden secret.

It irritated Mira. She looked back down at the medallion, so cool in her palm. And when she looked up—the crone was gone.

 Lenore grew up in Montana, and Alaska, and currently lives in central US. She is a member of Romance Writers of America, holds a BA in Sociology, from the University of Northern Colorado, with a minor in writing and is a student of the Shaman path. She is a wife, living her dreams, with her husband, as a writer. She is also the mother of four grown children.

I would love to hear from you. Look for me at Facebook, Myspace, LinkedIn and Twitter. Join my free newsletter to see what's new. You may contact me at lenorewolfe@gmail.com

Made in the USA
Monee, IL
05 January 2023

24352978R10154